And Then
There Was You

Also by
Nancy Naigle

Christmas Joy

Hope at Christmas

Dear Santa

The Christmas Shop (mass market paperback)

Christmas Angels

A Heartfelt Christmas Promise

The Wedding Ranch

Visit www.NancyNaigle.com for a list of all Nancy's novels.

And Then There Was You

Nancy Naigle

ST. MARTIN'S GRIFFIN

NEW YORK

First published in the United States by St. Martin's Griffin, an imprint of St. Martin's Publishing Group

AND THEN THERE WAS YOU. Copyright © 2023 by Nancy Naigle. All rights reserved. Printed in the United States of America. For information, address St. Martin's Publishing Group, 120 Broadway, New York, NY 10271.

www.stmartins.com

Library of Congress Cataloging-in-Publication Data

Names: Naigle, Nancy, author.
Title: And then there was you / Nancy Naigle.
Description: First edition. | New York : St. Martin's Griffin, 2023.
Identifiers: LCCN 2022060292 | ISBN 9781250794178 (trade paperback) |
ISBN 9781250794185 (ebook)
Subjects: LCGFT: Romance fiction. | Novels.
Classification: LCC PS3614.A545 A85 2023 | DDC 813/.6—dc23/
eng/20230105
LC record available at https://lccn.loc.gov/2022060292

Our books may be purchased in bulk for promotional, educational, or business use. Please contact your local bookseller or the Macmillan Corporate and Premium Sales Department at 1-800-221-7945, extension 5442, or by email at MacmillanSpecialMarkets@macmillan.com.

First Edition: 2023

10 9 8 7 6 5 4 3 2 1

Every change in your life can be a stepping stone to something precious.

This book comes with my hope that it may open your heart and light the way to unbelievably special moments ahead.

And Then There Was You

Chapter One

NO MATTER how wonderful the vacation, there's nothing better than getting home and sleeping in your own bed.

That was the exact sentiment on Natalie Maynard's mind as she stared out the window at puffy white clouds from the back of the taxi. The clear blue skies in Cancún the last two weeks had been picture perfect; she'd almost forgotten how beautiful feathery clouds could be.

Missing Marc, who'd had to leave two days early because of a business issue, she couldn't wait to thank him for insisting she stay. He'd even scheduled spa appointments to make sure her vacation ended on a high note. He always thought of every tiny detail.

It's only been two days. To think she'd sworn she'd never get serious with anyone after losing Jeremy following fifteen years of blissful marriage; it still surprised her that things moved so quickly after meeting Marc. As it turned out, her heart had a mind of its own.

Jeremy had been a Monday-through-Friday, nine-to-five kind of guy. Now, being with Marc, she realized she'd under-appreciated the time she had with Jeremy. Nights, weekends, were all spent together with him. It had taken some getting used to Marc being gone days on end and working late more often than not.

Change. It wasn't something that had ever come easy to her.

But after being widowed for two years, she'd gotten used to her own company, which probably had made it easier to accept when Marc was called away for work.

Her life with Marc was practically the opposite of her marriage. She and Marc attended fancy parties, ate at the best restaurants, and there were often unexpected surprises, like this trip.

The last two weeks they'd stayed in a swanky all-inclusive resort with shiny marble floors and upscale dining. Morning walks on soft white sand and romantic nights dancing in Marc's arms had been magical. Somehow, he'd even arranged private time with the hotel biologist to release baby turtles into the ocean under a starry moonlit sky. Bucket list stuff.

There was no comparing Jeremy and Marc, and maybe that's why it worked.

I'm almost home, Marc. What will you surprise me with tonight?

Wearing the sundress Marc had insisted on buying her at the resort boutique when they first arrived, her insides tingled in anticipation of the way his eyes would twinkle when he saw her. The soft fabric flowed around her body like a whisper, fancier than any outfit she owned.

Life had changed a lot over the last couple of years.

Two years, nine months, and three days. That's how long Jeremy had been gone, and as happy as she was now, she still missed him. A scar that would forever be a part of her.

She reached for her heart. The familiar ache pressing on her. Some days it felt like yesterday.

The phone call.

The accident.

No chance to say goodbye.

The flurry of funeral arrangements that left me unable to process reality until weeks later when autopilot shut down. The day I broke down. Thank goodness Sheila was there that morning.

Leaning back against the vinyl seat, she crossed her legs, settling in for the ride home. *Concentrate on today. On the good things.*

Finally, thirty minutes later, the taxi driver entered the gated community where she now shared a house with Marc. The high-dollar home had been going into foreclosure when Marc told her he was looking for a partner on it, it had been too good of a deal to pass up. Plus, he knew someone who'd rent her house for more than the mortgage. Profits all the way around. Marc was good with money and the deals had all come together as easy as their own relationship.

Meant to be.

The driver pulled the taxi into the driveway. "Here we are."

"Feels good to be home." Out the window she could see that Marc had found the time to finally neaten up the flower beds, even raising the profile of the front trees like she'd been asking him for weeks. The tired-looking pine straw that had once covered the flower beds had been replaced with fresh beautiful hardwood mulch. She'd never been a fan of pine straw.

Her heart danced. *He understands my love language. Gifts of service.*

"Forty-two fifty." The driver pressed the button on the meter. "Need a receipt?"

"Oh. Yes." She tugged her credit card from her wallet and

handed it to him. The ruby ring on her finger reminded her that his love language wasn't all that bad either.

The driver pushed the card into his handheld device, then shook his head. "Didn't go through." He handed her card back.

"Do you mind trying again?"

He shrugged and did so, but with the same results. "Sorry, ma'am. You have another card?"

"Um? Here." She pulled a fifty-dollar bill from the zippered compartment of her purse. "Here you go. Sorry. I was out of the country. Those fraud algorithms can be as much a nuisance as a help." It was the card they'd been using in Mexico. Maybe it had to do with being in two countries in one day. She tucked her credit card back into her wallet and got out.

The driver followed, wheeling her bags up the sidewalk.

She was so happy with how pretty everything looked. A little landscape love went a long way to improve the curb appeal of their home.

The driver hoisted the bags onto the porch.

"I can get those from here," she said.

"Have a good day, ma'am."

"Thanks for the safe travel." She put her carry-on bag on top of her big suitcase, then made her way to the tall double doors with an extra snap in her stride.

Natalie unlocked the doors, then stepped inside.

She sucked in a breath. Her eyes darted left, then right, trying to make sense of what she saw. "What?" It was more of a shriek than a question.

Her suitcase slipped from her hand and fell backward with a thud.

The taxi driver was at her side in an instant. "Ma'am. Are you okay?"

She spun toward his voice, still trying to take in the situation. Twisting back toward the foyer. The shiny floors still reflected nothing but sunlight.

The house was empty.

"No!" She swung her arms in the air. "Look." Her heart raced. "Everything is gone. Something is very wrong. It's not okay!" She didn't wait for his response, instead rushing inside, overwhelmed with concern. Had she fallen asleep and this was all nothing but a dream? She opened the hall closet door. Not even a dust bunny.

"Marc?" She called out more in desperation than anything, because if he'd been here she'd have seen him by now. There was nowhere to hide. Not even a place to sit. How does a lifetime of furniture and memories, two really, his and hers, all just go missing?

She grabbed her phone and called Marc. No answer, and she didn't wait for voice mail.

"Ma'am. Are you sure this is the right house? Maybe I put it in my GPS wrong."

The cab driver's voice was slow and steady, but his eyes were wide. He was giving her that slow, over-polite treatment as if she might explode. *I'm not crazy.*

"I used my key." Natalie ran to the porch. The Cancún sun hadn't baked her brain, causing it to misfire and fail her; this was her house. The numbers on the front pillar not only matched, but they were the ones she'd hand-painted on tiles and hung herself.

"I made those." She stabbed her finger in the air toward them. "What is going on?"

The driver pulled his phone from his shirt pocket. "We have a problem at 4410 Landover Lane."

"Who are you calling?" she asked.

"The police." He stepped away, turning his attention to the phone. "I don't really know for sure. A robbery, I think?" He shrugged, looking to her for concurrence.

"I guess." Her mind clicked through a virtual slideshow of everything she owned that had been here. From the cherry dining room hutch that had been her grandparents' to the blond mahogany dresser she'd splurged on with her first real paycheck. Her favorite handbag. More importantly, the things that couldn't be replaced. The silver frame that held the picture of Jeremy asking her to marry him that stayed tucked in the bottom of her lingerie drawer. Mom's Bible, and Daddy's watch that his father had given him when he graduated college.

A tear slipped down her cheek.

Through the cloud of confusion, a moment of clarity flooded her with fear. Things were things, but where was Marc and why hadn't he answered? Was he in trouble?

Chapter Two

N O LOGICAL explanation came to Natalie's mind. It had taken weeks to move everything in.

She walked back inside. "This is mind-boggling. I just don't get it."

"Ma'am, maybe you shouldn't go back in there until the police get here." The taxi driver begged her to stay put, his hand touching her elbow.

Natalie jerked her arm away. "It's my house. There has to be an explanation. A house doesn't empty itself, and—" She shrugged. "It's like it's never been lived in." She reached out and touched the wall. "There was a scuff on this wall. I hit it with my suitcase the day we left."

She started up the stairs.

The taxi driver followed a sheepish two or three steps behind.

"Marc!" Her voice echoed back. There wasn't a single picture on the wall, and for all the decorating she'd done over the past few months, you couldn't tell there'd ever been a nail.

"I lived here. Two weeks ago, this was my home," she said, but the driver just stood there with a look of bewilderment on his face. She tried to make him understand. "Furniture, paintings. Dirty clothes in the hamper."

She opened the bedroom closet. Stark beige walls and empty dark cherry shelving greeted her. One wooden rod on his side, two on hers. Not one single hanger. She flipped the light switch. Even the lightbulbs were gone.

A loud bang came from downstairs. "Police."

She ran down the stairs. "Thank goodness you're here." She almost slipped down the last step.

The taxi driver hightailed it right past her with nothing more than a nod to the officer. He was probably headed to the closest bar, if she had to guess. She hadn't tipped him near enough for all of this.

"My boyfriend is missing," she blurted out.

"How long has he been missing?"

"And my credit card didn't work." *Was that connected to this somehow too?* "Look! *Everything* is missing."

The officer looked past her into the empty house, then stared at her for a long moment. "How long has he been missing? An hour, a day, a week?"

"I have no idea. I just got home. That guy . . ." She pointed to the driver slipping behind the wheel of the taxi in the driveway. "He just dropped me off from the airport. We'd been on vacation."

The officer's brow lifted.

"Not me and the taxi driver. Me and my boyfriend, Marc. He left on Monday, because of an issue at the office. We haven't spoken since then, but that's not unusual. He's a busy man." She took out her phone and called his office. No answer there either.

"Yes, ma'am. Is this his house?"

"Yes. No. It's both of ours. We lived here together."

"How long do you think he's been missing?"

"Since sometime between Monday and this minute. Or yesterday. Long enough for someone to clear out this place. This house was full of stuff when I left. Everything I own. Marc's not answering his phone, and no one is answering at his office either. We have to find him."

The officer looked past her into the room. "And you lived here. Together?"

"Yes. For months now. What does that even matter?"

"Are *you* the owner of the house?"

"I told you we lived here together. It's investment property. We went in on it together. Both our names are on the deed. I own another house in town too."

He pulled out a notebook and clicked his pen. "What's your name?"

"Natalie Maynard."

"Marc's last name, and how long have you known him?"

"Marc Swindell. S as in Sam, w-i-n-d-e-l-l. Seven months, I guess. What does that matter?"

"Just trying to get the details. Were you getting along?"

"Definitely. He treated me like a princess. We were vacationing in Cancún. Things were great."

"You only knew him seven months." He looked around at the empty space. "And you already bought a house together."

"So things moved a little fast. That's not a crime, but some kind of crime has happened here. Look around. Everything is missing! He's missing."

"How did you meet?"

"We were on the same flights to and from Dallas a few times. Finally, we started talking and became friends. Does this really matter?"

"And then you bought a place together?"

"Yes. We've lived here a few months now. It was an excellent investment. That's what he does. Investments. Financial planning. That kind of stuff. You need to get people looking for him. He's not answering his phone and no one is answering at his office either."

"Can you give me those numbers?"

"Yes, sure." She swept through her contacts and read them to the officer.

"What's his office address?"

"Um, I'm not exactly sure. I know how to get there, but I don't have the address in my phone."

"And the crime you think has been committed?"

"I'm not even entirely sure. We've been robbed at the very least. Marc is missing. I can't even take this all in." Her body tensed at the possibilities.

And there it began, what felt like hundreds of questions. Or maybe it was only tens of questions that were re-asked in seven ways to a month of Sundays, because she felt like she was repeating what little she knew over and over.

From the corner of her eye, she saw her neighbor, Mrs. Brooks, approaching.

The woman race-walked toward Natalie. "I can't believe my eyes. I told Frank that was you." The woman turned to the officer. "Marc told us she'd been in a horrible accident. That she died!" The woman threw her arms around Natalie. "Thank God you're alive!"

Natalie stiffened under the crying woman's grasp. They hadn't been close.

"Pardon me?" The officer glanced at Natalie and then back to the woman. "You know each other?"

"She lives next door," said Natalie.

"Yes. Lived here since the houses were first built," Mrs. Brooks said.

She stepped back from Mrs. Brooks. "You've seen Marc this week? When?"

"He was a mess," Mrs. Brooks said, holding a hand to her heart. "Clearly, there's been some mistake. You look fine. Better than ever, I always thought you were too pale." The woman turned back to the officer. "I'm Joan Brooks. I sent my Frank over with a Tupperware of my famous cookies the day they moved in. They are such a nice couple. We've been friends ever since." She patted Natalie's hand. "She never returned the container, but you know people are like that these days. No offense, honey."

Natalie pulled her hands together. "He came back because of an issue at the office. Why would Marc say I'd been in an accident? He knew when I was coming back. He booked the ticket."

Mrs. Brooks withdrew. "I have no idea." Her eyes darted back to the officer. "Frank said, don't go over upsetting things, but I was just so happy to see that she was okay." She turned back to Natalie. "I wasn't sure why you'd be here, with the lease up and everything. I thought maybe you were confused after the accident or something. Is there something I can do to help you?"

"Wait. The lease? Mrs. Brooks, you're confused. Marc and I

own this home." The words came out in a rush. "More importantly, when did you see Marc? When? Tell us."

"Ma'am." The policeman raised his hand for Natalie to take a pause, which she did, but she wasn't happy about it. Her hands shook, her heart rate as unsteady as a balloon flying across the room when you let go before tying the knot.

It felt as if the more Mrs. Brooks said, the less Natalie knew for sure.

The officer scribbled on his notepad, then dipped his chin toward the mic on his shoulder, calling for backup at 4410 Landover Lane.

Her senses became like goo swirling in a way that left her unsure if she was up or down.

Chapter Three

NATALIE BLINKED, forcing her eyes open only to squint against the bright lights. Struggling to get a clear indicator of where she was, people talking nearby, the incessant beeping, and the scent of ammonia with undertones of soap. The undeniable scent of a hospital.

She raised her left arm, where the IV taped to her hand and a thingamabob with a red light glowing on her finger made her wonder just how long she'd been here. Her glowing hand brought back a childhood memory of pressing a flashlight to her hand to see almost right through it. Her tongue stuck to the inside of her mouth. *How long have I been lying here?*

"You're awake." A cheerful nurse stepped past the curtain that cordoned off the space for privacy. "Need some water?"

She nodded, the words not wanting to come just yet. "What happened?"

"By the time you got to me, you were sedated. You were dehydrated. I think you may have had some sort of panic attack. You're going to be fine, though. Your numbers are looking good now."

"As opposed to?"

"How your vitals looked when you got here." The nurse

raised the bed using the foot pedal and plumped the pillows behind her. "That's got to be more comfortable."

Not really. She inched up to get comfortable. "How long ago was that?"

The nurse handed her a styrofoam cup of ice water. "Here you go. They brought you in this morning. It's close to dinnertime now."

Natalie pulled the liquid into her mouth, letting it wet the inside before swallowing. "Thank you."

"There's a detective here who wants to talk to you."

Slowly the pieces of the day came back together. "Okay. Yeah, I was talking to an officer earlier. I was robbed."

"Oh my goodness." The flash of concern was followed by a delicate pat to her hand. "Well, everything here looks fine. Can I get you something else to drink? A soda, maybe?"

"No. Thank you."

The nurse cocked her head. "Can I call someone for you? A friend or family member?"

"How long will I be in here?"

"Well, I don't know. We don't have any rooms available at the moment, so we're going to keep you here for observation until the doctor can take another look at you. Wouldn't you feel better to have someone here with you? I know I'd want that."

"Yes. Thank you. My best friend, Sheila." Natalie scanned the room. "Her number is in my phone. Do you know where my things are?"

"You were brought in by ambulance. All we got was you. What's Sheila's last name or address? I'm very resourceful. I'll find it."

"Aldridge. It might still be under her ex-husband's name, Dan. Her number ends in zero-five-six-seven . . . no, two-seven. I'm not sure."

"I'll find it. You relax. The call button is tied to the rail on your bed there. Just press it if you need me." Her scrubs swished with each quick step out of the room.

Natalie rested her head against the pillow, letting her eyes close as the pieces started coming back to her. Still nothing made sense.

"Ms. Maynard?" The voice was deep. "May I . . . ?"

She opened her eyes. Right where that nurse had been only a moment ago, now a dark-haired man stood, hesitant to make a step. His suit was gray, but the paisley tie was nice.

"May I have a word with you?" he asked.

She nodded.

He entered, scooching a chair closer to the bed before sitting. "How're you feeling?"

"I'm not sure. You're not who I was talking to before." He didn't look the least bit familiar. "I don't know you. Right?"

"No, ma'am." His smile was warm. "You don't know me. I've been assigned your case to help sort things out."

"Has anyone located Marc?" She scrambled to sit. "We've got to find him. I'm so worried." Tears welled, one slipping down her cheek. How long had he been missing now?

"We have conflicting information. I still don't know exactly what's going on. I'm hoping you can help me connect some dots." He glanced at his notes. "Marc is the man you were living with?"

"Yes. We bought the house together. An investment. We'd been on vacation, and he got called back early. Some problem at the office. Why doesn't anyone seem the least bit worried about him?"

"Your neighbor said that you'd been in an accident."

"No. That woman is confused. I'm perfectly fine. Well, I was when I got home, before I realized everything I owned was missing. Maybe Marc was telling her that he'd been in an accident. That might explain why Marc isn't answering his phone." She sat up. "You've got to find him. Something has happened to Marc. Can you call the hospitals? Households of stuff don't disappear. What if he caught them in the act, and they got rid of the witness?"

The detective cocked his head.

Okay, maybe that was a little dramatic, but something has happened.

"Slow down." His voice was calm and comforting, even if she was a bit annoyed by the barrage of questions. "Tell me what you know. I'm here to help."

There was something in his tone that made her believe him. She sucked in a breath and retold the entire story, from how Marc left the resort early until she got home and found it empty.

He nodded, continuing to write in his notebook and circling something.

Frustration had Natalie on edge. "I still don't understand why Mrs. Brooks would say that Marc told her I had been in an accident or that the lease was up. We bought that house. Cash outright. No mortgage. No lease."

He lifted an eyebrow, which made her feel more like this was some kind of test she had to pass or fail.

"Natalie?" Sheila bolted through the doorway. "I came straight over when I got the call. What is going on?"

Natalie snapped her attention to the doorway. "Sheila!" Natalie gobbled back the emotion she'd been trying to control, relief rolling over her as her best friend ran to her side. "I don't know what the heck is going on. Everything is gone."

"Everything what?" Sheila looked over at the detective, then thrust her hand in his direction. "I'm Sheila Aldridge. I'm Natalie's best friend. I don't think we've met."

"Detective Randy Fellowes."

"*Detective?* Okay, y'all need to bring me up to speed here. You're starting to freak me out a little. Are you okay, Nat?"

"Physically, I'm fine," Natalie said.

"Then why are you in the hospital?"

"I think I got overwhelmed, and from what the nurse said I guess it was a combination of dehydration, the flight from Mexico, and all the chaos when I got home and my house was empty and I can't get in touch with Marc. Something's wrong, which is why he's here." She thumbed toward the detective.

The detective nodded in Sheila's direction. "Ms. Aldridge, have you heard from Marc Swindell in the past few days?"

"No. I haven't." She glanced over at Natalie. "Not that I would. I'm Natalie's friend, not so much his. I mean, we're friendly, but that's it. Natalie, did you say your house is *empty*?"

"Completely. Not even a hanger. Everything I own." Natalie twisted the sheet in her hand.

The detective locked his gaze on Sheila. "And you've been to the house on Landover Lane?"

"Yes." Sheila leaned back. "Several times."

"Mr. Swindell was at the house?"

"Yes. That's an odd question," Sheila said. "I talked to her while she was with Marc in Cancún too."

"Nothing seemed off?"

Sheila grabbed Natalie's hand. "Things seemed like they were going great between them. They were, weren't they?"

Natalie nodded, and just above a whisper said, "It was the trip of a lifetime."

Chapter Four

DETECTIVE RANDY Fellowes was good at his job, and it wasn't often that a case caught him off guard, but this one was off to a messy start. The officer who'd arrived at the scene had taken down some notes, but it was a very short list of details that didn't line up.

He looked back at Natalie. "You flew back this morning? Is that correct?"

"Yes. It feels like a year ago," Natalie said, pushing her hair behind her ear. "If I weren't still wearing this dress I might not be so sure." She smoothed the wrinkles with her hand. At least being stuck in the ER instead of being moved to a private room, she wasn't given one of those horrible hiney-exposing hospital gowns to wear. "This might be the longest day of my life."

He couldn't help but smile at that. He'd had days like that before. "I hear you. So, you were not in an accident. Not in Mexico? Not here?"

"No. I guess I fainted to land here in the hospital, but there was no accident. I've been vacationing on the beach in Cancún with no issue, and I had an uneventful flight until I came home and found my house empty."

"I see."

"Did the other officer tell you that even the lightbulbs were gone? Every nail hole was patched too, and you know how many pictures I had on the walls." She looked to Sheila for confirmation.

"I do. That is weird," Sheila chimed in. "I'm in real estate. I mean, seriously, I can't even get sellers to do that before they vacate."

Natalie clicked her fingers. "The landscaping had just been done too. I'd been on Marc to raise the profile on the bushes and put down some new mulch for a month. Remember me telling you that, Sheila?"

"I do. Yes." Sheila nodded.

"He did it. It looked great. I was so excited," Natalie explained to her friend. "I can't believe everything I own is gone. And I can't reach Marc. And my neighbor is saying she saw him the other day and he was telling her I'd been in some kind of accident."

"What have you found out?" Sheila asked the detective.

"Not much yet. I haven't been able to connect the dots on Mister Marc middle-initial-*I* Swindell. There's no driver's license with that name registered in the state. Do you know if he lived somewhere else previously?"

"No. Well, Texas, maybe? We were both on flights between here and Dallas when we met. I'd assumed he was from here, but he may not have ever specifically said."

"I can check on that. You told the officer that Mr. Swindell worked for a company in the State Street Building in Richmond." He flipped his notepad. "Global TMG?"

"Yes."

"What does TMG stand for?"

She blinked. "I really have no idea."

"You'd been to his office to see him before?" Detective Fellowes asked.

"Yes. Two, maybe three times. His office was on the fourth floor."

The detective shook his head. "No company by that name has a lease in that building. Do you recall which suite number?"

"It was to the right as soon as you came off the elevator. There were blue chairs in the reception area. The lady who answered the phone, her name was Dory. I spoke to her often. A young woman."

"You've called his office before?"

"Several times. Earlier today, even. From the airport, and then when I got home and everything was gone. No answer."

"Okay. Is that unusual?"

"Yes." Her voice rose a pitch. "Look, I don't know what they rented that space under, but I've been there. You can see the calls on my phone if you check. Do you know where my things are? My purse? Luggage?"

"Yes, we have it. I can get your phone for you." He leaned forward. "So, here's the thing. You told the officer that you and Mr. Swindell bought the house together. Correct?"

"Yes. We each paid half. Those houses go for over seven hundred thousand in that neighborhood. Nearing foreclose, we were able to get it for half that. It was a steal," Natalie explained.

Sheila nodded.

"A steal. Yes." Randy paused.

Natalie and Sheila shared a glance, then Sheila piped in. "Why did you say *steal* like that?"

He hated to be the one to break this to her. "Your neighbor was correct. The house on Landover Lane is a rental property."

Natalie shook her head. "No. That's impossible."

"Just hear me out." He paused, giving her time to take a breath. "The owners live overseas. I spoke with the property manager this morning."

"I signed all the papers. I saw the deed. It was in the safe in the closet." She turned to Sheila. "You know. Tell him."

"I know they went into that business deal together," Sheila said. "I didn't actually see the papers, but Natalie is a smart lady. It's not likely she moved out of her house to rent one."

"I checked the courthouse," Detective Fellowes said. "The same family has owned that house since it was built eleven years ago, just like your neighbor said."

"What does that even mean? How could—"

"Things are not always as they appear." He paused. "I believe you've been conned, or—"

"You think I'm crazy." Her lips quivered.

"No, ma'am. I don't, but there's no sign of foul play, and that leaves me with a lot of questions." He paused, watching for her reaction. "The house was left in tip-top shape. Your neighbors gave us the name of the moving company. I contacted them. They delivered the contents to a storage facility in Virginia Beach."

"Thank goodness." Her demeanor softened. "I'll be able to get my things back."

Randy hated to even say the words. "No. Actually, that storage unit has since been emptied. We've asked for the security tapes to see if we can get information on who moved them."

"Everything I have, except for what I had on vacation, is

gone? My car? My jewelry. My clothes. Pictures." Her voice got softer and softer with each word, and he watched the tide of tears rise until they slipped down her cheek.

"What can we do?" Sheila asked.

"I'm so sorry. This is not a good situation. I really don't think Mr. Swindell is missing. We've contacted where you were staying in Cancún to see if they can help us fill in some blanks on him, but they aren't being too cooperative so far."

"This can't be happening." Natalie pressed her fingers to her temples and closed her eyes. "Where am I supposed to live?"

Sheila sat on the bed and wrapped her arm around Natalie. "It's okay. You'll come stay with me."

"I can't even go back to my old house since Marc helped me rent it out."

"We'll figure out how to get the renters out of your house."

"What a mess! They'll figure this out. They have to. I won't be in your hair long. I promise," Natalie said.

"You are welcome to stay with me for as long as you like. Forever, even," Sheila said.

"No. You need your privacy."

"Not really," Sheila said. "All I do is work. You know that. The house sits empty except when I'm asleep. It's a perfect solution."

"Okay, so you have some options for the short term," the detective said. "That's good."

"I must be an idiot to let something like this happen." Natalie held her hands to her face, wishing that closing her eyes would make things go back to how they had been.

"Don't beat yourself up." Randy felt for her. "This looks like a professional job. It is in no way your fault. These cons, well, they could con anyone. They are just that good."

"This is like something you hear on television," Sheila said. "Not what happens to someone you know."

"It happens more than people realize," Detective Fellowes said. "I'm sorry this happened to you, Natalie." She seemed like a nice lady. He hated to ask, but he needed to know. "Did it ever cross your mind that something was off?"

Natalie sucked in a breath. "No. Never. He was good to me. A good Christian man who is thoughtful and caring."

"It's not the first case like this that has come across my desk. I bet things moved quickly."

"Very," Natalie said, "but in a good way."

"These cons can be extremely charming. Did he push you into buying the house?"

"It was something we had to move on fast, but he didn't coerce me. It was never like that, and we did all the paperwork. Everything to the letter. Marc was diligent about that. Making sure everything was legit."

Sheila's lips pressed tight.

"How about you? Any red flags?" he asked Natalie's friend.

Sheila gave a sigh. "Well, he was moving fast, and monopolizing all her time, but she was so happy, and after Jeremy died . . . she deserved to be treated nicely."

"You're a widow?"

She nodded. "Marc took care of me. Of everything. It was nice to not have a worry in the world for a little while."

"His name was *swindle*." Randy couldn't hold back the harumph. "I'm sorry, it's not funny, but if I'm right about the situation, he was practically advertising it. Cocky SOB." He regretted letting that last part slip out.

"Swindell." She enunciated the *ell,* refusing to pick up on the coincidence.

"Swindle . . . swinDELL. Tomato, tomAHto. You call it a tomAHto, and I'd think something was up. Probably a coincidence, but who knows. These guys are brazen."

"I still find this hard to believe." Natalie shook her head. "I think you're drawing the wrong conclusions. Please look for him." Another tear slid to her chin. "You have to find Marc. There's got to be an explanation."

"We're looking for him," he said. "I'm sorry if some of the questions make you uncomfortable."

"They do."

"He's just doing his job." Sheila patted Natalie's hand. "We understand, Detective."

Randy stood. "I think he had a plan before you even officially met him. They carefully select their targets."

Natalie ran her hand up and down her arm. "That's a little creepy."

"Yeah, it's what they do. If I can get you to go public and make a statement, we could possibly shake out some other victims. This is definitely not the first time he's taken advantage of someone. Not with the meticulous planning this took."

"I can't make a statement. I'd look like a fool."

"You're not a fool. You're the victim of a crime, ma'am."

"I don't want to be the victim either." She ran her fingers over the soft fabric of her dress. The one Marc had bought her in Mexico. A watercolor wash of orange and magenta and even a dab of yellow. The fabric had floated weightlessly around her as she walked out to model it for Marc that night.

He hadn't wasted one minute pulling her into his arms to tell her just how much he loved it on her.

I'd never felt as beautiful as that night. How can this be true?

"Unfortunately, that's why and how these cons can keep doing what they do," Detective Fellowes explained. "They count on their marks, men or women, to be too embarrassed to come forward."

"Can you blame them? There's no way I'm telling everyone that I was conned out of everything I own." She raised her hand. "Which is not what happened. It can't be. You need to go back and start from square one and look for Marc."

"Do you want your stuff back? Do you want justice?" The detective tucked his notebook in his pocket. "We're keeping an eye out for him. We aren't discounting anything at this point, but I'm pretty sure you've seen the last of him, and not because something happened to him. You're the victim here. If you don't want him to do this to someone else it would be best if you make a public statement so we can flush out any leads before he liquidates all of your stuff."

"He'd never do that to me. He knew how broken I was when he met me." She gulped back a sob. The machine monitoring Natalie began blipping and beeping. The nurse whisked into the room straight to the source, pressing buttons and adjusting settings.

"Please think about it," he said. "You don't want him to get away with this, do you?"

The nurse spun around from the machine, then glowered at him. "Detective, I will need to ask you to leave."

He got up and let out a sigh. "I'm sorry."

Natalie had her eyes squeezed shut, her hands at her mouth. She looked small and fragile in the hospital bed.

"I didn't mean to upset you," he said. "I really am on your side here."

She shook her head, and Sheila leaned in.

The nurse gave her some water. "Ms. Maynard. It's me. Nurse Cathy. I'm right here. Calm down for me, okay?"

The nurse stared him down, one brow arched. "Detective. Maybe you can come back tomorrow."

He walked out into the hallway. Natalie Maynard was still crying. A real boo-hoo session. Not the fake tears some people tried to fool him with. She believed every line that guy had fed her. Sadly, from where he sat it was pretty easy to see the gaps.

The worst part was if she didn't go public, they'd probably never find that con. He'd change his name and do it again and again.

The nurse walked out and gave him a look. "Tomorrow, sir."

"I know. I'm leaving. I just wanted to ask if she'd be here overnight."

"The doctor requested a room, but if they don't find one for her soon, I think he'll probably release her as long as the rest of the tests come back fine."

He handed her his card. "Can you give this to Ms. Maynard for me before she leaves?"

"Of course." The nurse took the card, pursing her lips. "Do you think that man really conned her out of house and home?"

"You were listening?"

"I was keeping an eye on my patient." She put the card in her pocket. "Fine. I was listening. She didn't look the type to do something wrong. I was curious, and they had her down for a psych watch."

"Well, then you know what happened. I don't think she's crazy. She seems to be telling the truth. Too bad too. These cons get away with it over and over, because their victims are too embarrassed to go public."

"That's terrible. How could she fall for that?"

He leveled his gaze. "Don't judge her. Con artists are a breed of their own. Very convincing. They say all the right things. Anyone could've fallen for it."

"He cleared out the whole house?"

Randy nodded.

"And she thought she bought that house, but really he just took her money, didn't he?"

"Appears that way." She really had been listening to everything.

The nurse lifted her chin. "I don't like seeing a woman taken advantage of."

"Me either." Randy turned to leave. He hated meeting people in the hospital. The maze of corridors in funky, outdated colors was dizzying. For a place that was supposed to be so sanitary, the smells were so intense it always left him feeling like he needed a shower.

The whole way back to his car, he thought of how Natalie Maynard's life had been dumped like a kitchen junk drawer. A scattered mess of mismatched parts that didn't make any sense.

The arrogance of that guy to use an alias like Swindell.

He wondered if that vacation to Cancún had been part of the plan. A finale of sorts. Or maybe a con man can find a smidgen of conscience along the way. At least he left her with a good memory or two. Even the best thief couldn't steal those.

Untangling this web of deception would be tricky. Like a puzzle with no corners and nothing but raindrops, it would take work—but then, he loved puzzles.

Chapter Five

NATALIE CLUTCHED the hospital sheet in her hands. "This is a nightmare. What do you think happened?" She pulled her knees up. "Is it possible Marc is responsible for all of this?"

"That he conned you?" Sheila walked over and sat in the chair where the detective had been seated. "I guess anything is possible. I'd have once said Dan would never cheat on me. And you know how that all ended."

"I still can't believe it. Maybe I'm just that naïve."

"You're not. You are one of the most level-headed people I know. And I still think Dan was having a midlife crisis."

Natalie knew that didn't make it any better. "And you haven't really moved on from that."

"I have to."

"When was the last time you went on a date?"

"Who needs to date? I'm perfectly fine alone," Sheila said.

"Better off than me. I guess I should talk." Natalie shrugged.

"Don't do that to yourself. It could've just as easily been me or any of our friends. I watched that documentary about the Tinder Swindler. Those guys are very manipulative, charming and good-looking to boot."

"Marc was all of those things. The charming and good-looking part, I mean. I never once felt manipulated."

"That's what makes them good at it. Let's talk about something else. We've settled where you'll be staying. With me. So, the trip was good?" Sheila asked.

"Amazing." Natalie rolled her eyes. "Until I got back. The whole time in Cancún was magnificent. I even sketched a whole series of note cards."

"That's wonderful. See, so something good came out of it, besides the island time. Well, two if you count Marc convincing you to concentrate on the cards and not worry about going back into nursing. You've really found your gift. I can't believe you didn't know you had such a talent for drawing all these years."

"I'm not sure I did have it before. Cancún was really inspiring. We released baby turtles, danced under the moonlight, took morning walks on the whitest sand."

"Morning walks? He turned you into a morning person too?" Sheila laughed.

"He did, and I didn't even complain." She leaned in. "Our time together was easy. He showered me with gifts and moments I'll never be able to forget, or regret, even if it all turns out to be a lie."

"You were in love with Marc?"

"Yeah, I guess I did fall for him, but not love." Spending two weeks in the most beautiful resort in Cancún, personal butler and all, had given her a unique taste of how the other half lived. Marc had definitely been a blessing, and she enjoyed his company, but it wasn't love. "It's not love like I had with Jeremy. It was different."

"Every love is different," Sheila said.

"I can't believe he'd steal from me, Sheila." She shook her head, still struggling to wrap her head around the possibility. "It's got to all be a big misunderstanding. He's a good man. He's charitable."

"I don't know." Sheila shrugged. "It all happened so fast. He always made me a little nervous."

"You just didn't get to know him like I did."

"Because he didn't allow you to spend time with me. He kept you on the go all the time."

"It wasn't like that." Natalie fidgeted with the sheet. "Did you know when he had to leave early that he scheduled the rest of the trip for me to keep me busy? He arranged spa treatments and excursions. Seriously, how many men would even think of that?"

"Not many. That's true." Sheila crossed her legs. "I'm just glad you're back and okay. I'm kind of excited to have my bestie in the house for a while. I've missed you."

"All I have are the things I brought back from Cancún. Vacation clothes. Some gifts, jewelry, and makeup."

"Well, you'd been talking about cleaning out your closet."

"This is a little extreme."

They both laughed.

"Maybe we've stumbled upon a new television series. *Extreme Life Makeovers*."

"I hope it has a happy ending."

Chapter Six

Four Months Later

Natalie Maynard walked down the hallway of the police station toward Detective Fellowes, who stood holding the now too-familiar conference room door open.

She wondered if the drab yellowish-gray color on the walls had been intentionally chosen or if it had faded into that color over the years. Wasn't it bad enough that no matter your reason for being here, the victim or the arrested, it was pretty dismal? Did it have to look that way too?

She itched to volunteer to paint it a lovely neutral blue. There was scientific proof that navy blue was the most relaxing color, but that would be too dark. Maybe a shade of cadet blue as cool as a pair of worn-out jeans.

A little artwork wouldn't hurt.

Her footsteps echoed, but she was used to it after so many visits.

When this all first happened, she'd practically camped out here just to make sure they kept looking for Marc. She was so sure that there'd been foul play and dear Marc had been harmed. She'd mourned him, praying for any tips that might help find him.

For a long time she'd thought Detective Fellowes was being just plain lazy by saying Marc was a con, and was just trying to close the case. But as the weeks went by, and the detective uncovered more and more things that just didn't add up, well, piece by piece the evidence outweighed her logic. Plus, there was still absolutely no sign of Marc anywhere.

Reality had finally settled in.

The bitter aftertaste of being manipulated, and conned, was tough to swallow.

Now she hoped they'd find him so they could lock him up and throw away the key. Chances seemed to be getting slimmer that they'd recover any of her things, or the money she'd paid into the house that was never hers.

The memory of how Marc had laid out all that paperwork for her to sign as if it was the real deal. An award-winning performance.

All this paperwork is such a hassle. Marc had leaned in with a tender squeeze as she signed those papers, reassuring her that her investment was safe.

One big hoax. The deed, blue paper on the outside and all, had come in the mail. Of course, she didn't have it, because it had been in the safe, which he'd packed up while she sat basking in the Cancún sun.

Don't worry. I'm taking care of you, he'd said.

That was back in May. Now it was almost the end of September, and the first day of fall was upon them.

Gone were the spring flowers and the summer sun. Hurricane Ike had blown through a couple of weeks ago, and now the leaves were beginning to change from green to gold and orange.

The holidays would start rolling in soon—a nonstop flurry

of parties, sales, and meals with their own color themes—Halloween, Veterans Day, Thanksgiving, and Christmas.

Detective Fellowes gave her an easy smile.

He was handsome if you liked that scruffy beard look. His eyes were so blue she still wasn't convinced they weren't colored contacts.

"How are you today?" he asked politely.

"Fine." She stepped inside, and he followed, closing the door behind them.

He was nice. Or he seemed so, but then she hadn't been the best judge of character recently, she reminded herself.

Self-doubt wedged itself between every positive thought she had these days.

"Well, about the same, I guess," she clarified. "Unless you have some good news for me in regards to what's-his-name." Hope tugged at her heart as she pulled out her own chair and sat, eager for some shred of a lead.

"Sorry, I don't have much new to share."

"Anything at all?"

"The Moritz Fund where your checks were being deposited. We've finally been able to get a little more information." He flipped open the folder on the table between them. "It belongs to a nest of small corporations. Do any of these names look familiar?" He fumbled through the pages and turned one toward her. "Here it is."

She scanned the list. "I don't think so."

"We're not having much luck getting in touch with anyone listed." His gaze held hers for a long moment, then he shrugged. "I know you think we're not trying. I promise I am, but these cases aren't easy to solve."

He'd told her the same thing the first day, but easy didn't mean impossible. She'd prayed, wished on stars, and had considered a Marc Swindell voodoo doll if it might at least hit a satisfying nerve. That wasn't a very Christian thing to do, though, not even after what he did.

"We've talked about this before," he continued. "Cons have been around for centuries. Unfortunately, the victims rarely come forward, because they don't want others to know what they've fallen prey to."

"Like me." He'd said that before too. She understood better each day why people kept quiet. "I can't. I'm not ready."

"I get it," Randy said. "But this wasn't a Judge Judy court case over a little loan mistaken as a gift. This was an elaborate scheme. He'll do it again."

His gaze was challenging. She didn't want to feel responsible for the next lady to get taken. "Lucky me. I got the royal treatment." She wished she hadn't said that out loud. Sniping at the one person who might be able to bring that rat scumbag to justice wasn't helping a thing.

"You don't have to come here all the time. You could call, ya know. I mean, I like that you drop in." He paused for a second, his smile quirking at the edge. "I've grown to look forward to your visits, but while you're spending your days driving across town to check in with me for an update, that guy is living the great life on your money and your belongings. You need to get back to living yours."

"I know."

"He's probably already reeling in his next victim, getting ready to do the same thing to someone else, if he hasn't already."

He knew how to press her guilt button, but she still had her pride. "I hate to think that's true." A queasy feeling hung in the pit of her gut.

"I'm going to connect those dots at some point. You won't be his last victim . . . unless someone finally speaks up and helps us. I'm not going to give up."

"I can't give up hope."

"I don't want you to." He let out a long breath and shook his head. "You shouldn't." He leaned forward, resting his arms on the table.

His well-muscled forearms didn't go unnoticed. Still tan, probably from summer activities, he looked the type to golf, fish, or maybe he had a boat. His watch wasn't expensive, just a black diver's watch. Too bad he'd met her when her life began to fold, spindle, and mutilate.

"I know you want answers. Natalie, you deserve them. I'd like nothing more than to be the one to help make that happen, but I don't want to give you false hope either. I honestly don't know if we'll ever find the jerk. I am keeping my feelers out on any other cases that might be similar. Right now it's my best chance for a lead."

Frustrated, she lifted her gaze from him to the ceiling. It wasn't his fault. It wasn't fair to get upset with him. She stared at the tired acoustical ceiling until the texture on the aged tiles reversed—looking like bumps instead of holes.

That was kind of how she felt today. Inside out and backward.

His voice was patient, but brought her back to the moment. "You need to concentrate on the things you can control," he said. "Your future. Recouping your savings. I don't know, maybe find a hobby to concentrate on. This guy took everything. It's bad, I get it, but he didn't take your life. You're wasting your energy on him. Don't let him take that too. You deserve better."

A tear slipped down her cheek.

She brushed at it. She really wasn't sad anymore. They were more tears of frustration and anger, and being tired of the whole mess.

He plucked a tissue out of the box on the desk.

She took it and dabbed at the corner of her eyes, then blotted the tears that had made it to her chin. "Look. I know you're busy, overworked, and I'm not helping by showing up like this. I need restitution to start over. Is that too much to ask?"

"It's not."

She swept a tear from her cheek. "I'm sorry. You've put up with more tears from me than if I was your girlfriend." She forced a smile, laughing to try to lighten the mood. "I told myself I wasn't going to cry this time."

"It's okay. I've got a whole box." He pulled out another tissue and waved it in front of her. "The situation sucks. What do you say we take a break, and get some air? There's a place around the corner where we can grab a cup of coffee."

"You're busy. You don't have to do that."

"I know I don't. Come on. I want to." He got up, and gave her an encouraging look. "No agenda. You can trust me. I'm a nice guy."

"That's what *he* said."

He nodded toward the door. "Probably true, but I'm not Swindle."

"Swindell," she whispered, correcting him for the fiftieth time. "Doesn't matter. Probably Jones or Smith this time." She managed a laugh and raised her gaze to meet his.

"Or Conway?" Randy teased, soft lines stretching from the corners of his eyes. "Seems to me the guy has a sick sense of humor. Like he's handing you a warning label with his name and laughing that you didn't catch on."

"Joke was on me. I never saw it coming. Even now, when I look back, there were no red flags. He seemed so sincere."

"I hear ya." He walked to the door, and she followed.

They walked outside, past the parking garage along the sidewalk. The fresh air eased her emotions. "Sorry again about the tears," she said.

"What tears?"

That made her laugh. "That was pretty convincing. Sure you're not a con too?"

"Definitely." He pointed to the street sign ahead. "It's just around that corner."

"Okay." He had a way of making her feel better. As they rounded the corner there was a shiny trailer parked across the parking lot. "Is that where we're going?" she asked.

"Yep. The best-kept secret of great coffee and tea in Richmond."

"Love it." As they got closer she picked up the pace and walked right past him. "Is it a horse trailer?"

"It was," he said.

And it wasn't the big fancy kind, just a simple two-horse bumper-pull deal, painted and decorated in a way that was downright adorable. "That is such a cool idea."

"Yeah, it was just a rusty hunk of junk her son had abandoned in her backyard. He's got a big fancy rig with the slide-outs now. She gutted it, decorated it, and added the barista counter."

"It's gorgeous. Not only unique, but functional." Natalie was impressed.

The barista counter was polished to a high shine. Live-edge wood added a rustic charm against the glossy paint and shiny accents on the trailer. The ramp, which once made it easy for the horses to load, now served as the walk-up entrance to place your order.

A sign on a black iron easel read:

GIDDY-UP AND GO
COFFEE AND TEA

The name was written in bright chalk paint against a black background that matched the logo on the side of the trailer.

"That is too cute." Natalie admired how the low-rent stop in the middle of a parking lot had all the touches to make it feel unique and somewhat luxurious at the same time.

"This is my favorite place to stop and take a breath. The caffeine kicks my brain into gear when I'm trying to work through a case."

"I bet it can be a stressful job, trying to make sense out of situations like mine."

"It can be." He walked up the ramp. "Hey, can I get two coffees?" He turned back to her. "Or would you rather have something fancy? They have it all."

"No. Don't need the calories. I'll just take a regular coffee with a dab of creamer if you have it," she said, directing the last to the gal behind the counter.

"Not a problem. Hazelnut, mocha, or vanilla?"

"Ooh, hazelnut sounds good. Thanks," Natalie said.

"You got it." The barista made short work of the order. "Anything else?"

"That's it. Thank you." Randy handed her a twenty and she counted his change back to him.

"Come on. We can sit over here." He led her to a little two-seater folding bistro table. "I hate to see you letting what this guy put you through weigh you down."

"I can't let it go. I really wish I could."

His smile was gentle. "Well, it's easier to give advice when you're not in the middle of it."

"But you're going to armchair quarterback anyway?"

"Want me to?"

She wondered what he would say if she declined. But she was curious too what his opinion was. "Okay. What do you think?"

"The way I see it, you have a couple of options. You can keep staying with your friend Sheila, licking your wounds, coming to see me for updates every couple of weeks, which I've sort of started looking forward to. Not the tears. I never like to see a lady cry, but you know what I mean."

She half chuckled at that. "What's my other option?"

"Put it behind you. I promise I'm going to keep this on my radar, but the odds aren't good that anything will turn up if you don't go public." He raised his hands in front of him. "I'm not judging. That is entirely your decision, but if that's the way you're going to go, I think you need to move on and live your life. You're a nice lady. Smart. Pretty. Don't let him do more damage than he's already gotten away with."

Is he flirting? "You make it all sound so simple."

"It's easier when you take the emotion out of it. Like I said, I'm not the one living it."

"It feels like I'm giving up if I *do* move on."

His head bobbed thoughtfully. "I guess I can see how it would feel that way."

"I've thought about going public more than once, but I'm not going to be the one to do it. I just can't."

"It's your decision. I respect that."

She took a sip of her coffee. "This is really good coffee. Thank you for bringing me here."

"I thought you might like it." He lifted his chin to the sun for a moment. "Sometimes you just need some fresh air to clear all the noise in your head."

"Yeah. I definitely needed this."

They sat quietly, which was nice—not feeling pressured to fill the space with small talk. Thoughts swirled in her mind. Yes, the problems piled up in front, but what he'd said was true. She was letting what happened take over her life. She'd been in a perpetual state of waiting ever since the day she'd returned from Cancún.

Finally things lined up like a checklist in her mind. "I need to concentrate on the assets I have left. Move out of Sheila's and find a new place, and get back to work."

"I thought you sold your art online. Note cards, right?"

"Yeah, but I used to have a real job. I was a geriatric nurse. When my husband died I really threw myself into it. Took on extra shifts and patients. I only started the online business to fill the time in between."

"I didn't know that. A nurse. I can see that in you. I bet your patients loved you."

"And I loved them. That's kind of why I ended up taking a break from it. I was grieving my husband, and then a few of my patients . . . well, they passed and I had trouble separating myself from the loss. They were old, had lived wonderful lives, and it wasn't a surprise, but in my state of mind it hit me hard."

"I can imagine. That would be a hard job on a good day."

"Honestly, I haven't done much but sell backstock since I met Marc and we started jetting off doing this and that. Then, after he left I haven't created one new thing."

"No new designs?"

"Nothing at all." Her jaw tightened. "You're right. He's still stealing from me, and he's not even around."

"I want to find that guy so bad."

"I hope you do, but you and I both know there probably won't be any updates." It was a harsh reality. One that Sheila reminded her of too. They'd even binge-watched a whole docuseries on Romeos who took advantage of women. Those cons were finding their prey through online dating, and that wasn't the situation in her case, but just the same, they were nice ladies who had been conned. Even with six women pooling together to track down the guy, they hadn't been successful. It was hard to catch a con. "I'm not going to be coming back and pushing you for updates."

Randy nodded in acceptance. "Can I check on you?"

"That's not necessary. I'll be fine. You have bigger cases to work on. Solvable ones. You're right. I can't let this situation continue to drag me down." She straightened, trying to feel as strong as the words flowing from her lips. "I gave this exact same advice to Sheila when she told me about her cheating husband years ago. It's way easier to dole it out than to live it."

"Always is."

"Marc can't continue to hurt me unless I allow it. I'm letting him do that, and he's vanished, as far as we can tell. Right?"

"Another town. Another target. They don't change." He shrugged. "Probably, another clever name."

"Like Conway, maybe?" Natalie teased, taking a page from his book on Marc's name being an intentional warning.

His eyes twinkled when he laughed. "Yeah. Conway would be a pretty good one. Sorry. It was a bad joke. Occupational hazard I guess."

"It was actually kind of funny. Maybe the best lead yet. I might start calling him Swindle instead of Swindell myself."

"It's fitting." He got up and reached for her cup. "Are you done?"

"Yeah, thanks."

He tossed both cups in the trash bin. "Look, I know you're hurt, but I wasn't kidding when I said I look forward to your drop-in visits to the station. I'll of course keep you up to date on the case."

"I know you will."

"This might seem inappropriate, but I'm just going to lay it out there anyway. Do you think maybe we could do dinner sometime?"

"Why? Because you've seen me at my finest?" He'd seen her at her worst. He'd insisted she call him Randy, but she'd stuck to her guns calling him Detective Fellowes. No sense risking falling for another good-looking guy on the heels of the big con. Which was unfair, because she knew he was no con. She still believed that Randy Fellowes was one of the good guys. "You don't have to feel sorry for this victim."

"No, Natalie. That's not it. This was nice, wasn't it?"

"Yeah—"

"I asked you to dinner because I enjoy your company. You're beautiful and nice, and it's a shame that someone would take advantage of that when honestly it's not a quality that's easy to find in people these days."

"I guess your worldview becomes a little jaded seeing the bad side of everyone in your line of work."

"It doesn't help, but I keep my focus on the right things. It's a good world. It's just that the rotten people overshadow the good stuff sometimes. And if you'll have dinner with me I'll put someone else on lead on this case, and just make sure it doesn't go cold."

"I'm sure you're getting a hard time over me pressing on about this."

"I am, but it doesn't matter. Maybe someone else will come forward, and together you might both get justice. My guess is the money is long gone or well hidden. I'm not sure how they could untangle ownership if he's trading things in as fast as he did with you. But you'd have to feel better that he couldn't do it again."

"I would." She sucked in a breath. "I wish I had the guts to do it, but I'm very private with my life. You know, I don't have any family, and maybe that has something to do with how hard it is for me to let other people in. It was one of the things that my husband and I had in common. He was really private like me."

"I like your company."

She got up and they started walking back toward the police station with that last comment hanging in the air until they reached the parking lot.

"Thanks for the dinner invitation," she said. "A different time and circumstance, well . . . thank you, but I need to pull myself together. That needs to be my focus right now. Thank you for helping me realize that."

"The invitation stands. You've got my number."

"I know it by heart."

"You should," he said with a smile. "I'm kind of glad you do. Move forward. You can still visit me. We can do coffee. That'd be good. Or just stop in to say hello. Even better."

"Or maybe that's just part of the cycle I need to break."

He stopped and turned to her. "I don't want to be part of the cycle you break."

His eyes locked onto hers, and she thought he was going to say something else, but he didn't.

"Thank you for saying the right things. It's a little hard to hear, but I know you're right." She was parked on the next row. She lifted her hand in a finger wave. "I'm parked here. Thanks for the coffee, and therapy session."

"Any time."

She turned to leave. *I don't need to be rescued. I can take care of myself, and that's exactly what I'm going to do.*

Chapter Seven

NATALIE WALKED out to the farthest edge of the parking lot, where she'd parked the Mustang that had been Jeremy's prized possession. If it got scratched, she'd never forgive herself. And maybe he wasn't here anymore, but she still felt just as nervous around it as she had when he was. It wasn't worth much, but Jeremy had cherished that car.

She'd hated to take the Mustang out of storage, but it was one of the few things Marc had no access to, and thank goodness for that.

The whole drive back to Sheila's house, she thought about Detective Fellowes's dinner invitation.

He'd asked her to call him by his first name a hundred times. If she had from the beginning, would she have perhaps felt inclined to have dinner with him now?

Randy.

He seemed like such a nice guy, but it was weird with him knowing all about this embarrassing mess with Marc.

Why would he want to take me to dinner?

Friends had rolled her status back to when she'd become a widow, making her relationship with Marc just a blip on their radar—like Marc had never happened. If only she could allow herself to forget that easily.

Jeremy had worked hard to make sure she was taken care of if anything ever happened to him, leaving her in a comfortable position. He'd planned it so well, except for the part where she put it all at risk.

Knowing she'd lost all he'd worked so hard for hurt the most.

She twisted the old-school knob on the radio to silence it.

Although all the evidence proved that she'd been scammed, she still wanted so desperately for there to be another explanation when they finally found Marc. She cursed herself for feeling that way.

With Marc gone, she missed Jeremy even more—maybe because Jeremy's honesty and trust had always been undeniable. Perhaps she'd never quit missing that. It had just been swept to the side in the flurry of travel, parties, and fancy dinners while Marc schmoozed her.

Randy called it love bombing. It has a name. A stage in a process.

She drove back to Sheila's house. Her home away from home.

Funny how things had flip-flopped. Originally, Natalie's plan after Cancún had been to help Sheila move on from her divorce, only Sheila had had to rescue Natalie instead. Coming to the hospital. Insisting she come stay at her house, and not even asking any questions for weeks.

True friends were irreplaceable, and she was so thankful that Sheila hadn't given her a choice except to move in with her.

The timing hadn't been horrible. They'd been each other's support system, and Natalie was glad she'd been there for Sheila following the complicated division of property with

Dan. Sheila was keeping the house, and she'd let Dan keep the lake cottage and big toys he loved more than he'd ever loved Sheila.

It was time for both of them to move on now.

Her mind wandered, trying to picture a new beginning.

Forgiveness. She knew she had to forgive Swindell to put it behind her. Like most investments, there's a risk. She should've just taken the whole wad of money that she put on that house with Swindell and instead gone to Vegas. At least that would've been a fantastic story to tell.

Natalie tried to picture herself in one of those cute little condos with a nice view of the James River with everything you need in walking distance. Some of them even had garages, so she could park the Mustang and walk most of the time. Plus, furnishing a little condo would be much easier since she was starting from scratch.

She could work from anywhere, though. It didn't even have to be around here, and properties on the outskirts of town would definitely be more affordable. When Sheila thought Dan would fight her for the house, they'd looked at a few really nice places that weren't all that far from here.

Maybe a small house with a yard. She could even plant flowers. She loved fresh flowers. One of her guilty pleasures was treating herself to a fresh bouquet each week, just like Jeremy had done for her when he was alive.

"Because it's Tuesday," he'd say. The memory still made her heart flutter.

She sat a little taller in the red leather seat of the Mustang.

It's not impossible. It might be a little tight until I get back to work, but I can totally do this.

She took the next exit from the interstate and zipped into the first supermarket she found.

With her key still in hand, she headed inside on a mission to snag every free home magazine and brochure from the racks that were always right there by the door.

A plan was brewing. Natalie wasn't exactly sure what her next step was yet, but she was taking back control starting right now.

She grabbed a shopping cart then wheeled it over to the wire frame display that held the freebies. Homes, houses, estates, even the ones with apartments.

One by one she tossed them into the cart. Feeling more confident as each one hit the bottom.

Off to the coffee aisle, she stocked up on her favorite light-roast toasted-coconut blend, then reached for a box of sugar dots.

As she held the box of sugar cubes, she heard Jeremy's voice as plain as if he were standing there with her. *Have you ever tried to chop up one of those dots in a bowl of Wheaties? Doesn't happen. You're left with nothing but soggy flakes by the time that thing dissolves.*

She pulled the sugar to her chest. They'd had that conversation a hundred times. She'd kept a big bag of sugar right next to his cereal box from that day forward.

She lingered there, glowing in that sweet memory for a moment, then whipped her cart around and grabbed a box of Wheaties. "For old times' sake," she whispered, feeling closer to Jeremy than she had in a long time. A longing for him filled her heart.

At that moment, his voice echoed in the back of her mind. *The mountain cabin. Babe, it's a place of peace. I know you always thought of it as mine, but you need that right now.*

She clutched the box of Wheaties, almost afraid to look to see who was on the front. Was it Jeremy? Talking to her from this box? Her hands clamped tighter, then she relaxed.

"The cabin? Yes, the cabin. You're right." The words poured out. She turned, half expecting him to be there. "It's furnished. Simple." She turned to see if anyone had heard her talking to herself. Thank goodness she was alone in the cereal aisle. "Oh my gosh. Jeremy, you always take care of me." Her nose tickled. She sniffled, trying to maintain control.

She resisted the urge to start apologizing to Jeremy right here in the store, because that would certainly leave her in a sobbing heap on the cereal aisle floor. Maybe even get her a ticket to the loony bin.

"I'm going to the cabin in the mountains," she whispered.

Jeremy's family had lived in Chestnut Ridge for generations. The cabin on No Business Mountain had been there for longer than that.

She remembered his enthusiasm as he told her how the cabin had been built from a single chestnut tree. The ridge had once been covered in the giant trees. Now, they were all but extinct from blight brought in from some imported tree long before anyone realized the damage about to ensue.

He'd taken her fishing there a couple of times. She'd caught her first fish on the stream in front of the cabin, and he'd cooked it over an open fire in a cast-iron skillet. Jeremy came alive in the mountains, like there was something in the air that he couldn't get enough of.

It didn't take long for her to understand why the cabin was his sanctuary, a man cave of the very best kind. After that trip, she'd politely rejected future offers, to allow him to get together with old friends there.

She turned her cart to the cracker aisle and tossed in a box of Triscuits. They'd always been Jeremy's favorites. She snagged the reduced-fat version, always trying to eliminate unnecessary calories since it was a battle to keep weight down on her short frame.

Reliving moments when she'd shopped in preparation for Jeremy's hunting trips with the guys, she felt a strange sense of déjà vu. Crackers already in the cart, she snagged peanut butter, turkey jerky, and marshmallows, then over to the deli to get cheddar hoop cheese. More cheese than any man should ever consume in a short time. More than she would, for sure, but hoop cheese meant cabin to Jeremy, and if she was going to head that way, why not carry on the tradition? Protein bars and a case of water rounded out her provisions.

When she got back to Sheila's house, she packed her suitcase. She didn't have much since she'd only bought what was absolutely necessary since she got back from Cancún, thinking and hoping maybe the police would track down Marc and all of her belongings.

It was time to shift out of neutral and get back to living. Thank goodness she'd refused to commingle all of her money with Marc's.

I have enough, and I'll make more. I'm capable. For the first time in a long time, she believed the words.

As long as she could get a decent internet connection, she could work on her note cards and fill orders from the cabin. She could go back to eldercare too. Gerontological nursing was challenging, but also meaningful, and she loved being a part of her patients' lives. Her visits were a guaranteed happy moment in their days.

If Jeremy were still alive, she had no doubt she'd still be doing that work. It had just been too hard to face more death after losing him. It had been self-preservation that had led her to the leave of absence and accidentally falling into making hand-painted note cards and selling them online.

Everything happens for a reason.

It was so clear she had no idea how she hadn't thought of it before.

"Oh my gosh. I think I know what I'm going to do."

Unsure if the butterflies in her stomach were dancing in excitement for the new direction or fleeing for freedom, she vowed to move forward and never look back.

Jeremy's hunting cabin was paid for, and it was hers now. Taxes and insurance would be due in December, but they weren't much. There was absolutely no reason she couldn't live there. It was modestly furnished, but that was fine. It was more than she had now, and no one would ever take *this* from her.

Natalie packed and put her suitcases in her car, then went back inside and made a cup of chamomile to wait on Sheila to tell her the news.

Sheila strolled through the front door like clockwork with a "Yoo-hoo, it's me!" at 5:25.

"In here," Natalie called from the sunroom. "Want a cup of tea?"

"Tea? Make mine wine."

Natalie had already poured a glass of wine for her. She wanted one herself, but she never drove after even one drink, which was why she was drinking tea.

She met Sheila in the hallway with the wine.

"Thank you." Sheila slipped her hand beneath the goblet in one swift move, then plopped down in the chair, lifting her feet onto the ottoman. "How was your day?" She took a long sip.

"The best one in a long time."

Sheila sat up—her feet on the floor now. "You went to see the detective today, right? Did they finally make some progress? I hope it's good news."

"It is, but nothing to do with my case or my stuff. I think those hopes are drying up."

"Oh." She settled back in the chair and took another sip. "It's rotten that it happens so often, and these same men just keep getting away with it."

"I agree, but I'm taking control of my situation. I'm done focusing on what I lost." Maybe moving out of town would help her get closer to the day she'd be strong enough to take that stand and go public.

"About time. Not judging." She lifted the glass in the air. "Just saying."

"I also came to a realization today." Natalie's mouth was suddenly dry. It had seemed like a perfect plan while she was stocking up on snacks to take, but now as she began to spell it out a wave of nerves came over her.

No turning back. I promised myself.

Natalie flexed her fingers and forged ahead. "I still own Jeremy's cabin in the mountains. I'm going to move up there for a while. Kind of get a fresh start."

Sheila sat there staring at her for a long moment.

"You remember it, don't you?"

She blinked and set down her wineglass. "Yeah, absolutely.

I remember now that you mention it. You went fishing there. Rustic man cave and all that. But I don't want you to leave. You know you're welcome here."

"I know, but I also know I need to move forward, and staying with you is enabling me to live on the hopes that they'll find all my stuff when I should be working toward tomorrow."

"I think . . ." Sheila cocked her head. "I understand. I do."

"I've been in neutral, waiting for something to roll back time and undo this mess I got myself into. I want to get moving. Get my feet back under me. Restore my confidence."

"I get it."

"But?"

"It's in the woods. And winter is coming."

"So?"

"You are not that kind of girl." Sheila laughed.

"What kind of girl?"

"You know, rugged. Going without a manicure. Building a fire. I don't know. What mountain skills do you have?"

"None, how many do I need?"

"I have no idea. I'm not that kind of girl either."

They both laughed, and Natalie was glad the conversation was getting more lighthearted. "I'll be fine. It has electricity. It's not like I'll be sleeping in a tent."

"I'll miss you. I like you being here. I'm not ready for you to leave."

"I know, but we're going to turn into the Golden Girls before we know it. We both need to move on."

"What's so wrong with that? You do pour a nice glass of wine. Didn't they always eat cheesecake? I do love a good cheesecake."

"Yeah. Me too. I promise to have a wine rack well stocked at the new place just for you."

"Are you sure you'll be okay up there?"

"No," Natalie said. "But I'm sure I want to try."

"When was the last time you were there?"

"Five, maybe six years ago."

"Maybe we should take a road trip and check it out before you go moving out."

"I can make it work. I know I can."

"Well, you know what? I'm not going to argue this. I like that the fiery friend I've known and loved for so many years showed up today. There's nothing you can't do if you put your mind to it." She snapped her fingers in the air and let out a hearty laugh. "One little mouse and I'd be back in the city. I wouldn't do it, but I know you can."

"Thank you for believing in me, and thank you for being there for me through all of this. You are the best friend in the world."

"You were a saint helping keep me coolheaded through the whole separation and divorce from Dan. Why is it so easy for us to place blame where it belongs when a man cheats, but when he milks you for all you've got . . . you think it's all your fault?"

"I don't know. I guess I'd like to believe I was smarter than that."

"You can't out-con a con, Nat. He probably loved that you were a challenge for him."

"Well, I doubt we'll ever get the chance to know that, from what Randy said today."

"The handsome detective." Sheila sat back in her chair. "He likes you, ya know. He's a good guy."

"Maybe in another place and time, but it's just business."

"Doesn't have to be."

"We're not having this conversation." Natalie thought of his dinner invitation. She'd keep that to herself, or else Sheila would have her in a little black dress and out the door on a date. "Besides, I'm heading up to the cabin tonight."

"Already? Tonight? It'll be dark by the time you get there, and I haven't had a minute to get used to the idea."

That was the point, but Natalie didn't say that out loud. "I'll be a phone call away."

"If you even have service."

"I'll check in when I get there, even if I have to go back down the mountain to get a connection. Deal?"

"I have a feeling you've already packed. Am I right?"

"You are."

Sheila got up and hugged Natalie. "Deal. Don't you go silent on me. You need to call and check in every day for a while. Not just for you, but for me too."

"I wrote the address down on your calendar. I'm here for you, Sheila, no matter where I put my pillow."

"That goes both ways."

"We're both going to be okay."

"You don't have to convince me of that. I'm proud of you, Natalie. You have more guts than I do."

We'll see. Almost giddy with excitement, Natalie got up. Sheila slugged back the rest of her wine, and then the two of them walked out to the car.

Natalie got in, and parade-waved as she backed out of the driveway. "To new beginnings," she yelled out the window.

Chapter Eight

RANDY SHUFFLED through the case files. His caseload was impossible to keep up to date during regular hours, so he spent many nights like this trying to catch up on the paperwork.

The phone on his desk rang, interrupting him for the fourth time tonight. *Seriously?* Sometimes he wished he could take it off the hook so he could catch up. He glanced at the paperwork stacked on the corner of his desk with a sigh.

He pressed the speakerphone button and begrudgingly answered, "Detective Fellowes."

There was an awkward beat of silence, then a tentative, "Hello, Detective." Another momentary pause was chased away by a giggle. "Um, sorry, I expected to get your voice mail tonight."

He'd recognized her voice immediately.

"It's Natalie Maynard," she said.

That antagonistic mood evaporated. A smile spread across his face. "Hey there." He laid his pen down and picked up the phone. "It's good to hear from you. How are you?"

"Doing good. Thank you. I was calling for . . . well, I was hoping you could do me a favor?"

"If you're going to ask for a favor, you could at least call me Randy." He heard her sigh across the line. Not like he hadn't asked her to do that a hundred times since he was put on her case.

"Fine. You're right. Hi, Randy." Her response held a playful lilt.

"Better." He sat back in his chair and spun to the left. *Call it a victory lap.* "Thank you. Tell me you changed your mind about dinner, and you'll make my night."

This time, the nervous giggle came across the line more clearly, giving him an inkling of hope.

"No," she said. "First, I want to thank you. I took your advice. I'm moving out of Sheila's house and going to refocus my energy on something positive."

"That's great. Good for you."

"You're to thank. My husband had a hunting cabin up in the Blue Ridge Mountains. It's paid for, furnished, and just sitting there."

He straightened in his chair. "Wait? You're moving?" He hadn't meant for that to happen.

"Not too far away. Fulton County."

"Just like that? Wow. You're moving fast."

"No time like the present. In fact, I'm on my way there now."

One man's hunting cabin could be another woman's palace, possibly. Or not. Maybe it wasn't as small and primitive as what was in his mind right now, but deer heads on the wall and a woodstove for heat didn't seem her style. Not that she appeared high maintenance, just girly in a way that was hard to imagine in flannel, handling mousetraps.

He knew it was none of his business, but he had to ask. "Are you going alone?"

"Yep. Just me. I'm going to take some time and get back up on my feet, and start looking for another job in nursing."

"You sounded like you really loved that career."

"I did."

That jerk who conned her had tested her confidence. A little alone time would probably do her good, but a hunting cabin just seemed like a weird route to get there. He wanted to talk her out of going, but that was self-serving. "The mountains. That's a big change from Richmond." And a huge difference from the neighborhood she was living in when she got robbed.

"It's been a while since I've been up there. It's rustic, but the mountains were peaceful. Caught my first fish right there at that cabin. I'm excited about it."

"At the risk of crossing a line, I have to say I'm going to miss you dropping in. Can I call?"

"Yeah. That would be nice."

She hadn't even hesitated. He liked the sound of that. He wouldn't be the first detective to fall for a damsel in distress— was that what this was? She'd gotten past the worst of it now, but she'd be hard-pressed to trust anyone again.

Until these last few months when he'd taken on her case, he'd been perfectly content being married to his job. Only Natalie's impromptu visits to check on her case had started an onslaught of daydreams of what-might-have-beens with someone in his life. Someone like her.

Randy grabbed a pen and pulled his notebook in front of him. "What's the new address?"

Natalie rattled it off for him.

"How far away is it?" He was already googling it, though.

"Only a couple of hours away if you go the speed limit."

"Which you will, right?"

"Always do," she said. "Although I'm going to admit I feel fast in this Mustang."

"I saw you leaving in a sixty-six Fastback. Nice ride. Yours?" She could've borrowed it. He hadn't been able to track down the ones Marc had stolen along with everything else.

"It was Jeremy's. It's been in storage."

Made sense. "You'll stay in touch?"

"Count on it," she said. "Although I'm really going to try to put this behind me, so you're not going to hear from me nearly as often. I'm sorry I've been so insistent. Probably a royal pain in your you-know-what."

"You weren't a bother at all." He missed her visits already. "It just takes one person to get people talking. When you're ready—"

"I know."

He could hear her shifting the phone, rustling.

"And Randy. Thank you for being so kind. If my judgment means anything anymore, I believe you're one of the good ones."

"I'll take that." He liked the way she said his name. "Wait. You said you were calling for a favor. What's the favor?"

"To still keep me in the loop. Maybe wish me luck?"

"I will, and I do, but I don't want this to be goodbye."

"Me either."

Her words had him nodding. "Then it won't be. I'll talk to you soon."

"Definitely."

He hung up and stared at the address on the pad in front of him, then checked the area for crime and sex offenders. Nothing much of anything. She'd be safe.

A few more key clicks, and he had the plat pulled up. Eighty acres up a pretty steep incline on a mountain called No Business that was pretty much otherwise owned by an LLC.

There were a couple of homes at the mountain base, although they were spread out. *Should have asked Natalie if she knows how to shoot a gun. Isolated like that, she needs protection from bears, if not from people.* He was tempted to call her back but held off.

He'd give it a week. Maybe she'd go up and realize that wasn't the best place to start over. What strength she'd suddenly mustered didn't need to be rattled.

He finished entering updates on his new cases, then updated her contact information in her file.

Turned out to be a good night after all.

He grabbed his coat and headed for the gym.

If there was one thing he found comfort in, it was routine. Every morning started with push-ups, sit-ups, and prayers, all before even a sip of water. Then coffee, and off to work. He wrapped up each day with an intense weight workout, and then home to do a few case reviews before the next day. Unless it was softball season. Then he could be found out on the field two nights a week with the guys.

He stayed busy, and he liked it that way. Living alone was easier. No one to answer to, no one to mess things up or to pick up after, and he'd never liked anyone picking up after him. He could pick up his own towels and socks, and wash them too.

Using the key fob to enter the twenty-four-hour gym, he went to his locker and changed out of his suit. With a towel over his shoulder, he walked over to the treadmill, knocked out five miles to warm up, and then went straight to the weight bench.

Caldwell wasn't there tonight. Married just over a year now, his workouts had slumped the week after his honeymoon and became more infrequent.

They'd been best friends since the academy, but like with most guys, once he got married, the fun and games came pretty much to a halt.

Caldwell worked vice. How he had time to find a wife like Tess was still a mystery, and they seemed happy. Randy didn't mind being treated to a home-cooked meal over at their place now and again.

Tess treated Randy like a brother and mercilessly teased him that he was so set in his ways he'd never get married. She seemed worried about that, but he couldn't care less. Watching Mom and Dad make each other miserable had convinced him that it wasn't in his DNA to be married. Their marriage had been more like a cutthroat political debate that never ended. *No thank you.* Besides, he loved his job, and the long hours and unpredictable schedule would drive any woman nuts. Even the independent types.

Probably just as well Natalie is leaving town. She needs a new life, not just some fun nights out on the town, and that's all I have to offer.

He pumped out two more sets of twelve, placing the heavy dumbbells back on the rack with a clank and a huff. Out of breath, he swept the back of his hand across his sweaty brow.

So then why am I thinking about her?

Chapter Nine

NATALIE FOLLOWED the GPS on her phone to Chestnut Ridge. Jeremy's '66 Mustang was adorable, but it lacked the frills most people considered standard in a car these days. Like navigation, power windows, and locks.

When Jeremy was alive, he treated this car as great as he treated her, and that was saying something. Jeremy had always been a caring and supportive husband, and he'd always done the driving. It wasn't unusual for him to walk in the door shaking his keys, which meant they were about to drop everything and go for a ride in the Mustang. With nowhere in mind, they'd head out, stopping at hole-in-the-wall diners, and see what they'd stumble upon around the next turn. Some of their best meals had been happy accidents.

The throaty motor revved like a race car through the hills, although she was careful to go the speed limit. Unfortunately, the AM radio signal was so weak it couldn't drown out the engine noise.

The main thing she remembered about the cabin was how much Jeremy loved it there. The cabin wasn't big, but it had the basic necessities. Although they'd cooked over a campfire so maybe it didn't have a kitchen. She couldn't be sure.

Didn't much matter. If not, she'd get a microwave. Problem averted.

The sun dipped lower in the sky as she drove.

Autumn nudged the sun into its holding spot for the next season. The shorter days made her long for summer again already.

She hadn't considered the timing of this trip—with autumn's days so much shorter, she should've waited until morning. Driving the mountain roads at night could be tricky.

Too late to turn back now; she'd find a place to stay in town rather than chance getting lost trying to find the cabin in the dark. Then get an early start and check out the cabin tomorrow. That would have to be soon enough.

When you don't have a thing, anything is better than nothing. I can make the cabin do for a little while. This doesn't have to be forever.

But it could be.

Worst-case scenario, termites had made the place dinner, or it had been blown to smithereens by a tornado. But with eighty acres, she could build something new. A tiny house, maybe. They were becoming more and more popular.

Or I could take the easy route and pull a camper on-site until I decide what to do. She had options. It was a better starting point than a lot of folks got.

Traffic was heavy, but her motivational chat with herself had lasted long enough to get her out of the city limits.

Finally, traffic thinned and they were moving at a good clip, but she doubted she'd reach town before dark now.

Finally, a green sign with "Chestnut Ridge 30 miles ahead" came into view. She gave a victory shout. "Won't be long now."

The speed limit dropped down to just thirty miles per hour, and every yellow sign she encountered had a different squiggle and speed warning. The closer she got, the more her gut twisted and turned like the mountain roads.

The poor little Mustang chugged up the steep inclines with everything she had.

She patted the dash. *Come on, girl.*

The road curved so sharply to the left Natalie held her breath as she gripped the steering wheel to stay on her side of the road.

Maybe it was to her advantage that it was dark, because she had a feeling the edge of that pavement fell straight off down the mountain to nowhere.

Driving these roads was going to take some getting used to.

Finally, her headlights reflected off a large sign between tall white poles. "Welcome to Fulton County" in bold, straight letters between the outline of green mountains and blue sky.

She let out a breath. *I made it.*

The speed limit dropped to twenty-five in town.

She took a sip from her water bottle to settle her nerves.

She and Jeremy had never discussed his will, just that he had one. His lawyer was from here, and he'd talked her through it step by step. She'd been surprised at how much detail had gone into it, especially regarding the property and the cabin. He'd made detailed provisions for the cabin to be maintained by someone local. She hadn't even had to worry about it.

She couldn't remember the caretaker's name, and since all of her papers were gone she figured she'd just have to drop in on the lawyer and ask a few questions. How many lawyers could there possibly be in a town this size?

Certainly someone in Chestnut Ridge would be able to help her connect those dots.

At the next turn onto Main Street, it was a welcome sight to see streetlights.

Two blocks of brick buildings, all in varying styles of architecture, held a variety of merchants. She pulled into a parking spot in front of the Trout & Snout Restaurant to get her phone out and look for a hotel nearby.

Only two places popped up on the search. One was back about twenty miles. The other was just up the road.

She clicked on the link to the Mountain Creek Inn website. The beautiful white Colonial Revival–style home with colorful baskets of flowers on a Southern wraparound porch looked like more than she could've dreamed of. There was no online reservation system, but it did show pictures of the rooms they rented, and they boasted the best tea around. The tagline read *Fulton County's Best-Kept Secret.*

How did one prove they were the best-kept secret without giving the secret away? Sounded a bit of an overpromise to her, but the Mountain Creek Inn seemed to be her best bet. Hopefully they'd have a room available.

She pulled back onto Main Street and drove slowly down the block, looking for the address. From the numbers, it should be on the right-hand side.

On a well-lit lot, a huge magnolia tree graced the front yard, and there it was. It looked just like the picture. Single-bulb candlelight glowed from every window sill of the large house like she'd only ever seen at Christmastime in Colonial Williamsburg.

From the driveway she could see that mums in autumnal

oranges and golds had replaced the pastel colors in the hanging baskets from the picture. A row of carved pumpkins lined the walkway to the porch. Not silly jack-o'-lanterns, but fancy designs of swirling paisley patterns glowing brightly. She'd seen similar projects on Pinterest and had thought to try making one herself. She'd never found the time, though.

I'll have time now.

Although she had every intention of going back to work, and continuing painting her note cards on the side, she planned to maintain good life balance this go-round. Something she hadn't been so good at in the past, but this was a fresh start. Yes, a fancy pumpkin was definitely in her future.

She pulled her keys from the ignition.

There wasn't a sign, which certainly lent credence to this place being a best-kept secret, but with nothing indicating they still rented rooms, her heart sank.

That was the problem with the internet. Sometimes things were way out of date, and there was no way of knowing it until you showed up to find out in real time.

Suddenly tired and second-guessing her hasty plan, as she got out of the car she whispered a little prayer that they'd have a vacancy.

Halfway up the walk, she turned and pressed the lock button. *Can't be too careful.* It would probably be a while before she could trust folks again after Marc's betrayal. *I'll work on that.*

A bird chirped from a tree nearby, and something, hopefully a little bunny rabbit, skittered into the pine straw just to her left.

She followed the walkway to the porch and reached for the

doorbell. Before she could press it, something flew around her head and then dipped down toward her shoulder. With a squeal, she stepped back, almost off the porch, before she realized it was simply a moth. She leaped toward the front door, away from the light where that moth still darted around like a drunken bat.

Natalie rang the bell, keeping one eye on the moth.

She waited and then knocked.

Just as Natalie was about to give up, a petite woman with a meticulously coiffed silver bun peered out from the window next to the door. She knitted her brows together before sharing a big toothy grin and opening the door.

The woman pushed her glasses up on her nose. "Well, hello there. I thought I heard something. What can I do for you?"

"Hi. My name is Natalie. I own some property up on the mountain. I hadn't planned to arrive so late, and with it getting dark already, I was hoping I could rent a room for the night. Maybe a couple of nights, depending on . . ." *Why am I telling her all of this?* "I saw on the internet that you rent rooms."

"Oh?" Her lips pulled tight, almost disappearing.

"It was my husband's getaway," Natalie added. "I haven't been there in years."

The woman looked confused.

Had she not heard her? Natalie spoke slower and a little louder. "My late husband. He passed away a couple of years ago. He used to come up here all the time."

"I'm so sorry, dear." She pressed her wrinkled hand to her heart. "So young. I just lost my husband four years ago. Still miss him every day."

"I'm sorry for your loss too." Natalie regretted being in this situation. When had she become so careless with the details? "Do you have any vacancy?"

"Oh, that." She let out a heavy sigh. "My granddaughter lived with me for a while. Wanted to turn this old house into a bed-and-breakfast until she realized that was a lot of work, and she'd have to clean the house and cook breakfast. Kids these days. They don't have the work ethic we did in my time."

"You're not the only one saying that these days. I'm sorry to have bothered you. Do you know of anywhere nearby that I might be able to rent a room?"

The old woman sighed. "No. There's no hotel for miles, and honestly, the closest ones aren't too nice. You'd probably have to go clear back to Roanoke to find something decent."

"I'm not that particular, as long as it's safe." Roanoke was a much longer ride than she wanted to make on roads she'd never driven. "I'm sorry to have disturbed your evening. Thank you." Natalie turned to leave.

"Where is this place you're going?" She stepped halfway out of the doorway, propping her hip on the doorjamb. "If you don't mind me askin'."

"My cabin?" She stopped and turned. "On No Business Mountain."

The woman stepped onto her porch, letting the screen door close behind her. "There's not much up on that mountain but trees and the old fire tower."

"My husband used to hunt there. The cabin was in his family since before he was born."

She eyed Natalie as if she didn't believe her, then raised an arthritic finger. "Are you Jeremy Maynard's widow?"

Natalie took a step back. "Yes. How did you know?"

"I know everything and everyone in this town. Jeremy's passing hit this town hard. So young. I'm so sorry for your loss, dear."

"Thank you."

"We had dinner at the church in his honor. His momma passed on years ago, his dad . . . well, he was just a mess. Not a good bone in that man's body, but Jeremy was a good boy. I'm truly sorry for your loss."

It struck Natalie as odd for this woman to say such personal things about Jeremy, not knowing her from Adam's house cat. "I'm thinking of moving into the cabin. Sort of a fresh start."

"Aren't you adventurous?"

"I'm not sure. I guess I'll know tomorrow when I go see it. I'll be honest, I don't remember too many details about the place."

"It's too late for you to go up the mountain to the cabin tonight. There's a road but no streetlights." She shook her head. "It's not paved either."

"It was a last-minute decision. I'll call and see if I can get a reservation in Roanoke. Maybe I'll grab a bite to eat before I go."

"That's a long ride. How far did you drive?"

"Couple of hours."

"Well, Natalie, you must be famished. The Trout and Snout is right up the block, and it has great food. Tonight's special is their fried pork tenderloin. It's my favorite. Good ol' comfort food."

"Comfort food sounds perfect right now," Natalie said.

The woman stepped toward her. "I'm Orene. I've lived here

all my life. I was born up in that front bedroom." She pointed to the upstairs, and sort of gave Natalie the once-over. "You seem like a nice young lady. My husband would've liked you at first sight. He had such a good sense of people."

"Thank you. It's nice to meet you." Natalie took the first step down from the porch. "Thank you for the information." She walked toward her car, wishing she'd made a better plan. This was not how she wanted to start the most significant change in her life.

Disappointment hung on her like a weight, making her tired. Hopefully, a good dinner would perk her up enough to drive to Roanoke to find a room.

Chapter Ten

NATALIE COULDN'T believe she'd put herself in this position. She'd call the hotel as soon as she got to the restaurant. If she couldn't get a room and had to sleep in the car, it was her own fault. Hopefully it wouldn't get too cold tonight.

"Natalie, wait a minute," Orene called out from the porch. "Hang on there."

She stopped and saw Orene waving her hands in the air. "I mean, it's not like I could take your money, but dear, I have plenty of bedrooms. I can give you some clean sheets to put on the bed. Why don't you settle in here for the night? Or two, if that's what it takes. We can play it by ear."

"Really?" Gratitude flooded over Natalie. "I'd be so thankful. I can pay you."

"You'll do no such thing. You have roots in this town, even if it is by marriage." Orene pursed her lips. "That still counts. It's the neighborly thing to do."

Natalie swallowed back thankful tears. "I appreciate this so much. I'll clean up after myself, I promise. Thank you."

"Get your things, and I'll show you to your room."

Natalie didn't waste a second, jogging the rest of the way to the car to get her overnighter.

Orene stood at the steps. "You can walk down to the Trout and Snout from here. You probably passed it on your way in. No sense in driving, plus a nice walk is good for the digestion, you know?"

Natalie hitched the bag on her shoulder as she joined Orene on the porch. "I appreciate your hospitality."

"It's my pleasure, dear. Sometimes things just happen the way they're supposed to."

And sometimes they don't.

Orene opened the front door and held it for Natalie. "Come on in, dear."

Natalie stepped inside. Years had worn the century-old front door smooth above the old metal hardware. She pushed the heavy door closed behind her, taking in the beautiful old home. The ornate millwork adorning the high ceilings was like nothing she'd ever seen.

"It's good to finally meet you, Natalie. We all wondered why Jeremy didn't bring you around."

It had never crossed her mind that people here might know who she was. He never spoke of anyone except his hunting buddies, but even that was just in passing.

"Hunting was really Jeremy's only hobby," Natalie said. "It wasn't the kind of thing we'd do together. It didn't seem right for me to tag along."

"Very wise of you," Orene said. "Women know the value of good friends. A lot of men never experience that. Come on in."

The original hardwood floors told of years of faithful service to the people who lived here and probably lots of friends and family over the years.

"Your home is beautiful." Natalie admired the chandelier

74

that hung in the foyer. It illuminated the front hall and a grand staircase. She could imagine a bride dressed all in white descending the staircase on her wedding day.

"All original, I bet." Natalie felt her cheeks redden as she realized she'd spoke the words out loud. "This house is absolutely gorgeous. I adore old architecture."

"It's home." Orene sniffed and wiggled her glasses back up on her nose. "And yours for a day or two as well."

"Lovely."

Orene pressed her hand against the thick banister and climbed the stairs to the second floor. The stairs creaked and groaned beneath them.

At the top, Orene opened the double doors on an armoire that nearly reached the ceiling. Solid wood, it had to have been a bear to get up those stairs. The ornate woodwork around the mirrored door reflected the light from chandelier.

Orene retrieved a neat square of white sheets and handed them to Natalie. "There are fresh towels in the bathroom. Use whatever you like. I'm not one of those 'hang 'em because they are pretty but don't use them' types. I've always thought towels just got better with use. A little washing never hurt one that I ever heard."

"Excellent point."

Orene walked to the end of the hall, and opened a door that faced the front of the house. "I think you'll be very comfortable in here."

The four-poster bed was so tall there was a step next to it. Natalie wondered if she got points for sticking the landing on the dismount. It was an unusual-style bed. Very simple, yet elegant.

"Orene, it's beautiful. I feel like a princess. Are you sure I can't pay you something for my stay?"

"I wouldn't hear of it."

"Will you at least join me for dinner?"

"I ate hours ago." Orene tossed her head back, peering through her bifocals, then with a tsk, said, "Yes. I think I'd enjoy that. I'll join you."

"Wonderful." Natalie dropped her overnight bag in the rocking chair next to the door. "I'm starving. You've got me salivating over that fried pork loin already."

"I'll just make a quick call so they can be preparing it as we walk down. They like it when I do that."

"Well, then, by all means."

They went back downstairs, and Orene used the phone on the wall in the kitchen to call the restaurant. Natalie couldn't quite make out the conversation, but the little lady came out grinning. "You're in for a treat. He's putting aside two dishes of fresh cobbler for us too. He makes the best. Follow me."

They walked out of the house and down the street like a little parade of two.

Natalie paced herself to Orene, who took two and a half baby steps for every one of hers, leaving Natalie wrestling with a crude cha-cha trying to keep from rushing her. Having worked with geriatric patients for years, she used to be pretty good at it. As she took another half step to slow down, it bothered her that she was out of practice.

She hadn't thought about that job in a long time. Sometimes it was hard watching someone's body wear down while their mind was sharp, but she loved working with her patients to navigate the complications of growing old. She never tired of hearing their stories and found it interesting the memories that lasted the longest.

A whiff of something savory hung in the air outside the restaurant, making her stomach rumble.

She grabbed the Trout & Snout door handle and let Orene lead the way inside. They were met with a wave of hearty hellos as they made a beeline for what was clearly her regular table.

"Hey there, Miss Orene. I'm guessing you already called your order in ahead?" The smooth accent was way more Southern than anything Natalie had heard in Virginia before, but it was nice. Almost like a song the way each word stretched out, and despite the fact the place was packed, the waitress was cool as a cucumber. Not in a hurry at all.

"Of course, darlin'. You know me." She patted the girl's arm. "Amanda, honey, this here will be a new neighbor of ours. First time I've ever set eyes on her, but she's practically family already. This is Natalie."

Natalie hitched a breath. Apparently, the old wives' tale about everyone in a small town knowing everybody was accurate. *I prayed for a fresh start. Here we go.*

"Well, hello there, and welcome to Chestnut Ridge." Amanda's smile brightened as she lowered her order pad to her apron with the Trout & Snout logo embroidered across the front. "Always nice to make a new friend. You're going to love this town."

"Oh, she's been here before, only a time or two. Amanda, Natalie here was married to Jeremy."

"Jer—" Amanda's mouth dropped wide. "You're . . ." Speechless, she stood still as if her battery had just died, then grinned and clapped her hands together. "My goodness. It is nice to finally meet you." She slid into the seat across from her, scooching Orene over with a nudge. "Welcome. This is the best place on earth. We loved Jeremy. Everyone misses him so much. I'm sure you do too."

"Every day," Natalie said. "Nice to meet you." No wonder Jeremy loved coming here to escape. It was like a warm hug, which was what she needed right now.

"Jeremy's wife? I can't believe it," Amanda said. "I'm so glad to finally meet you. This is just great. Dessert is on me tonight, ladies." Amanda got up and snagged a tea pitcher, topping off glasses at every table as she headed to the kitchen.

The words "Jeremy's wife" played on a loop in her brain. Not widow. Wife.

"Wow, she is a bundle of energy," Natalie stated, realizing that may have come out wrong. "And very nice."

"Yes, she is. An extraordinary gal, that one." Orene smiled and waved to someone else across the room. "That guy over there, he runs the gas station and garage down on Mills Street. He took it over from his daddy about ten years ago. A little bit of a blessing, really. His daddy didn't know a thing about these new cars with all the computers and stuff. Like that Mustang of yours, take him an old classic—he could take it down to the lug nuts and rebuild it like nobody's business."

"Good to know."

"The woman in the red shirt over there. That's the new pastor's wife, Janet. Don't know her too well yet. If you ask me, she's a little shy for a pastor's wife. I'm sure she'll warm up. Pastor John tells it like it is. Even makes you a little uncomfortable sometimes, as if he knows your secrets. I like that about him. You should come to church with me sometime." Orene turned her attention back to Natalie. "You go to church, right?"

"I used to." It wasn't that they'd intentionally stopped, it just sort of got easy to skip service with everything going on, and then it just didn't hit the radar. "Haven't been in a while."

"Perfect timing then. I can introduce you to everyone."

"I'm getting a little overwhelmed."

That cracked Orene up. "Oh, honey. We ain't even got started."

At that moment, Amanda slid their dinners onto the table. "Eat up. I'll be back with dessert, so save you a spot."

"We don't have to tell her that we already had dessert arranged." Orene reached across the table and took Natalie's hand in hers. "Lord, thank you for this food, that it may strengthen and prepare us to do your work. Thank you for bringing this lovely woman to Chestnut Ridge. We are so happy to welcome her as a loved neighbor. Amen."

"Amen," Natalie said through misty eyes. She pushed her fork into the tender meat. Didn't even need a knife. Orene hadn't oversold it at all. Comfort food, richly laden in butter, ham fat in the veggies, and more carbs than she'd eaten all last year in this one meal.

"I heard we had a special guest tonight." A man wearing a Kelly-green polo shirt stopped and stood at the head of their table.

Natalie looked up from her plate. He had to be over six-foot-five the way he towered above them.

Orene jumped right in. "Yes, we most certainly do. Isn't this great? Natalie Maynard, this is the owner of this fine establishment. Folks 'round here call him Stretch. You can see why." She raised her arm in Vanna White style to his graying hair.

"And you too can call me Stretch. Nice to meet you, Natalie."

"Thank you."

"You're in good hands here with Orene, but if you need any connections or information, you can always give me a call. Happy to help in any way."

"Thank you. I'll take you up on that."

"So, where are you going to be staying? Up at Rock Castle?" He looked toward Orene with a raised brow, then back to Natalie.

"I don't know anything about a castle. Orene said there weren't any hotels nearby," Natalie said.

"Oh, there aren't. None I'd recommend, anyway. No, it's just a big old castle of a house that sits on top of the mountain. No one I know has ever been inside it. Little girls in this town have princess dreams about it their whole lives." He shrugged. "I was just joking around."

"Oh. I'm staying with Orene tonight."

"Of course you are."

"Just until I can drive over to the cabin tomorrow," Natalie explained. "I need to see what I need to do there. I haven't been there in a long time. I'm anxious to see what shape it's in."

"The cabin over on No Business Mountain?"

"Yes. That's the one."

His eyebrows darted up. "It should be in fine shape. As far as hunting cabins go, it's one of the finest. You're planning to live out there all alone? It's kind of separated from everything."

That made Natalie a little nervous. "I don't mind a little

quiet. It's not that far from here, is it? I thought it was just a few miles."

"Yeah, no, it's not that far as the crow flies, but it's unpaved. A good rock bed in most areas, but not all. With winter coming, that could be a little bit of a problem, but not if you stock up, I guess." Stretch laughed. "You'll figure it all out, but if you don't, you can call me. I'll help you find what you need."

"You've got a deal."

"Enjoy the rest of your meal," he said, then walked over to the next table and started talking to them.

The clanging pots, the hum of conversation, and the whir of the heat closed in on her a bit. It was like she'd been swept off into a dreamworld.

Amanda brought out dessert. "Told y'all to leave some room. Hope you listened."

"You know I'm going to take at least half of mine home," Orene said.

"Yes, ma'am." Amanda laid two little containers on the table. "I know you like the back of my hand. Plus, who has room after fried pork tenderloin night? Brought you both a box." She gave them a wink and spun around to tend to someone else.

"That woman is singlehandedly handling this crowd. And with a smile, no less." Natalie nodded with appreciation. They were probably about the same age.

Orene agreed. "Oh yeah. She works circles around others. Always has."

They both took a few bites of the still-warm cobbler, then packaged the rest. "We'll have it for breakfast with our coffee," Orene announced. "The best thing about getting old is eating dessert for breakfast."

"Count me in on that."

Stretch wouldn't let them pay on the way out.

"I wanted to treat you to dinner to thank you for your kindness," Natalie said as they walked out of the restaurant.

Orene threw her hand in the air. "It'll all work out. A thank-you goes a long way around here."

"Thank you." They walked in silence back to Orene's house.

When they got back to the house, Orene said, "I don't know about you, but I'm ready for bed. You can make yourself at home. TV is in the living room over there."

"I'm ready for some rest too. Thank you for such a warm welcome tonight. I feel like it's proof that I'm doing the right thing."

"Of course you are. Trust the journey, dear." She lifted her chin toward the heavens. "He'll steer you in the right direction. All you gotta do is give him space to talk to you."

Natalie wasn't sure if it was a God reference or if Orene was referring to Jeremy, but either way was okay by her. "Good night. I'll see you in the morning for coffee and cobbler."

Orene went around the corner, and Natalie climbed the stairs to her room on the second floor. She'd eaten way too much tonight. She made up the four-poster queen-sized bed with sheets so soft she couldn't wait to climb in. She changed into her pajamas and then crawled up on the mattress with her belly full and hope in her heart.

She pulled the vintage bedspread draped over the footboard up over her. It was like the one her grandmother had on her bed, white with the little nubs and fringe at the bottom.

She stretched out, grateful for the way things had turned out tonight.

She wished she'd called Sheila earlier. She had a feeling sound carried in this house, and she didn't want to disturb Orene. She texted Sheila to let her know that she'd arrived and was safe and sound in a beautiful room on Main Street.

> SHEILA: Thank goodness. Was getting ready to send out a search party.
>
> NATALIE: I'll call tomorrow. Promise.

She texted Sheila a picture of the beautiful room.

Thankful for the safe place to lay her head tonight, Orene's open invitation had diluted the worry Natalie felt earlier.

She closed her eyes with a smile in her heart and a tear on her cheek.

For there is a right time and way for everything.

Chapter Eleven

NATALIE ROLLED over and gave a long stretch as she inhaled the smoky aroma of coffee.

Mmm. Those cup-at-a-time coffee makers don't fill the air like that.

Sunshine streamed into the room. Shadows from the huge tree outside her window danced across the walls. The rhythmic image reminded her of a couple waltzing in fancy attire.

I haven't slept like that in a long, long while.

She reached for her phone on the nightstand to check the time. It was still early. Taking joy in the shadowy image dancing on the wall in the rays of light, she lay there for a long moment before climbing out of bed.

She'd forgotten how high the bed was and almost slipped to the floor, catching herself mid-fall.

She changed clothes and headed downstairs.

By daylight, the house was even more opulent.

Natalie ran her fingers along the banister, stopping at a niche on the landing she hadn't noticed last night.

An oil painting in vivid autumn hues hung slightly crooked, just a smidge to the left.

She straightened it, sweeping the dust from the frame as she did so.

A brass plate below the picture read *Fairy Stone State Park 1936*. Propped in an easel like a best-selling novel, a shadow box with a yellowed, handwritten note from 1917 highlighted the fluid script of a time when people took pride in their penmanship. Faded, but still legible, was a thank-you note, and if she didn't know better, it looked like it was signed by Woodrow Wilson. A small cross-shaped rock had been matted below the letter.

Natalie wondered about the connection between those things as she followed the caffeinated aroma to the kitchen.

"Good morning," Natalie said softly, trying not to startle Orene, who was sipping a cup of coffee at the table.

"Hello, dear. You're an early bird." Her expression brightened. "I wondered. I've always been an early riser myself. Coffee is on. Make yourself at home."

"Thank you." Natalie poured herself a cup and added a splash of cream from a tiny pitcher that matched the cups. The china was so fancy she felt the need to lift her pinkie as she took her first sip. She was going to need at least five of these tiny cups of coffee.

"Sleep well last night?" Orene asked.

"I did." She carried her cup to the table and sat. "The best night's rest I've had in months."

"I'm not surprised." Orene put down her cup. "This house is known for restful stays."

"I noticed the note next to the picture when I was coming down. That was from someone who had stayed here? It looked like it was from 1917."

"Yes. We've had lots of important guests stay over the years. That letter was from Woodrow Wilson. He stayed here many times. Before, during, and after his presidency. As did others."

"He stayed here? In this very house?"

"Oh yes. In the same room that you slept in, to be exact. At one time, this house was known for its hospitality to many influential people. My family had connections to the best pre-Prohibition apple brandy around. Word travels fast about things like that." She giggled, quite pleased with the story. "A coveted secret that wasn't really all that secret when you think about how many people happened through this little town. We've been known to enjoy a nip or two. Just for good health, mind you." Orene's laugh was as playful as wind chimes. "The biggest apple tree in the nation was right here in Fulton County. It might still hold the record."

"You don't say." Sounded like another one of those exaggerated bragging rights no one could ever confirm, but who was she to judge?

"I do," Orene said. "It's documented, though."

Was Orene a mind reader on top of it all? "So, people came for the apples?"

"Some." Orene's lips pursed. "Others for the apple brandy. I'd say more came for the fairy stones."

"Fairy stones?"

"Darlin', did your husband not tell you anything about this town?"

"It wasn't something we talked about much, except when he was headed here for a hunting trip with friends. Our home wasn't here, so it didn't come up much."

"Well, it's part of the heritage in these parts. I guess you spent most of your time with your family and relatives."

"No." She shook her head. "I don't have any family."

"None? Surely you have some family. Aunts? Uncles? A couple cousins?"

"No one."

"Not even a brother or sister?"

"I was an only child. I guess having no family is what brought Jeremy and me together. Something in common."

Orene's brow quirked, and she didn't say a word for an awkwardly long moment.

Don't feel sorry for me. People did when they heard. The thought made her miss her parents, and Jeremy too. There's no promise of the time you think you have with someone, but she'd never imagined that she'd be living without Jeremy, especially so suddenly.

She missed him more than ever at that moment. Chasing the blues before they settled in, she asked, "So, what's a fairy stone?"

"High up on the mountain where Fairy Stone State Park is now, but for many years before too, there'd been stories told of the miracle of the precious fairy stones. They are only found in a few spots in the world. It's a natural occurrence that is very rare. Legends tell of fairies weeping when they heard of the crucifixion of Jesus, and their tears crystallized into tiny cross-shaped stones."

"Like the one below the letter in that shadow box?"

She nodded. "Shaped like crosses, they are said to bring good luck and fortune. You can best believe guys like Woodrow Wilson, Theodore Roosevelt, and even Henry Ford carried them as good-luck pieces."

"I was born and raised in Virginia, and I've never heard of them."

"It's well known to the locals, and now you know too."

"There's so much to learn and see."

"Oh yes. People think living in a small town can be boring. You could spend a lifetime learning about this county's people, places, and history."

"Meeting you has been a good start." Natalie knew she should head on over to the cabin, but it was nice chatting with Orene about the town that would be her new home.

"I took the liberty of heating up our breakfast." Orene pushed back from the table. As soon as she opened the oven door, the sweet scent of cinnamon poured through the kitchen.

Natalie took in a breath. "It smells so good, but I think I'm still full from dinner last night."

Orene smirked. "Looks like you could use a few good meals. You're too skinny." She grabbed a potholder and lifted two white ramekins out of the oven and carried them straight to the table. "Careful. That dish is hot."

This woman had known her less than twenty-four hours and she was already mothering her. It was kind of nice.

"Smells heavenly." Natalie closed her eyes for a moment and took in another breath. "Okay. I'm hungry again."

"Thought you might say that. Let's say a blessing right quick." She took Natalie's hand into her own and started. "Lord, thank you for this beautiful day. For bringing Natalie here to us and helping her find her way to what she's looking for. Bless this food, our town, our nation, and our president, and nourish us to help do good work in your name. Amen." Orene lifted her head and nodded.

"Amen." Natalie waited for Orene's lead to pick up her fork.

"Don't wait for me. I want to grab something to show you."

Orene left the room but returned before Natalie got the first steaming bite of cobbler to her lips.

"I did this cross-stitch when I was a young girl. Far from perfect, but my mother treasured it. I must've poked my fingers a hundred times working on it."

"Oh gosh. Let me see." Natalie took the frame and read the poem.

May the charms of the Fairy Stone make you blessed,
Through the days of labor and nights of rest.
Where ever you stay, where ever you go,
May the beautiful Flowers of the Good Fairies grow.

"That's sweet. Did you write the poem?" Natalie loaded her fork with the sweet, gooey concoction. She could get used to this kind of breakfast.

"Oh, no. I'm no poet. I was never gifted in that way. Not cross-stitch either. This is the one and only piece of needlework I ever did. Not my cup of tea."

"I was never good at that kind of stuff either," Natalie admitted.

"Oh, I don't mind sitting still. Needlework just wasn't my thing, as much as Mother loved it. I had other interests."

"Like what?"

"I collected teacups. Anything to do with tea. I used to dream of turning this place into a tearoom. Tea really is my cup of tea." She laughed at her own joke, which made Natalie laugh too.

"And yet here we sit drinking coffee," Natalie teased.

"Tea isn't for everyone, and I wanted you to get your day off to a good start."

"That was so thoughtful of you. The coffee is perfect, but for the record, I'm always up for a good cup of tea."

"I'm looking forward to that. I hope we have many to-gether." Orene topped off her coffee and sat down again. "You don't have to be in a hurry to rush off. That cabin has been there since the late 1800s. It's not going anywhere."

Chapter Twelve

NATALIE FELT bad for being so anxious to get out of there to see the cabin. Orene had a point. What *was* her hurry? "I'm excited to see the cabin. I barely remember what it looked like."

"Doubt it's changed, except for some dust."

"Jeremy was so relaxed here. Did I tell you he taught me how to fish there? I'll admit I wasn't all that excited about it, but it was nice with him." Her voice caught. "Everything was good with him."

"Sounds like you remember the most important parts, dear."

"Yes. You're right." Positive thinking and determination drove her this morning. "We were all each other had; I mean aside from friends."

"What happened to your folks?"

"I lost them when I was in my second year of nursing school." It was still hard to talk about. Maybe because she never did. Jeremy was the same way. "I almost dropped out of school when they died, but they had been thrilled when I was accepted into the program. I forced myself to finish for them."

"You're a nurse." Orene clearly approved.

"I am. Licensed with a specialty in geriatric care."

"That must be very rewarding."

"It was. I took some time off after Jeremy died."

Orene's eyes flashed understanding. "I'm sure that can be difficult. Don't you become attached to your patients after spending so much time with them?"

Natalie struggled to swallow past the lump in her throat. "It's very hard when they leave us, but it's so rewarding knowing that I was helping make every day count."

"I have a strong feeling you've been a blessing to many people."

"Thank you. I like to think so." She blinked, hoping the tears wouldn't fall. "And I'm blessed to have bumped into you," she added, trying to lift the mood.

"God has a way of bringing the right people together." Orene gave a quick nod and a wink. "I believe that." She reached over and touched Natalie's arm. "Will you be looking for work here in Fulton County?"

"Yes. I plan to go back into nursing. Hopefully there's a need for my skills here, but I could do lots of other things. I'm flexible."

"I know someone who could use that kind of help. I don't know what it pays, but I can connect you if you like."

"That would be great." She hadn't expected to start looking so soon, but you couldn't turn down a good lead when it fell into your lap.

"I'll write down the contact information for you. I know you're in a rush to get going, but before you do, would you like to see my collection of teacups?"

How could she say no after Orene had been so kind? "Sure. I have time for that."

Orene was already on her feet. "Bring your coffee with you." Orene carried hers too, darting through the door off the back of the kitchen, through the butler's pantry, to a formal dining room. One entire wall was a built-in with glass shelves floor to ceiling of teacups, tea sets, and pretty little teaspoons displayed like jewelry.

"You weren't kidding." Natalie turned slowly, trying to take it all in. "I can't imagine having to dust all of this."

"Ha! Me either." Orene walked over and tugged open one of the long doors. "My sweet husband made this cabinet for me. He and a friend picked out and chopped down the trees, milled and cut the boards, and planed every one of them. People just don't do that kind of thing anymore."

"Wow. From a tree to this?"

"Sure did. Everything except the glass. He had to hire that out with a guy in Norfolk who was the nephew of his momma's sister's cousin. Each piece of glass was cut perfectly to size and trimmed inside and out. No way any dust is getting into this thing. It's about airtight, I think. Even the silver doesn't seem to tarnish like it should."

"That's true love."

"Every woman deserves that kind of love." Orene stepped back, looking at the cabinet and shaking her head.

"You miss him," Natalie said.

She nodded. "Every single day."

"But you've got this to remember him by."

"And so many other things. I miss him so much, but knowing what I know about heaven . . . I'm okay with it."

Natalie wished she felt that same comfort.

"Sometimes I'm almost a little jealous he got to go first,"

Orene went on, "but then I still have stuff to do, I suppose. He's in the most beautiful place there is. Which is really saying something when you live in a place as magnificent as Chestnut Ridge." She touched Natalie's arm. "You know about missing that kind of love. I know you do."

"I do." She nodded. "I haven't gotten to the peace where you are on it yet, though."

"You'll get there." Orene clicked her fingers. "Ah. You might be interested in this." She hooked her finger as she darted toward the stairs.

Natalie followed, feeling a bit like a duckling ambling behind the mama duck. "You were asking about the letter on the landing. This," she said, taking a book from a shelf, "was the registry people would sign upon visiting. Not really sure why. I don't think it was an official record for bookkeeping or anything. I think it was more tradition at some point. Or maybe just bragging rights." She flipped open the book to the first page. In bold letters the year "1886" was written. "Look how many people visited."

"No wonder your granddaughter wanted to reopen this as an inn. It must've been quite successful."

"Our family lived a very comfortable life sharing house and home with others." She lifted her chin. "My granddaughter's motivation was far less genuine. I think she thought she'd just pop up a website and let me run everything while she raked in the dough."

"Oh, I'm not—"

"Oh, yes, that's exactly what it was. I know it, and you can believe it or not, but don't just say it to be polite." She flipped through the book, to a date in 1967. "Look at this."

Natalie leaned in closer to read the entry. "Harrison Maynard?" Her mouth dropped open.

"That was Jeremy's daddy. He stayed here for a full week before he and Jeremy's mother got married. Back then there was no shacking up. A couple didn't live together until that ring was on the finger. Her father would've shot Harrison Maynard before he'd let him break that rule. Harrison stayed here until their wedding night."

"That's so romantic." She pressed her hand to her heart.

"Well, truth be told, her father would've done anything to stop that wedding. He never did approve of that relationship. We all thought he was being overprotective at the time, but his misgivings about that man being a lousy excuse for a human proved to be spot-on. Anyway, there's lots of history here."

"Yes. There certainly seems to be." In less than twenty-four hours Natalie felt like she knew more about this town than she did the one she'd grown up in. "I'm so glad I came here. It's so interesting. The town. The history. Chestnut Ridge is a really special place."

"Honey, we ain't even begun to crack the chestnut on this place. I can't wait to share more with you, but I know you're anxious to move along and see what you've got ahead of you."

"I am. I'm dying to know what shape the cabin is in."

"You'll get it all worked out. But please, don't go being too proud to ask for help, and if that place isn't as cozy as where you slept last night, you bring your fanny right back here to sleep tonight. Deal?"

"Yes, ma'am. Thank you. I'm just going to get my stuff."

"Run along."

Natalie went upstairs to get her things. She stripped the bed so she could bring the sheets down with her to put in the wash as she'd promised. This had been a wonderful way to start her transition. She felt a bit like a butterfly coming out of her cocoon for a fresh look at the world.

Before heading downstairs, she dialed Sheila. No sense taking the chance there'd be no service at the cabin.

Sheila answered on the first ring. "I've been waiting for your call. Tell me everything."

Natalie filled her in on the ride up, the curvy mountain roads, and the inn. "It is the most amazing house. I can't wait for you to meet Orene. She's so sweet. You won't believe her teapot collection. I've never seen so many. It's like the teapot museum or something."

"You've only been there a few hours. How on earth did y'all get that much talking in?"

"I have no idea."

"Well, I'm glad things are off to a good start. Good luck with that cabin. I feel better knowing you've got Orene's place to crash."

"I'm not going to do anything impulsive. If it's not habitable, I'll admit I was wrong."

"No you won't."

"Why would you say that? I always admit when I'm wrong."

"True, but you are absolutely hell-bent on making this work. I know you. When you get your mind set on something you're like a pit bull. You won't let go."

Natalie laughed. "Okay, guilty, but I will not live in my car. I can promise you that, and I *will* call and keep you posted."

"My door is still open too," Sheila said. "I already miss you."

"Thank you for being the best friend. I'll keep you posted. Don't worry." She hung up the phone with a heart full of gratitude. She was lucky to have such a good friend, and she had a feeling Orene would become one too. With her overnight bag on her shoulder she carried the sheets downstairs.

"Orene?" She looked around the corner. Orene was back in the kitchen, fixing another cup of coffee. "There you are. Where's the washer? I want to get these started for you."

"Well, I guess you're feeling pretty optimistic you won't need to stay tonight. The laundry room is right through that door."

"Nothing wrong with a little wishful thinking," Natalie said with a laugh as she walked out of the room. Not surprising, Orene had a blue tin of laundry powder with little teacups painted on it, and a washer that still had the hand-turn dial on it. *Do they even make these anymore?*

Water filled the tub and the sheets were already swishing when she went back to say goodbye to Orene.

"All set," Natalie said. "I promise I'll stop back by later to let you know how it went."

"I'd like that, and I'm serious, if it's not lady-ready over there, you bring yourself right back here. For as long as you need. You've been a delight."

"Thank you." She started for the door, then stopped. "You wouldn't happen to know the best way to Grand Creek Road from here? My GPS only showed a route to the edge of Mountain View, then woods."

"That's pretty much where it is." Orene pressed her lips together. "You should go by the fire station first. Go back past the restaurant then up three blocks, turn left at the light blue truck filled with pumpkins, and then it's one block up on the right. Red metal building. Brand new. Can't miss it."

"Pass the restaurant, left at the pumpkins, then on the right."

"Exactly. Get Tucker to take you to the cabin. He's been taking care of things there. He can get you up there and show you the ins and outs of the place. Tucker's a good guy. He'll get you situated."

"That's very helpful. I wasn't quite sure what I'd be walking into, but I'm feeling a little less concerned knowing how helpful everyone is around here."

"You'll be fine. This town is filled with them."

"I guess I shouldn't have expected anything less. Jeremy was good people."

Orene nodded. "Folks are going to be happy you came here."

"I can't thank you enough for letting me stay last night. Are you sure I can't pay you?"

"No, ma'am. It was enough that we shared a meal last night, and I truly enjoyed your company."

"Can I bring you anything when I come back?"

"Not a thing."

Natalie took the last sip of her coffee and carried it to the sink. "Well, I'm going to see if I can hunt down Tucker."

"Have a wonderful day exploring, dear. I think you're going to find Chestnut Ridge a wonderful place to settle. We could use some new faces around here."

Chapter Thirteen

NATALIE WALKED outside to fresh cool air, and sunshine that warmed her cheeks. Energized by the colorful foliage and high hopes, she headed to her car.

Driving the Mustang down Main Street, she wondered what it must've been like for Jeremy when he was young. They'd been so happy living in the present, never bringing up the past or looking too far ahead, and she'd never regretted that until now. Now, she wished she knew everything about every second of his life.

Chestnut Ridge was welcoming by the light of day. The buildings were old, but cared for, by the looks of the colorful paint and bright awnings.

Wooden benches lined the street in front of almost every business. Each one was painted in a different way, some of them almost like miniature murals. The one in front of the hardware store had been painted like an American flag waving in a breeze. In front of the ice-cream shop the bench had been painted in the colors of Neapolitan ice cream—pink, chocolate brown, and a creamy vanilla.

She followed the directions Orene had given her to the fire station.

When she pulled in front of the bright red metal building, two guys sitting in lawn chairs sat watching two others roll up huge hoses from the fire truck. It didn't look like light work.

She parked and walked over. "Good morning," she called out with a wave. "I'm looking for Tucker."

The guys in the lawn chairs nudged each other, then one hollered back, "Is he expecting you?"

Despite their childish yukkity-yuks Natalie approached with a polite smile. "Could you please get him for me?"

The guy didn't budge; instead, he stuck his fingers between his teeth and let out a whistle, then yelled. "Tucker!"

A tall, lanky, dark-haired man wearing a T-shirt with the fire department logo marched out and pulled his hands to his hips. "Why can't you walk inside to get someone like the rest of us? That's just plain rude."

The man looked about her age, but he hadn't noticed her yet.

"You got company, man." The whistler nodded in her direction.

"Hi." Natalie walked over and extended her hand, pleased to see he didn't look any more impressed with those goobers than she was. "I'm Natalie Maynard."

"Oh?" His brows pulled together for a hesitant moment, but then his eyes widened. "Hey! Jeremy's wife. Wow. It's good to see you. I can't believe you're here." He pulled her into a hug. "Welcome to Chestnut Ridge."

She felt like a rag doll in his arms and, for some reason, she did a dorky half curtsy as she stepped back, freeing herself from the bear hug. "Thank you."

"This is great. Come with me." He pressed his hand to her shoulder. "Let's go talk where these clowns can't eavesdrop."

She followed Tucker inside. His office was all the way in the back of the fire station past the fire trucks, small but orderly.

He sat down behind the desk, and she took the seat across from him.

On the wall there were scores of pictures of him hunting, and fishing with friends. Her breath caught at Jeremy's smile. He was younger, probably a teen in the picture, but there was no mistaking his grin. Tucker was on the other side of a trophy so big it took the two of them to hold it up. She quickly averted her eyes, hoping to keep her emotions in check.

"I should've called before I came up here, but it was kind of a last-minute decision. It's a long story that ends with me staying with Orene last night."

"You know Orene?"

"I do now. Happened to see an old ad on the internet and stopped to rent a room."

He laughed. "Yeah. That worked out, though. Orene loves company."

"It was really nice. She said you could show me the best way to get to the cabin." Natalie slid the index card with the cabin address on it over toward him.

"Yeah. I'm your guy." He picked up the card and laughed, handing it back. "You can keep this. I know where it is. One of the roads is pretty bad, but I've kept the other one clear. It's on a good rock bed too. What are you driving?"

"A Mustang."

"Not Jeremy's sixty-six Fastback?"

"That's the one."

"Nope. I can't let you drive that up that road. Jeremy would haunt me sure as I'm sitting here if anything happened to that car on my watch."

"You and me both," she said with a laugh.

"He did love that car."

"I know. That's all I can think of when I'm driving it. Another long story."

His lips pulled into a thin line. "I'll drive."

"Do you really think it wouldn't be good for the car? Or are you kidding?"

"When it's dry, it's not a problem, but the least bit of bad weather and you'll want to have four-wheel drive. You could get a four-wheeler to leave at the road, but that would be a miserable ride to the house. Out of respect to Jeremy, because he loved that car as much as he loved you, I recommend you find a place to park it, and use it as a Sunday driver."

"I wasn't planning on having to buy a truck." That would make things tight, and there was no way she could sell this car.

"You don't seem the truck type. Now, Jeremy. He was the truck type. What happened to his truck? Or is that part of the long story too?"

"Yeah, it is."

"Jeremy and I grew up together. We were like brothers. Did you know that?"

"It's really good to get to know you."

"I never thought he'd leave Chestnut Ridge, but one day he just up and left. He'd never talk about it. Thank goodness for the occasional hunting weekends, but you know there weren't that many of those."

"And now he's gone," she said quietly.

"Yeah. Still can't believe that either." There was a long silence until he cleared his throat and changed the subject. "You came up here with him a few times. I remember."

"That was before I realized the cabin was the unofficial man cave. I thought it was best to let him enjoy that. He always worked so hard. He loved coming up here."

"He missed you when he did. Talked about you nonstop. I feel like I know you, even though we only met that once."

She didn't remember meeting him before.

"Are you thinking to sell the place?"

"No. Actually, I thought I might stay up here."

"By yourself?"

"Yeah. Why? Do you think that's not a good idea?"

He eyed her. "I don't know. It's just kind of rugged terrain out there. A little bit of a hike from where you can park—" He got up and walked around the desk. "Doesn't matter what I think. I don't even know you. It is one of the most beautiful places on this mountain, though, and we've done a lot with the place since the last time you were up here. Come on. I'll take you up there."

"Thanks." She followed his long strides out to a fire-engine-red Ford F450 pickup. He opened the passenger door for her and shut it once she was buckled in.

It was a nice truck. The whole King Ranch package and all. It smelled of new leather still. The truck was as neat and orderly as his office. A phone cord lay coiled next to the cupholder, and there wasn't a single thing on the floorboard or littering the seats.

He hopped in, and they sped off down the road. "Your GPS would probably take you this way and tell you to turn here." He pulled off the side of the pavement where a dirt road trailed off to the right. "Don't follow that. You *can* get there from here, but a few places flood, and it can get a little iffy. I'll show you how I go."

Back on the pavement, he drove about another four miles. The road twisted and curved as they climbed the mountain.

She tried to memorize landmarks to help her retrace this route later.

Gravel crunched under the giant tires as they turned right off the state road.

Dust lifted around them, rocks popping against the wheel wells.

She could see why it wasn't a great idea to drive the Mustang down here. The trees became more dense on this side of the mountain, shading the way, with magnificent oranges, reds, and golds peppering the landscape between the evergreen pines, but it wasn't a smooth ride even in this big truck.

He patted the steering wheel while he talked. "This road isn't nearly as steep as the other way. We're climbing the mountain now, but we'll cut back across. There's a right-of-way on this side of the property now too. Jeremy had given me a power of attorney to take care of any cabin-related things while he was getting plumbing installed years back. Legal stuff with the city and all that. I requested the access after . . . you know. I hope you don't mind."

"Of course not."

"It was finally granted by the landowners after about a

six-month full-on press. People in this town spoke their minds and forced them into giving in after the news of his death. I doubt they'd have ever agreed to it for any other reason."

"I knew about the power of attorney from my discussion with the lawyer."

"Don't worry. I'd never take advantage of it. We were buddies. Although we didn't see each other often, when we did, it was like we hadn't been apart a single day." He looked over. "We really were the best kind of family."

"I get it." *When you don't have family, found family and friends are that much more precious.*

"Okay, we're going to take this turn right here. You can use that water tower as a landmark." The white tower rose from the middle of nowhere. A mountain scene that had probably been beautiful at one time was painted on the old tower, but now the colors had begun to fade. "I could help you post some little signs along the way to help you navigate this, maybe even some with reflectors if that would help."

He turned on a dirt lane that wasn't much more than two rock paths enough for the tires to track.

"How much farther?" Nothing around here looked familiar, and for a fleeting moment she prayed she hadn't just done something stupid, trusting this guy she'd never met.

"Almost there." He drove just another minute and then stopped in front of a long wooden bridge, not quite wide enough for the truck. "This is it."

"I don't remember there being a bridge."

"It wasn't here the last time you came with Jeremy. The guys from the hunt club helped Jeremy work on it a few years before he died." He opened his door and climbed out of the truck.

"It was spring, and man, the biting flies were torture. Funny, I don't ever remember them being a problem since."

She got out of the truck and followed Tucker to the bridge. It looked sturdy enough. The silvered wooden boards didn't have big enough spaces to see between them, and she was thankful for that, because she wasn't one for heights.

He strode forward.

She slowed, peering over the edge. It wasn't too far down, but still, she hoped the bridge didn't wobble when she walked on it. The water rippled in the stream below.

The bridge itself was about five feet wide. She centered herself, preparing for the first step.

He turned back. "It's safe. We drive four-wheelers over it all the time." He jumped, landing with a thud. "See?"

"If it's sturdy, why didn't y'all make it big enough for the truck?"

"Well, if we made it for vehicles we had to go through a lot of red tape. By keeping it to UTVs we could do what we wanted. But it would've held a truck. I can promise you that."

It would be an adjustment, and a pain in bad weather, but it wasn't the end of the world. She took another step out onto the bridge. It didn't even wobble.

Satisfied, she held her hand just above the wooden handrail so as not to get a splinter but to have something to grab on to if she needed to hang on for dear life, because it was still high enough to make her nervous.

It only took her a moment to get comfortable and jog forward to catch up to Tucker.

"Not so bad, right?"

"No. Actually, the bridge is sturdy as can be. That railing sure helps." She turned around. "It's even prettier here than I remembered."

"Spring is beautiful too. The rhododendron and wild azaleas practically take over in some places. I've always loved fall the best, though. The trees shed lots of their leaves, and you can see things you didn't see all spring and summer."

And he wasn't kidding. The land opened up on the other side of the bridge to a view that was like a painting. "It's beautiful. How could I have forgotten this?"

"You were probably preoccupied with other things. Y'all were still dating back then."

"True." It had been romantic stealing away to the mountains with Jeremy. Like living in a storybook.

"It was definitely love, because this cabin was kind of a dive the first time he brought you here. It's why he was determined to fix it up. He loved you so much. I'd never known him to be so happy."

"I felt the same way. It was the real deal." Her heart pounded just thinking of him. She'd never lost that feeling. It lived in her heart with every beat. "We loved each other . . . so much."

"Sorry for your loss. Not sure if I said that. Everyone in this town hurt when we got the news."

She didn't really want to get into all that with him. "I'm kind of backward, so where did the old road come in?"

"You would have come in over there." He pointed across the way.

Just beyond a big stand of trees, the edge of a structure rose above the wildflowers.

"Don't tell me that's the cabin." The words hung in her throat. The vast timbers were impressive, but it looked more like a picnic shelter at a park. *No walls?*

"Ha. No. The cabin is over this way. You would have come in on the backside of that building."

She breathed a sigh of relief.

They walked down a wide path to another clearing where a red pole gate hung from an old tree. A locked padlock dangled from a chain that Tucker simply lifted over the pole. "It's just for looks. Keeps people from nosing around, but no one ever comes up here." He opened the gate, and she walked through.

A lock she had a key to would be the first thing on her list.

Her hopes lifted when she saw the cabin ahead. It was much bigger than she remembered, and it was rustic, no question about it, but it had walls and didn't look half bad from here.

Chapter Fourteen

NATALIE STOOD there taking it all in. She was so grateful the cabin was at least a sturdy building with four walls.

"Are you okay?" Tucker asked.

She swept her hair behind her ear. "Yes. I . . . I'd forgotten what it looked like."

"Disappointed?"

"No. Quite the opposite. It's charming. Rustic, but really inviting. Did the deck always come out that far?"

"No. That's where the firepit used to be."

"Right. We roasted marshmallows." She laughed, remembering how few they ate. "Mostly, we had a marshmallow fight, but a couple ended up on long sticks over the fire that night."

"When we widened the path the way we came in, we repurposed the bigger trees into lumber. One of our buddies has a sawmill. We used the rough-cut wood for the bridge and the deck. All of the stumps are in a circle around the back for seating. That's where the firepit is now."

"Neat."

"Folks 'round here don't much like letting things go to waste. The guys have shared a lot of stories around that firepit."

Natalie felt a bit like an intruder, but she needed this place.

She lifted her feet above the tall grass, praying there weren't any snakes. The live-edge boards on the cabin ran horizontally on the side of the house, stacked one atop the other like you'd expect on a log cabin. Over the front porch, the boards ran vertically to the tall peak, adding some interest. On each end of the porch, logs as big as a hug supported the porch structure.

"I do remember these big log posts." She walked to the backside of the one at the far-right end of the porch. "It's still there." Her fingers grazed the indentations where Jeremy had carved their initials and "TLA." *True Love Always.*

"Huh. All the time I've spent here, and I never noticed that."

"We had no idea on the day he carved this that forever wouldn't be that long." *You were taken too soon, Jeremy.* "I'd pictured us old and gray, stooped over and slow, rocking in chairs here someday." She chased the chill with her hands along her arms at the thought of being here without him on this perfect blue-sky day.

I miss you still every day, Jeremy.

Tucker stared at the carved initials. His smile spread into a lazy grin. "Jeremy turned into absolute mush after he met you."

"I remember him carving this like it was yesterday."

"The mind's a funny thing. Sometimes you just need a re-minder to open up the old memories. Hope you don't mind we made a few additions to this place over the last couple of years." He pointed to the furniture on the porch and deck. "One of the guys had those chairs and the wooden chaise. When he moved, he didn't have room for them, so they kind of ended up here. Better than the dump, but if you want me to get rid of this stuff, I can do that for ya."

"Mind? No. It makes it look homey. Thank you." *A few*

brightly colored pillows would do wonders. Something off near the trees caught her eye. "Is that your horse trailer?" she asked.

"No. That was Jeremy's."

"He had a horse?"

"He rode when he was a kid. Everyone around here does."

"Hmm." It was strange to hear things about him that she'd never heard him speak of.

She walked over and sat on the edge of the chaise. It faced the sun and had a spectacular view of a mountain. Tall, skinny trees sprouted from the top of the ridge, giving it the appearance of a crew cut. "What mountain is that?"

He sat in the other chair, leaning forward with his elbows on his knees. "That there is Bull Mountain. It's kind of a famous place, actually."

"How so?"

"Well, there's about fifty acres on that mountain where you can find rare fairy stones."

"I thought that was in Fairy Stone Park. Orene was telling me about them this morning."

"Orene knows everything there is to know around here. She's right. The park was built on Bull Mountain."

She got up and walked toward the door of the cabin. "It's safe up here on the mountain, right?"

"Yeah. Absolutely." Then he turned and said, "Do you have a gun?"

"A gun? Heavens, no." Not only didn't she have a gun, she pretty much had nothing after what all Marc had stolen, but that was not a story she intended to share.

"You'll want to get one. Guess I could lend you a shotgun."

"I don't know how to shoot."

"You're telling me Jeremy never taught you how to shoot?"

"He didn't."

"I might need proof you were his wife before I release this place to you."

A jolt ran through her, but he started laughing, and she realized he was joking. "Funny."

"Well, you might need to scare off a bear, or if God forbid some rabid animal happens along, you're going to want to take care of that, pronto. There are coyotes up here. We get a bounty for 'em, so I could set a trap or two if you like."

"Are you trying to scare me?"

"No. Nothing to be scared of, but you want to be smart about living up here. I mean, this is their home too."

"Are there really bears up here?"

"Yeah, a few big ones. They don't much bother anyone, but it's been dry. If we don't get some rain, they might happen down looking for food. Drought messes up their supply of berries, and they got to eat."

Dread coursed through her, making her heart heavy. "I really want to make this work."

"It's doable. You'll be fine here. Since Jeremy and I added the well and bathroom, it's actually posh for a hunting cabin. I'm pretty sure he only did that for you, anyway."

"He never even told me about the improvements."

"Well, technically he hadn't finished them when he died. The guys and I finished the project. I can't leave things half done. It's my flaw."

"Good flaw to have."

"Yeah, that's only because you're not waiting on me to finish a project to start yours."

"True. I can see where that could become a problem."

"It happens. My old girlfriend used to hate that." He walked over and opened the door for her. "Let me show you inside. Wish I'd known you were coming. I'd have opened the place up and turned on the heat and everything."

"Please tell me there's more than a wood fireplace."

"Oh yeah, but the woodstove comes in handy when the electricity goes out, and that does happen. You've got plenty to burn just in the small trees that naturally fall. The electrical panel is all set for the mini-split, but it hasn't been installed. I could help you get that set up. The units are still boxed in the storage shed." He pointed to the smaller wooden building. "You've got plenty of wood stacked up to get you through the winter."

"Looks like a great place for snakes to hang out."

"Better there than over here by the house, don't ya think?"

She hadn't considered that.

He reached up over the porch light and used the key there to open the door. He reached in and turned on the lights. "After you."

She stepped through the doorway, knowing this was a new start.

Inside, the cabin was clean and neat. Devoid of feminine touches, it was still welcoming in its own way.

The black-and-white buffalo-check comforter on the bed was the one she'd ordered for Jeremy the first year they were together. *Was it for Christmas? Maybe his birthday.*

She recognized a few other things too. The wooden gun rack

was hand-carved by an artisan in Gatlinburg. Jeremy had gone on and on about it when they'd seen it while on vacation, but wouldn't buy it because it was so expensive. She'd surprised him with it for Christmas that year. It was so big she had to use two rolls of wrapping paper to cover it and practically a whole roll of tape.

Tucker walked through the cabin, turning on the lights. "Everything is in working order."

"You've really taken care of the place. Thank you."

"Happy to do it. There is more than enough money to ensure everything is kept up in that fund. There's not much to it. Whatever is left over each year, I use to upgrade something. I like piddling around with the place."

She felt a pang of guilt that she'd be taking that from him. "I feel bad. I mean—"

"No. Don't. It's good you're here, and I'm happy to continue helping with whatever you can't do."

She walked into the kitchen. Pots and pans hung from a rack on the wall, probably out of necessity since there weren't many cabinets. An old woodstove with burners on the top was the focal point.

"Do y'all use this?" she asked.

"A couple of times, but honestly, mostly for heat. We did our cooking outside."

She pulled open one of the drawers. "Everything is here."

"Yeah, you could move in today. None of us kept anything personal here except for Jeremy. There are a few of his things in the drawers. I didn't disturb them."

The water ran clear when she twisted the handle.

"Good spring water," he added. "Oh, and there's a ceiling

fan." He walked over and flipped the switch. "Keeps things really comfortable pretty much year-round."

She turned and leaned against the counter. "It's more than I'd hoped for."

"Not much closet space, but this is a great place. I'm sure you could add some nice little touches here and there. One of the guy's wives made a wreath for the door at Christmas last year. We begrudgingly hung it to make her happy, but it did look nice."

There was a fireplace on the other side of the cabin with stuff piled in the old firebox. "Not in working order?"

Tucker shook his head. "No. It's original to the house. There was no sense in risking catching the place on fire when there's the big one in the kitchen. It's sealed up, just decorative."

"Are you in a hurry?" she asked. "I'd like to look around for a bit."

"Not at all. If you're okay here, I'll just take a ride out to check on a few of the traps, then come back and get you."

"That would be great."

He left, and in the cabin alone, the emotion hit her. Tears streamed down her face in the quiet moment, and although they were in part for Jeremy and all they'd shared here, it was also sweet relief.

Thankful tears for a soft place to land after the mess she'd been through. *I'm so grateful for the memories of Jeremy that still live here.*

She wrapped her arms around herself, eyes closed; she slowly turned, then opened her eyes, taking it all in as if it were home.

"Thank you, babe. I can do this. I can live here."

It was so quiet that it was hard to listen. A bird squawked in the distance, reassuring Natalie that life was nearby.

Above the closed-off fireplace, pictures of the guys with trophy deer lined the mantel. Tucked catty-corner behind two others, she found an unframed photograph of her and Jeremy fishing. It had been so windy that she'd pulled her hair up into a messy bun to keep it out of her face.

She carried the picture over to the bed and sat on the edge. Laying the picture on the nightstand, she slid the top drawer open. His Bible. She'd wondered what had happened to it. She lifted it, and a picture fluttered to the floor.

Our wedding picture.

Their love spilled from her heart, memories flooding back. She held the picture in her shaking hand, then tucked it back inside the Bible.

Grief rushed over her, but there was a strange comfort in this moment too. She put the Bible back in the drawer and then caught a glimpse of that stupid bucket hat with the lures stuck in it that he used to call his lucky hat. It was hanging on the coat tree along with a slicker and some waders. They'd probably come in handy. Well, not that hat.

The sound of Tucker's diesel truck approaching was a welcome interruption.

Soon after, he gave a quick double-knock and walked inside. "Hey, it's me."

"Better than Smokey the Bear," she teased.

"They don't knock."

"I'll remember that. I was wondering about all those deer heads on the back wall. Did Jeremy shoot all of those?"

"Not all of them. I shot that one, and this one over here,

well, we shot this monster one day when we were out together. We used to argue about who actually took the kill shot."

"Someone hung another pair of horns on that one," she said with a laugh.

"No, actually, two bucks had fought to the death, and the loser was hung up in his antlers. This big guy had been dragging that buck around, and we'd caught sight of him a few times but could never get a good shot on him. Finally, one early morning, he was down at the stream trying to drink water. A tough thing to do when you have a couple-hundred-pound dead animal hanging off your head and antlers. He was getting tired, and I'm sure that rotting, stinking carcass was weighing on him. He couldn't run faster than our guns that day."

"Oh no. I can't imagine. I had no idea that could even happen. Hunting was a side of Jeremy I never really understood. He was such an animal lover, and so gentle."

"Well, we ate what we killed. It wasn't just for sport. And truth is, if we didn't hunt, this place would be overpopulated with them."

"I've never eaten deer meat. I never let him bring any of it home. I guess that was silly."

"He'd let us have it all. When we have too much, we take it down to the shelter. Lots of hunters donate to feed neighbors. I'll have to fix you some venison sometime, though. You'll be surprised how good it is."

"Is it a requirement for living here?"

"No, but I think you'll be pleasantly surprised, and it is a natural resource."

"I'll have to give it a try. What's right is right," she said.

"Speaking of what's right, I guess I can turn the checkbook

from that fund to take care of this place over to you now if you're going to be living here."

"Or maybe I should let you hang on to it. I might need a little help now and again."

"You don't know how happy it would make me if you'd let me help. I owe that much to Jeremy."

"You don't owe us a thing, but I would appreciate it."

"The guys and I have enjoyed being able to use it, but it's yours."

"I feel a little funny about this. Like I'm taking something from you."

"Don't. We knew it was okay to use, but we also knew it would end one day. We're even. Don't think another thing of it."

She couldn't contain her joy. "I can really live here." Sheila was not going to believe this. She'd have to come up and see for herself. She lifted her phone and took some pictures.

"You can definitely live here," Tucker said. "You should. It's a great town. I'd always hoped you and Jeremy would move back."

"I'm excited." She looked at her watch. "Oh gosh, the time has flown. I didn't mean to keep you away from work for so long. Take me on back. Now that I know the way, I can get here. I'll just drive really slow until I figure out something about the car."

Tucker raised his hand in the air. "You'll figure it out. If rain moves in before you get the car situation taken care of, give me a call. If I'm too busy, one of the guys from the hunt club or the fire station will shoot up here and take you where you need to go. Really, it's no bother."

"That's very generous of you. Thank you." She had no intention of being helpless, no matter how many things she had to look up on the internet to figure things out.

Chapter Fifteen

WHOEVER STARTED that *out of sight, out of mind* rumor had never met someone like Natalie Maynard. Even though Randy hadn't spoken to her since the day she decided to move to the mountains, she was always on his mind.

He'd been hoping for a lead or some reason to call her to see how things were going. It would've been nice if the excuse would've come a couple weeks before Natalie decided to leave town for that little cabin hours away from here, but finally he had some good news and that made him happy just the same.

Maybe she hated it up there in the mountains and had already nixed the plan entirely, to come back to Richmond.

That's a terrible thing to hope for.

He understood her wanting to move on and put this whole thing with Swindell behind her. Living with a friend, even a best friend, would get old after a while.

Natalie had been the bright spot in a lot of his weeks this year, and just knowing she was miles away had played on his mind more than he liked to admit.

Yeah, it sucked to be the one to tell her over and over there wasn't much hope in running down that con man, but knowing he was trying to help her made him feel good, and in this case he was realizing it was more than just doing his job. He liked her, and the last two weeks he'd had to admit that to himself.

If only they'd met under different circumstances . . .

Bad timing. That's my specialty.

He picked up his phone and dialed her number.

It only rang twice before it went to voice mail. Just hearing Natalie's voice made him smile, though.

She'd warned him that she might have spotty connectivity in the mountains. *Guess you're still there.*

The voice mail message ended, and following the beep, he kept it short and all business.

"Natalie, this is Randy, yeah, uh, Detective Fellowes. We've made some progress. It's good news about one of your stolen vehicles. Hopefully this will help us get a little closer to finding Swindell too. Give me a call when you have service." He got ready to hang up, then added, "Hope you're doing okay. Are you still in the mountains? Look forward to talking to you. Bye."

He hung up, wishing he'd stuck to the facts and hung up when he'd meant to.

He tapped his keyboard to bring his computer screen back to life, and typed in the make and model of her other vehicle. If Swindell was in a rush for money, maybe he'd sold the other one too, or even ditched it by now if he caught wind they'd recovered the truck.

Not today.

Turning away from the screen, he flipped through the notes on his desk. They'd gotten lucky recovering this vehicle the way they had. Maybe Marc Swindell was getting sloppy. He'd make another mistake, which was good news for the good guys.

Randy left messages for the contacts they'd gathered from

the car dealership. According to the paperwork left in the glove box, they now had the person who'd traded in the vehicle and information on who'd done repairs on it recently. No one was answering his calls, though. He hated days like this.

He started down the list of calls to make on the new case he'd been given this afternoon. It came with the same results. Nothing.

All due diligence aside, he finished up the paperwork on Natalie's vehicle and went to refill his coffee cup.

It was shift change for most of the guys, so things were quieting down. He went into the break room and lifted the coffeepot. The pungent smell nearly choked him—clearly this pot had too many hours on the burner. When he swirled the liquid, it moved like sludge.

I'll pass on that.

"Fellowes! What are you still doing here?" Kirk was a vice cop. One of the big beefy guys who looked like he could lift criminals by the elbow with one hand.

"Working. Why aren't you?"

"I have a date." Kirk's Hollywood smile shifted into a smirk. "I'm meeting her across the street at the tavern. You need to get a life outside work, man. You know what they say about all work and no play."

"I really don't think anyone says anything about that anymore."

"How would you know? Far as I can see, all you do is work."

"I'm fine with that." All his hard work had earned him a detective position in record time, and Randy was proud of that. He didn't mind working twice as hard to prove himself to the older, seasoned detectives. "I've got things to do."

"Not tonight, you don't. You *are* coming to the softball game, aren't you?" Kirk was the best hitter they had on the department team. Most people called him "Moon" because that's where he hit most of the pitches to on a good day.

Forgot all about it. "Lost track of time." He glanced at his watch. "Don't know if I have time to make it home to get my gear and back out there now."

"We're playing the Twelfth Precinct. Chief will never let you live it down if we lose because you're not there. Speed if you have to. I know a guy who can make the ticket disappear for you."

"Yeah, right." Randy laughed at the joke, but speeding wasn't entirely out of the question. There was a long rivalry between the two departments, and if he didn't play tonight, the chief wouldn't be doing him any favors anytime soon. "I hear ya. I better hustle up."

He shoved his mug in Kirk's chest. "Make yourself useful. Put this in my office. I'll see you on the field."

"That's more like it." Kirk tossed Randy's favorite mug in the air, sending it reeling end over end straight up.

"Don't drop that mug."

Kirk caught it and tossed it again, higher this time.

The guy was too cocky for his own good.

Randy jogged out, hoping his mug would crash against the tile floor. It would serve Kirk right.

He jumped in his truck and took the back way home. The interstate would take twice as long this time of the evening. Any other day he'd have had his ball bag in the truck. Prepared. *I'm always prepared.* But not lately. The only ducks he had in a row these days were the ones that pertained to Natalie's case . . . or Natalie in general.

An hour and twenty minutes later, he was on the ball field in his uniform, warming up.

Kirk was leaning against the fence talking to some blonde. He rarely warmed up with the team. No one counted on him for anything but the home runs anyway, which required no running, just a little shoulder jog around the bases and a few high-fives.

The team came together in the dugout for a resounding promise to quickly take the other team down, ending in a rousing *rah!*

They jogged out to take the field and were able to shut them down—three up and three down. No thanks to any great fielding, just a series of pop flies that just about anyone could have caught, but they'd take it.

Randy led off the batting order with a solid double, and by the time Kirk came up for cleanup, they had the bases loaded.

By their last at-bat, the game was tied, they only needed one run to put this game to rest, and with two outs, it was Randy's turn to bat.

He grabbed his bat, swinging it to exert some of the excess energy on his way to the plate. He kicked the dirt and slid into his stance. His hands gripped and re-gripped the bat. Eyes leveled on the pitcher, who shook off whatever the catcher was signaling. The guy finally got ready to throw the pitch.

Randy let the first one roll on by.

A woman's voice rose from the crowd. "That's it, Randy! Make him pitch to you."

Randy choked back a laugh. *Courtnie.* His sister had come to the game. She was always the biggest voice in the bleachers.

He repositioned his stance. It never paid to swing on the

first pitch, no matter how good it was. He'd learned that early in baseball, and still stuck to it. He shook it off and got ready.

The next pitch was a little on the inside for his liking, but he took the swing anyway.

He didn't even have to look to know that ball was going right over the fence. The sound it made when the ball hit the bat was perfect.

His sister screamed, and he'd know that two-fingered whistle anywhere. "Run!"

Randy dropped the bat and headed for first base in a sprint. His team was cheering. He looked to the outfield, and watched that ball sail like it was driven by hurricane-force winds.

He pumped his fist in the air and rounded the bases, taking care to stomp squarely on each bag. The whole team was at home base when he got there.

Oh yeah, the chief will be a happy camper this week.

After the handshakes, the guys headed out to the parking lot, and Randy went over and hugged his sister. "What are you doing here?"

"Haven't talked to you in a couple weeks, and I was wondering what you were up to."

"You could've texted me for that."

"True." She propped a hand on her hip. "But you're hard to read on the phone."

"Uh-oh. What's going on?"

"I don't know. You tell me."

"Me?" He shrugged. "Nothing going on with me."

"Who was the girl you brought over for coffee?"

He paused, and that was the nanosecond Courtnie needed to go all in. "I knew it. That was not just a casual cup of coffee," she said. "You two looked all interested in each other, with your heads together." She slugged him on the shoulder. "Tell me! Who is she?"

"It's nothing. She doesn't even live here anymore. She moved to the mountains. That was the last time I saw her."

"What mountains?"

"Blue Ridge."

"That's not far."

"If she was interested, she probably wouldn't have moved."

"Did you tell her you were interested?"

"No, but—"

"Well, then don't put it on her. This is on you. As your big sister, I have the right to point that out."

"Which you are enjoying a little too much."

"That is not true, but my kids are grown and out of the house. You haven't even had any yet, and if you don't do it soon, you're going to be too old to be out there playing ball with your son. Just because that last relationship was a bust and sent you into workaholic mode doesn't mean you have to stay there. It's time you shifted your life into high gear."

"If it's meant to be it'll happen, if not—"

"Oh man," Courtnie groaned. "Now you sound like Mom."

"Hey, don't be disrespecting Mom."

"I'm not. She was a great mother, but by the time you came along she was old and tired and leaving everything in the universe's hands."

"Did make it pretty nice for me."

"Yeah, I never got away with anything." Courtnie slugged him in the shoulder. "It's like we had completely different parents."

"Thanks for breaking them in for me."

"That was not my pleasure, I might add. Which, by the way, I heard from Mom last night. She's already planning Thanksgiving and Christmas."

"Of course she is."

"She wants us to host Thanksgiving," Courtnie said. "Would you fry the turkey if I do it at my place?"

"Sure. I can do that. At least dinner will be on time if you host it."

"Right? You'd think as many Thanksgiving dinners as that woman has cooked she'd have it down to a science by now. Hey, maybe this year you can bring your new girlfriend and get some of the focus off of me."

"We're back on that again?"

"Never left it. What's her name, by the way?"

"We're doing this?"

"Yes."

"Natalie. Her name is Natalie."

"And you met this Natalie where?"

"Work."

"Cop or criminal?"

"Real funny. She was conned. Jerk took her for everything she had. Took her on this expensive vacation. He went home early, supposedly a business emergency. When she got home, everything was gone."

"No way."

"True story." It still griped him that something so bad happened to someone so nice.

"You better catch that guy."

"Doing my best."

"To catch the guy or the girl?"

"Both, if I'm lucky, but the timing is off for her. She's still sort of reeling from it all."

"You like her." It wasn't a question, but more like an accusation. Courtnie's eyebrow arched high.

"Fine. I'm interested. Yes." *Can't deny it. She always could read me better than anyone.*

"I can see that."

"She's nice. Different."

"Not just a damsel in distress?"

"She might be that at the moment, but no, she's smart, capable, kind. I don't know. She . . ."

"Makes you want so shift your life into high gear. Right?"

"But the timing is all off," he said. He knew better than to rush a woman, and he didn't want to complicate Natalie's life.

"Doesn't mean you can't still pursue it if you think something of her. You're the most patient guy I know."

"I'll take that as a compliment."

"It's meant to be one. You know me. I'm not patient at all."

"Like Dad."

"Yup. On that note, I gotta go, but are you going to call this Natalie who has you all in a twist?"

"Actually, I left her a message earlier today. I finally made some progress on her case. We recovered one of her vehicles."

"That's great."

"It was legit. Not a move."

"Well, either way, it *is* a move. You should go for it."

He sucked in a breath. "I'm going to go have a beer with the guys."

"All right, well, good luck with Natalie. Be charming."

"I'll try."

"Try harder than that, or you're going to become a work-aholic."

"Too late."

"That's true." She turned and waved.

He picked up his ball bag and walked over to join the guys. He hadn't missed a thing. They were still reliving every play of the game. He dropped his bag to the pavement and grabbed a beer from the cooler.

The stories became more elaborate with each sip.

Kirk was the first to peel off with his backstop babe, and it only took one to go before everyone else started heading home.

Randy gathered his bag and put it in the passenger seat of his truck. He took off his cleats and clapped the red dirt from them before placing them in the floorboard.

The only thing on his mind for the last few hours had been the ball game, and it felt good. He still loved game nights.

When he was a kid, he'd dreamed of being a major league ballplayer, but then didn't they all?

It wasn't in the cards for him. He was good but not excep-tional, and that's what it took to make it.

Randy headed for home, but not without a quick stop to pick up a bucket of fried chicken, as was customary on winning game nights. For the most part, he tried to eat healthily, but fried chicken was his comfort food, even if it wasn't nearly as good as what Momma used to fix. The family deal would feed him the better part of the week.

He was overdue for a Sunday dinner with his parents. He'd call tomorrow and coordinate a date to make that right.

Date. He shook his head. He never had been able to hide any-thing from Courtnie.

He dug his phone out of his ball bag. It had died sometime during the evening, so he plugged it in to let it charge as he drove across town to pick up his dinner.

He ordered a bucket of chicken at the drive-thru, and when he brought it into the car, it smelled so good he couldn't wait to get home to dig in. As he pulled from the window, he took a leg right from the top of the bucket and ate it while he drove. Tossing the bone in the bag, he wiped his greasy fingers on his pant legs best he could, so as not to gum up the leather on his steering wheel.

When he got home, his phone had finally recharged. A series of tones and whistles flooded in all at once.

He'd missed a call from Natalie during the game.

Her ears must've been burning from all that talk with Courtnie.

He played back the message. Her voice carried a bounce that made him happy. She was thrilled with the news and was on her way.

"I'll meet you in your office in the morning," she'd said.

Yes.

It had turned out to be a good day. *Maybe the Blue Ridge Mountains aren't too far away.*

The following morning, he showered, shaved, and took way too long deciding which tie to wear.

He wondered if Natalie would stay in town with her friend for a few days.

Stick to business first. Although Courtnie's prodding hovered in his mind, arguing the contrary.

When he got to his desk, he could hardly concentrate on his email for glancing at the clock and wondering when Natalie would show up.

It was after nine when his desk phone rang.

"Detective Fellowes," he answered.

"Mrs. Maynard is here to see you."

"Send her on back." With a nod of satisfaction, he pushed back from his desk. As he did every time he got a call like that, he stepped out and leaned against his doorjamb.

She walked down the hall, but this time she wasn't wearing the high heels that he'd gotten used to clicking down the hall. He didn't bother to hide his smile. He was glad to see her.

"How are you?" he asked as she got closer.

"I'm doing great after getting that message from you. I can't believe it."

"I told you I wouldn't give up."

"Thank you, De . . . Randy."

"Come on in." He led her into his office rather than the conference room where they usually met. It was small, but he wasn't ashamed of it.

She made a beeline for the pictures on his bookcase. "Is this your family?"

"Mom and Dad. Yep, and that's my brother with the surfer dude's hair. He's kind of a free spirit."

"He looks like you. Sort of. Like a Saturday version of you," she said with a laugh.

"I tell him he looks like the milkman."

"That is so wrong!"

"It's a family joke." He sat down and leaned back in his chair. "Me, Mom, Dad, and that's my older sister, Courtnie . . . we all have brown hair and blue eyes, and then there's Freedom. Black curly hair and brown eyes. Seriously. Where'd that come from?"

"Stop."

"It's probably where I first got my skills to become a detective. I love figuring stuff out, and as a kid, I was convinced he wasn't a Fellowes."

"You're too much."

"I guess I was lucky I was the first boy. I got named after my grampa. Who can blame a guy for being a bit of a hippie when his mom names him Freedom? Then again, the ladies love him. Maybe there's something to the name."

"I think I prefer Randy," she said.

His lips spread into a smile. "I was hoping you'd say that someday." He hoped the inuendo landed a little smoother than it felt coming out, because it sounded like a cornball line from here.

Her smile reached all the way to her eyes, but she didn't remark. Just a polite little nod and a half snicker that, in a stretch, he planned to consider flirty.

Trying to recover from the awkward comment, he blundered on. "So, let me tell you what I've got for you and why you drove hours to see me."

Damn, I'm out of practice. Maybe all work and no play really does hurt a guy. A beautiful woman is sitting in front of me, and I don't even know what to say. Get back to business. You haven't lost that.

"It wasn't but two hours. Not bad at all."

"Right. Good." Randy lifted a folder and pulled the one beneath it to the top. "Now for the good news."

Chapter Sixteen

NATALIE HAD just about let go of any hope that Randy would be able to make progress on her case. Even sitting here in front of him, she couldn't believe it. All the way here she'd been afraid to get her hopes up. "You really found something?"

"Sure did."

She leaned forward, resting her forearms on Randy's desk. "I still can't believe it. Is the car in one piece?"

"Yes. Well, not the car. We recovered the truck." He flipped open the folder and slid it across his desk to her. "I really hope this is just the beginning."

It looked like Jeremy's pickup truck, but without the personalized tag.

"Are we sure it's mine?"

"Yes. VIN matched. We've already checked everything out. It passed through a couple of hands, but this small dealership felt like the too-good-to-be-true price sounded fishy. Rather than shuffle it along and make money on the deal, he checked and found that it had been stolen. We got very lucky. I can't even take the credit for it."

"So it wasn't because of your awesome detective skills?"

"Afraid not. But I've always been kind of lucky."

"And Marc?"

"He's luckier than me, I guess. The kid who tried to sell the truck to the dealership had bought it from someone else, who didn't match Marc Swindell's description, but we're working our way through a list of people to see if we can trace it back to—"

"Marc." She didn't even like to utter his name anymore. The bitterness hung in the back of her throat. "Where did the guy buy the truck?"

"Williamsburg."

"That's not far away." She blinked in realization. "He could still even be here in town, couldn't he?" The thought of him possibly being nearby, or showing up again, made her thankful she'd taken the step to move.

"We don't know if that means he's in Williamsburg. I'm still working through the leads."

"Do we have to go there to get the truck?"

"No. I had it transferred to the impound lot here. I've got the paperwork all filled out. We'll just need a couple signatures from you, and it'll be yours."

An overwhelming feeling swirled around her, and she hoped she wasn't about to break down and cry. *This is good news.* "Thank you. The timing couldn't be better. The roads to the cabin in Chestnut Ridge aren't really fit for a car. There's not a speck of pavement, and it's a long trail back to the cabin from the main road."

"Well, this truck should get you there just fine. You'll need to sign here, here, and there."

She picked up the pen and scribbled her signature.

"So, the cabin? It was everything you remembered?" he asked.

"Better, actually. It's rugged but definitely livable. Everyone I've met so far has been so nice. I think it'll be a good place to live, and I have a lead on a job already."

He shifted his glance to the papers on his desk, or was he avoiding eye contact with her?

She tried to fill the hanging silence. "It's a nice little town."

"So you're going to stay up there?"

"That's the plan." She sucked in a breath. "Can't mooch off my friends forever. It's my first step to moving on." She lifted her chin, hoping she looked more confident than she felt right now.

His lips pressed into a thin line, then he placed both hands on the top of his desk and stood. "Well, then I guess we'd better go get your truck." He gathered the papers and gestured to the door. "After you."

She hopped to her feet and went down the hall, self-conscious of him being behind her. She slowed to force him to walk next to her instead. "I used to bellyache every time my husband made me drive his truck. Now, I'm just thankful to have it."

"A little practice, and you'll be fine," he reassured her. "I can help you practice in a parking lot until you get comfortable."

"I know you're joking, but it's not a bad idea. I might take you up on that."

He slowed, looking down across his shoulder at her. "I wouldn't mind."

"Thanks." They walked out, and Randy held the door on his unmarked navy-blue sedan for her.

She slid into the passenger seat and buckled her seat belt.

When he got behind the wheel, he said, "Impound lot is just on the other side of town. Shouldn't be much traffic this time of day."

Her mind raced as they drove through the city. This seemed above the call of duty, but she really appreciated it. Ubering around town to get this done would've been a pain.

When they finally pulled into the impound lot, there were hundreds of cars lined up behind the tall chain-link fence. "This is not what I expected. It looks like an auction. This many cars get stolen?"

"Not all of these were stolen. Some were impounded for being used in the process of committing crimes, or abandoned, illegally parked, or someone was driving on a suspended license or under the influence."

"Apparently, there's more of that going on in this city than I ever realized."

Randy pulled his car into a spot right by the door, marked for police. An hour later, she had possession of Jeremy's truck again.

When the clerk at the impound lot handed her the papers, she cried, and the tears wouldn't stop.

"I'm so sorry." She swept them from beneath her eyes, black mascara smearing on her fingers. "I don't know why this is hitting me so hard."

"It's okay." Randy led her outside. "Take a breath. Look, you've been through a lot. You're the victim of a crime. You don't have to apologize for experiencing emotion about this. It's justified."

"Thank you." She sniffled, trying to pull herself together. "You've been so nice to me. Patient. Kind. Accommodating. I know I've been a pain in your—"

"No. Really. I've enjoyed your company. I almost hope I never solve the whole case."

She laughed. "Better not let your boss hear that."

"I don't really mean it. I'd love to recover every last thing that man took from you. Nothing would make me happier."

"You're a good cop."

"I try to be, but in this case it's because I'd like to think I helped you. That would make me happy."

"You and me both." She swallowed back the last of the tears. "I'm so thankful you were the one assigned to my case that day. I have a feeling I'd be on the back burner by now for most over-worked detectives. Thank you."

"You're welcome." He spread his feet apart and folded his arms. "So, it's lunchtime."

"We've blown half the day already? Oh my gosh."

"I wouldn't say we blew it. It was a pretty big accomplishment. How about you let me buy you lunch to celebrate?"

"I—"

"Quick celebration, and then I'll give you a lift to the DMV to get tags for the truck."

"Oh, I didn't even think about the missing tags."

"Can't drive it without tags. Not legal. So, lunch?"

Natalie couldn't argue with that. "Something light?"

"Sure. Whatever you want," Randy said.

"Really?"

"Sure."

"You know what I really want?" She knew he would think she was making a cop joke, but she wasn't. She'd seen the "Hot Doughnuts Now" sign when they drove past the Krispy Kreme on the way in.

"No idea."

"A doughnut. And a cup of tea."

"Seriously? Are you trying to be funny? Because, believe me,

I've heard a million doughnut jokes since I took this job." He shook his head, but he was laughing.

She shrugged. "I promise it wasn't a cop joke. Besides, you're a detective. Does the doughnut thing even apply to detectives?"

"Not to this one."

"Well, I can't resist hot Krispy Kreme doughnuts. They are lighter than air when they are hot."

"And more calories than air no matter what." He opened her car door. "Get in the car. I'll get you your Krispy Kreme doughnut, but I get to pick the place for that cup of tea to go along with it. Deal?"

"You're on."

Randy pulled into the Krispy Kreme lot. There were about a half dozen cars already in the drive-thru. "How many should we get?"

"A dozen." She didn't even hesitate.

"You gonna eat half of them?"

"I can." And she didn't even apologize for that. "Oh, don't try to tell me you can't eat six of them."

"I haven't ever tried."

She rolled her eyes. "You won't have to try too hard. They are that good."

"We'll see."

"How far away is the tea shop? We don't want them to cool down before we eat them."

"Boy, you are really serious about this doughnut thing, aren't you?"

"Hey, this is serious business."

He placed his order at the intercom, then pulled up and

took the green-and-white box at the window and handed it off to her.

She held the warm box in her lap, taking a deep breath of the sugary-sweet aroma.

"They do smell good," he admitted.

She nodded. "You're going to thank me for this."

He smiled and stepped on the gas to make the light and get back on the interstate. One exit up, he took a right and pulled to a stop, parallel parking along the curb next to the park.

"Hey! You promised me a cup of tea."

"I don't break my promises." He got out of the car and walked around to the front of the vehicle. "Trust me."

"You know what happened the last time—"

"I'm not Swindell."

She got out of the car, still clinging to the box of doughnuts. "I'm well aware of that."

"Well, then just follow me."

She jogged to catch up with him. "These are cooling down." She tried to quicken her pace, but that wasn't easy while carrying a wobbly cardboard box of hot doughnuts. If he wasn't so handsome, and fun, she'd be ticked off.

All she really wanted right now was a doughnut. Randy was treading on thin ice now that she was hungry and still hadn't had a hot doughnut when she had a dozen of them in biting distance.

She sighed, trying not to be hangry with him.

Chapter Seventeen

RANDY NOTICED the set of Natalie's mouth, and he wasn't entirely sure he wasn't about to get an earful from her.

"Oh!" She cocked her head, laughing. "This must really be your favorite place."

He nodded. "It is."

"You're not going to believe this, but there's a rusty old trailer on my property. Do you think I could paint and repurpose it like she did?"

"You going to open up your own coffee and tea shop?"

"Would you drive up to try it if I did?"

"Don't tempt me with a good time." *Darn right I would.* "No, really, what would you do with it?"

"I might make a little art studio out of it to paint my cards. I could haul it to craft shows. That would be fun. I don't know. Maybe something else. I could sell it to someone else to run a coffee and tea shop like this one."

"My sister owns this one."

"Does your sister want to franchise?"

"She's actually been talking about it," he said. "It was out of necessity that she started Giddy-Up and Go." He nodded toward the counter. "Let's order. I'll let her tell you. It's her story to tell."

"Okay."

They walked up the ramp. "Hey, Courtnie," Randy said, waiting for her to look up.

"Well, hello." She almost choked when she saw who was standing next to him. "This absolutely makes my day."

"I'm sure it does. What kind of tea do you recommend to go with half a box of these?" He pointed to the Krispy Kremes.

"You already ate the other half?" she teased.

"No, but we intend to split them," he explained. "Meet my friend, Natalie."

"We are definitely splitting them," Natalie chimed in. "Can you believe he's torturing me like this? Not even one nibble yet."

"That is just wrong," Courtnie scolded him playfully. "What is wrong with you, man?"

"Hey, I was trying to turn the snack into a nice little meal with some ambiance."

Courtnie laughed. "You've got to give him points for that," she said to Natalie. "Giddy-Up and Go does have a special ambiance all its own."

"That is true. We stopped by when you were over by the police station a couple weeks ago."

"I remember. I'm Courtnie, by the way."

"I love the Giddy-Up and Go concept. This is such an innovative idea. I can see why it's Randy's favorite."

"Did he mention that I also happen to be his sister?"

"He did." Natalie laughed. "Not the first time, but just now."

She leaned forward. "I have all the inside scoop on him if you have any questions."

"I'll keep that in mind," Natalie said. She and Courtnie exchanged a glance.

Randy waffled. "I feel like I might be in trouble with the two of you putting your heads together."

Natalie smiled. "Is your tea as good as your coffee, Courtnie?"

"You will not be disappointed. I can assure you of that." Courtnie didn't seem to mind the challenge. "Why don't the two of you take the table with the blue tablecloth, and I'll work up something perfect to go with hot glazed doughnuts for two."

"We're starting without you," Natalie said, then turned and led the way to the table.

She and Randy sat, and Natalie opened the box, not even offering him a doughnut before taking one and biting into it.

"Okay, Randy. You're officially forgiven. They are still hot, plus I just love this bistro on the go."

"Mmhmm." He lifted a doughnut from the box and then tilted the box back in front of her. "Go ahead. Get another."

She leaned in and took a big bite of his doughnut instead. "Oh my gosh. So good."

He snatched it back and took an even bigger bite of it. "Yeah, you eat your own."

They'd already downed a couple by the time Courtnie made her way to their table carrying a blue tray with matching blue teacups and teapot, cream, sugar, lemon, and honey nestled around a perfect peony in a short flower vase. "Here you go. This is my personal favorite. It's a strong, bold, black Assam tea. It'll balance the sugar rush you're probably experiencing right about now." She poured two cups for them.

"Tell Natalie your story about Giddy-Up and Go and how you started it," he said.

"Sure, I love to tell that story." Courtnie held the empty tray. "I owned a bakery over on Fifth. I was known for wedding cakes, and specialty sweets. I even sold to most of the restaurants in the area."

"I remember that place." Natalie's eyes widened. "It caught on fire."

"It sure did. I lost everything."

Natalie's mouth dropped open. "I'm so sorry. Sounds kind of like my story."

Randy nodded.

Natalie said, "I know how that feels. To have to start from scratch. It looks like you're doing great."

Randy put both hands on the table, tempted to reach for her. "You're going to be fine too. You know that, right?"

"Thank you."

"Courtnie made a new beginning with what she had. This old horse trailer had once belonged to her son. It was sitting in her backyard rusting, and she gave it a whole new life."

"That's exactly how the old horse trailer at my cabin is."

Courtnie laughed. "There are a lot of these old steel ones abandoned for the new lighter-weight aluminum trailers. I called in some favors from old customers, family, and friends to help make this a reality. I love it."

"I think you're on to something big here," Natalie said.

"I'm thinking about franchising," Courtnie said. "I don't want to expand myself, but franchising and getting others to follow my lead would be amazing."

"I agree. It's such an awesome idea. I still can't imagine losing a whole storefront, though."

"This is even better than owning my own bakery because

now I don't work twenty-four/seven. I'm happier, and with this lower overhead I'm making more money with less effort." Courtnie shrugged. "You just never know why things happen, but good things can come from any situation."

Randy looked at Natalie. *Truer words were never spoken.* Had he not been assigned to the case, had Natalie not suffered at the hand of that con man, he might never have met her.

"Thanks for sharing your story."

"You're welcome," Courtnie said. "I've got customers. Let me run."

"Want a doughnut?" Randy asked Courtnie. "You can have one of mine."

"You can't turn that down," Natalie said to her.

"No thanks. I'm a sugar-free girl." Courtnie gave him a look and then turned to Natalie. "He must like you a lot, because he never eats that kind of stuff either."

Randy choked.

"You okay?" Natalie patted him on the back.

"Yeah, fine." Randy shook his head. "Guess none of my secrets are safe with my sister around."

"Got that right," Courtnie shouted as she walked away, clearly listening in.

Randy picked up another doughnut and held it in midair in front of Natalie, trying desperately to ignore his sister. "How about a toast?"

She giggled as she picked up a sticky doughnut and tapped it to his. "Okay, what are we toasting?"

"To sweet justice, new beginnings, and long friendships."

"Wow, that was nice. After all that joking around you've caught me off guard. I was expecting you to say something funny."

"You're welcome." The words came out quiet, but they'd landed quite deftly on her. "Thank *you* very much for being such great company today."

Natalie sipped her tea. "Oh, now that really is perfect." She spun around toward Courtnie, who was watching from the counter, and raised a thumbs-up. "Perfect combination!"

"Great! I hope that means you'll be back."

"As often as I can," Natalie said.

"I think that deserves another toast," Randy said. "To unexpected turns, and knowing when to let the journey lead you where you're meant to be."

"Absolutely." Natalie ate her sixth doughnut.

"Can I tell you something?" *Why did I ask? I should've just said it. Don't chicken out.* He blundered forward. "I really wish you weren't moving to the mountains." He paused, taking in a breath and the courage to go on. "Because I've never met anyone like you. I would've liked spending time with you, Natalie."

She sat there looking flabbergasted. She took a sip of tea, and he worried that he'd upset her.

"Randy, I'm flattered. That was unexpected."

"I'm not saying it because you're leaving. I mean it."

"Where were you before you-know-who came and stole everything?"

"Maybe that's why it happened. So we'd meet."

She didn't agree, and before he knew it he was talking again to fill the quiet space. "You can't just close the door completely because of a professional con. You can trust yourself. You can trust me."

"But I fell for it."

"Anyone would have."

"Randy, after losing my husband and everything he'd worked so hard for, to make sure I'd always be taken care of, how could I? It wasn't just material things that the swindler took. He took my confidence and my good judgment. It's really frightening."

This wasn't going how he'd hoped. Trying to lighten the mood, he said, "We got your truck back."

"I know, and I really appreciate everything you're doing, but the last thing I can do is trust myself to choose someone to date. You seem so nice, and you've been so helpful . . ."

"But it's too soon?"

"And maybe there'll never be another man in my life. I just don't know."

"Don't say that."

"I'm just being realistic. I had a wonderful marriage. Maybe thinking that can happen twice in one lifetime is just not realistic."

"Don't say no. Do tea or coffee when you're in town. Check in once in a while on a nonofficial-business kind of way? I would come see you if you'd let me. Just see where things go?"

She tilted her head. "That sounds like more than just friends."

"Says who? You'd do that with Sheila, right?"

"Yeah, but—"

"But then let's just be good friends." *For now.*

She sat there looking at him. Then she slowly nodded. "No harm in that, I suppose. If you can ever pull yourself away from work long enough to get away, come up to Chestnut Ridge and experience it. The fishing is great."

"Don't tempt me with a good time," he said.

"Is that what I'm doing?"

"Maybe not intentionally. But friends, yes, definitely friends, and I *will* come and fish at your house."

"Great." She looked pleased.

He was glad he hadn't completely ruined the pseudo-date, no matter what she wanted to call it.

"So, tell me about this little mountain town that has you all excited."

She poured another cup of tea from the cute blue pot and settled back in her chair. "It's amazing. I fell in love with it instantly. I feel so at home and safe there."

"Because your husband was from there."

"No. I don't think so, because we'd only gone there a couple of times, and he never spoke of Chestnut Ridge. It's more than that. I feel empowered there. Maybe it's because it's kind of rustic. I have to walk, like, a football field to get to the house from where I park. And there are animals and birds. I don't know. It's really hard to explain. It's just really different there."

"In a good way?"

"The best. I don't exactly know what it is about that place yet, but I'm going to give living there a try. I've got nothing to lose but some time, and that's something I have plenty of."

"It's kind of like Courtnie. Being brave enough to try something new. I admire that in you. I think it's a great plan."

"I do too. I feel really at peace about it."

"I'd love to come to see the cabin."

"You should. It's so relaxing. It's quiet in a whole different way. Actually, it's really not quiet at all." She laughed.

He loved her infectious laughter.

"I guess it's just different from city or neighborhood noise." She stopped, her eyes drifting off for a moment. "I think I actually hear the wind. Every little rustle of the trees." Looking him right in the eye, she said, "I may have heard the grass grow."

He laughed out loud. "Now that *is* something different!"

She shrugged. "That's how it feels. You'll see."

"I can't wait." Randy wasn't in any hurry to leave. "How did you and your husband Jeremy meet?"

"We met through Sheila."

"Sheila. Your best friend?"

"Yep. Jeremy and I hit it off right from the start. We had a lot of things in common, among them he had no living family, like me. Not a grandparent, uncle, aunt, or cousin. I was still reeling from losing my folks, and I felt so alone until I met him."

"Sounds like you were really happy together. I'm sorry you lost him."

"Me too. From really early on we promised each other that we'd always focus on the present. Not the past. We took our future together one day at a time."

"I can't imagine not having any family. I mean, don't get me wrong, I wished I was an only child before. But having no relatives? No built-in unconditional-love support system? That would be . . ."

"Different. Hard. Lonely." She nodded. "Yeah, all those things, and Jeremy and I were inseparable almost immediately. He was my everything. We were going to have children, but . . ." Her eyes glassed a bit, but it only took a moment for her to move on. "We'd just started trying when the accident happened. There are so many days when I wish we hadn't waited, but then, raising a child on your own isn't easy either."

"I thought I'd have kids by now too."

"You want children?"

"I do. How many do you want?"

Natalie's eyes narrowed. "At least three. Being an only child is lonely, but there's all those middle-child theories, so probably two or four." She shrugged. "If I'm lucky enough to have a family of my own."

Victims of crimes like the one she'd been through were scarred in ways others couldn't see or understand. That was the part he couldn't fix. "Your friend Sheila is like family."

"Yeah, maybe. We're definitely best friends, but that's different from family."

"You really think so? They say chosen family can be even better than those you're born to. I tell you what, if you ever need family time, I can share mine. You'd love my folks."

"I already love Courtnie. She's great."

"I'm very fortunate. I don't take my family for granted, but you should know sometimes family is problematic."

"You're going to have a hard time convincing me of that one."

"My brother and sister are both married and starting families, and then there's me."

"All-Work Randy?" She slurred the "w" and "r," making it more of an *All-Work Wandy.* "That's hard to say. Try that three times fast."

"I'll take your word for it."

"Try!"

They were both laughing so hard by the third try that they nearly knocked the little table off-balance.

"Ooops." Randy steadied the table. "I'm not all work. I play softball. Go to the gym. I do stuff."

"Then why is a good-looking guy with a good job like you still single?"

She thinks I'm good-looking. Randy absently rubbed the scruff on his chin. "I just haven't met the right woman." But in his heart he was beginning to think he had. "My friends haven't introduced me to a girl like you yet. You clearly had better friends than me in that department."

"I got lucky. What are you looking for?"

You. "I have no idea."

"That might be part of the problem," she teased.

"Yeah. Probably, but I know that we'd better get to the DMV and get those tags while we have the chance, or they'll be closed and you won't be able to drive your truck."

Chapter Eighteen

NATALIE LOOKED on as Randy squatted in front of Jeremy's pickup truck, twisting the last screw to secure the new Virginia tags. "Thanks for doing all of this. I have a feeling none of this has a thing to do with your detective duties."

"Happy to do it." He stood. "All set. Do you want to practice driving and parking in the lot first?"

"No. I'll just follow you, if you don't mind."

"Not at all, but how are you going to get both vehicles back to the mountains?"

"I'm going to put the Mustang back in storage. Technically, I still have that storage unit paid up until the end of the month anyway. I'll just extend it."

"You know, it's not good to leave a car in storage. It needs to be started, if not driven. I know a guy who might be able to help you."

"I can't sell it."

"I wasn't suggesting that you sell it. My buddy owns the Bay Area Automobile Gallery and Tap House. They rotate custom cars through the display every other month. He has a huge warehouse with a bunch of classic cars. I bet he'd let you keep the Mustang there if you let him put it in the rotation inside the brewery. The guy is a real gearhead. He'll make sure it's taken care of, and he probably won't charge you what you're having to pay for storage."

"Really? Why would he do that?"

"Well, he's a friend, but he's also a Mustang nut. He'd be thrilled to have this one on display. Just an idea. I could ask if you want."

"That would be great. Thank you." She shook her head almost as soon as the words came out of her mouth. "No. Not great. Look. I know you mean well, but I'm about to have an anxiety attack over this already. I don't think I can let this car out of my control. I know in my mind that everyone is not out to take advantage of me, but I just can't risk it."

"It's okay. You've got some healing to do. When you're ready, I can ask him about it."

Embarrassed by her reaction, she asked, "Do you really think a person recovers from this? I mean, I know it's not logical to think this way, but I can't help myself."

"Give yourself a break. You're going to be fine."

"I hope you're right."

"Come on. Follow me to the precinct, and then I'll follow you in your truck to put the car back in storage."

"That would be great. Thanks for understanding."

"That's what friends do," he said, then walked back to his car.

Yeah, they do. She climbed into the truck and waited while Randy got back into his car.

She was thankful the truck had been recovered. Randy was

turning out to be more than an acquaintance. She waited for him to get to his car, her thoughts wandering to his sister, Courtnie, and her new beginning. Natalie would've never guessed that woman had lost everything and started over in such a short period of time.

Maybe I can get my giddy-up and go back too.

Natalie straightened herself behind the wheel, ready to get this big ol' truck back on the road and hopefully between the lines.

She followed Randy back to the precinct, and the drive went quite well, but she didn't chance trying to park between two cars. She drove to the far end of the lot and parked. It would take some practice, but until she got it mastered a little exercise never hurt anyone.

She locked the truck and jogged over to meet Randy, who was waiting where he'd parked next to the Mustang.

"You did good," he said.

"Yeah, not as bad as I remembered."

"I'll follow you over to the storage unit."

"If you have to get back to work, I could get an Uber. You don't have to—"

"I want to."

"Okay. Then let's go. It's the new storage place over by the stadium. Do you know where that is?"

"Yeah, but I'll follow you."

She took the key from her purse and unlocked the car. She'd miss the sporty ride. She patted the steering wheel and then started the car.

Natalie pulled into traffic, with Randy right behind her.

Traffic had gotten heavier now that it was afternoon, and she was happy to be in this car rather than the truck in the stop-and-go traffic.

Finally, she got to the storage facility and pulled up to the garage bay door. She punched in the code, and the door rose. She slowly pulled in.

"Guess this is goodbye again for a while," she said to the car as she walked out to push the button to close the door behind her.

Randy pulled his car up right beside her. She waited until the garage door completely closed, then got in.

"We really got a lot accomplished today." She let out a breath.

"Are you in a hurry to get on the road?"

"Well, I'd planned to go back to Chestnut Ridge tonight, but it's getting late now. I'm going to see what Sheila has going on and see if I can stay with her. Why?"

"I've got a softball game tonight. If you don't have any other plans, you're welcome to tag along."

"Just as friends?"

"Of course. Sheila can come too."

"Gimme a sec. I'll text her." Natalie sent the text, certain it was not a problem, but Sheila was probably showing a house or something, because she didn't respond.

"Don't know if Sheila can make it or not, but I'll come to your softball game with you on one condition."

"What's that?"

"Can we get a snack on the way? I'm starving."

"I'm not eating doughnuts twice in one day." He patted his flat stomach. "I don't have time for another thirty minutes in the gym."

"No. I meant real food."

"Good, because I wouldn't be able to fit in my suit if I ate like that all the time. How about a burger?"

"Deal. Also, here's a little something you don't know about me that might come in handy. I used to keep score for our softball team in high school. I could keep score for y'all tonight if you want me to."

"Aren't you full of surprises?" He glanced over his biceps at her, his lips quirking into a smile.

When he looked at her like that, it made her insides tumble. *Just friends*, she reminded herself. This was all she needed. Safe and easy.

When they got back to the precinct, he pulled up next to the truck. "I can pick you up at Sheila's house."

"That would be great. I'll text you the address." She typed it into her phone and sent it.

"Got it. I'll see you in about an hour?"

"See you then." But as soon as she got on the road she was kicking herself for agreeing to it.

She dialed Sheila's number, thankful she answered on the second ring. "Hey, Sheila. I texted you earlier. I've got the truck. Can you believe it?"

"Natalie! That's great. It's just the beginning. I know it. You're not going back tonight, are you? I don't think I like the idea of you driving that truck in the mountains in the dark."

"No. That's why I was texting. Do you mind if I spend the night at your place?"

"Of course not. You know you are always welcome. I'm still at the office, but you make yourself at home."

"Great. I'm headed there now."

"I wish I could get out of here early so we could do dinner."

"Well, actually," she said, with her stomaching spinning, "I agreed to go to Randy's softball game."

"So you're finally going to admit there's a spark there?"

"No. I am not, and honestly I'm regretting agreeing to it already. I'm about to throw up. I don't know what came over me. We got my truck. He even took me to the DMV to get the tags, and followed me to put the Mustang back in storage."

"That's way above the call of duty. I mean, I'm not sure I'd have even done the DMV with you, and I'm your best friend."

"I know. Right?"

"I hate the DMV. So, you've got tags on the truck. You're driving that beast, and now you've got a date?"

"No. Not a date. Just friends. Softball. A big crowd, and I'm already thinking of canceling. Why did I say yes?"

"Because he's hot? Nice? Got your truck back?" Sheila's tongue clucked. "If you don't go for it, I will!"

"And I'm crazy."

"No, you're not. You're showing signs of being human again. Thank goodness. Look, if you are sitting on my couch in your pajamas when I get home instead of out with that detective I'm going to disown you. Go. Have fun."

"I'm afraid I'm going to throw up on his cleats."

"You will not. Quit being dramatic. You'll have fun."

"You really think I should go?" *Why did I think for a second she'd tell me to cancel?*

"Yes! Quit overthinking this," said Sheila. "It's softball. Just go and enjoy yourself."

She let out a breath. "Fine. I'm almost to your house."

"Have a glass of wine. Settle down. I'll see you tonight and I want to hear every detail. Or if you don't come home until morning, I'll not even sing the walk-of-shame song. I'll be cheerleading. Pom-poms and all."

"You are not helpful."

Sheila boasted, "I'm the best wingman you could have."

"I'm hanging up." She disconnected the call, laughing and feeling better already. Friends like Sheila were irreplaceable.

By the time Randy showed up at Sheila's place, she'd had a glass of wine and settled her nerves. Pretty much.

A flurry of nerves came back when the doorbell rang, but when she opened the door they settled quietly. Randy looked really good standing there in his softball uniform.

Who knew polyester pants and a jersey could look so good on a guy? He looked great in a suit, but somehow that camouflaged the wide span of his shoulders. For a hot second she pictured herself with her head nuzzled in the crook of his neck.

Stop.

"Ready?" he asked.

"Yeah. Let's go." It was out of her mouth and she was closing the door behind her before she could give it a second thought. *Thanks for the pep talk, Sheila.*

Sheila would be happy when she got home and saw that Natalie had indeed gone to the game with Randy. She'd try to remember to text a picture when they got to the ball field.

It took about thirty minutes to get to the park. There was a slew of men all in the same uniform as Randy, but none looked as fine as he did. She walked with him over to the field. He went to warm up, and she climbed into the bleachers.

Was it her imagination, or were a couple of those men staring at her? She hadn't considered some of his work friends might have seen her at the precinct before. Self-conscious, she pulled out her phone and texted Sheila.

> NATALIE: At the softball game with Randy.
>
> SHEILA: Hope you score a run.
>
> NATALIE: Funny. Just friends.
>
> SHEILA: Doubtful.
>
> NATALIE: Stop.
>
> SHEILA: I have a feeling about this guy, and not the creepy Marc feeling. Just give it a shot.

She swept the messages away, laughing.

"Hey, Natalie!"

Natalie spun toward her name.

Courtnie stepped over the first seats and climbed up to join her on the bleachers. "I didn't know you were coming tonight."

"I didn't either. It was sort of a last-minute decision." Courtnie sat down beside her and the guys came together in front of the bench, hailed a big *rah*, and then ran out onto the field.

"Here we go!" Courtnie yelled, and whistled.

Courtnie's enthusiasm made it even more fun. It was contagious.

The score was only separated by two runs for the first few innings, but finally Randy's team hit in a run and they started knocking balls over the fence. One run after another, they were bound to win.

Natalie and Courtnie cheered with such enthusiasm that everyone in the bleachers had joined in.

"This is great," Courtnie said. "I'm usually the only one cheering them on. I like your style."

"They're good!"

"Randy was always good at sports," Courtnie said.

"Seems like he's pretty good at everything."

"He is. Sports. Games. He's pretty handy too. He gets that from my father."

"Your family sounds really close."

"We are. If you aren't doing anything at the holidays you should get Randy to bring you over for Thanksgiving. I'm cooking this year. Would love to have you join us. We always have enough to feed an army, and it's fun to have someone new for Dad to tell all of his old stories to."

The batter hit a home run, and Natalie and Courtnie leapt to their feet, cheering.

Randy's team won by a landslide and as the guys came off of the field one of the players pointed at her. "You! You better plan on coming to all the games. We haven't had this kind of luck since Caldwell washed his lucky socks."

"Not my fault," Caldwell said. "Tess didn't know that was bad luck. I always did my own uniforms. She thought she was helping."

"Doesn't matter. Now we have a new good-luck charm. You hear that, Randy? You have to bring her to every game."

She was blushing, her cheeks burning from all the attention.

"Works for me," Randy said.

Chapter Nineteen

I T HAD been nearly a week since the night Natalie had gone to the softball game with Randy, and the guys weren't letting him live it down. Randy found himself working overtime and off-hours, trying to find some connection somewhere that would give him a reason to call her again.

Nothing this well thought out could have been someone's first con. This guy was making a pretty good living just from what he'd gotten away with of Natalie's. No telling how many others he had on the line at the same time.

How did someone store and get rid of that much stuff?

It was a lot to manage.

He'd requested call logs from Swindell's phone number months ago.

In this morning's email, he'd finally received the cell phone data. After hours of review, Randy had revealed the possibility of multiple other targets even while he was with Natalie. The phone had been issued to Mike Connors.

Connors? Con? Again with the telltale name? Got to love the audacity of this guy to dangle his ill intent right out in the open like that.

Randy remembered joking with Natalie early on that the guy was probably going by the last name of Conway. That hadn't been so far-fetched after all. He'd been closer than he thought all along.

Ballsy. That's what Marc Swindell-Connors-whatever-name-he-borrowed-now was.

This kind of criminal really crawled under his skin. And that he'd target recent widows just made him madder. Was that part of his pattern?

Randy wrote the word "widows" with a question mark next to it on the blotter where he scribbled thoughts and ideas to follow up on.

It would've been unlikely she'd escape the con on a good day, but to reel her in when she was dealing with grief and pulling herself back together? That was just low in anybody's book.

Randy had come up empty looking for a Mike Connors fitting the description Natalie had provided.

He jotted down the counties in Virginia where he'd found touchpoints, then sorted all the phone calls to see what other states were being called with any frequency.

Mostly it was here on the East Coast. Virginia, North Carolina, Georgia, then two in Texas, and one in Tennessee. He circled Tennessee. Maybe he'd get lucky and find a family member who wasn't a fan of this guy who was ready to share something.

"Hey, aren't you coming to the baby shower for Caldwell and Tess?" Hutchens was the oldest detective, more grandfather age than father.

"Yeah, hey, thanks for stopping. You headed that way now?"

"Sure am. Want to ride with me? I have to come back this way on my way home."

"That'll be great." Randy shut down his computer, locked

the screen, and picked up a box wrapped in white paper with a springy pink, blue, and yellow ribbon.

"Tell me you didn't wrap that yourself," Hutchens said.

Randy glanced down at the box. "I did. Why?"

"That looks great. You don't even want to see my package." Hutchens grimaced. "Looks like, well, looks like it was found next to a dumpster. I bought a bag and stuffed crumpled paper in the top, but it didn't turn out anything like any of the gift bags I've received. It's not as simple as people make that look."

"It's the thought that counts. Besides, why do men have to go to baby showers nowadays? What are we supposed to do at one?"

"Bring presents and hopefully drink some beer. There better be beer."

"If Caldwell wasn't such a good guy, there'd be no way I'd go to this," Randy said.

"You, me, and at least six others I can think of," Hutchens said with a snicker.

But despite the grumbling, no one else had bailed either. There were cars parked up and down the block.

"Did this many people even go to their wedding?" Hutchens climbed out of his car and grabbed his package.

Randy tried not to laugh at Hutchens's gift. He hadn't exaggerated. It was a mess! "Don't know. I was working."

"Lucky you, but this time, buddy, your luck ran out. Come on. We're going in."

It's their *luck running out with the looks of that gift bag. Hope Tess is one of the it's-the-thought-that-counts believers.*

Inside the house, every room was crowded. There had to be

some kind of fire code being broken with all these people piled into one place.

As Randy walked past the living room, he saw the very pregnant Tess with a plate of food resting on her uncomfortably large belly. The high-pitched chatter coming from that room made his ears ache.

Thank goodness, the closer they got to the kitchen, the conversation carried a lot more bass. Giggles were replaced with grunts and high-fives. Much more his speed.

"I see the beer," Hutchens said. "I'll get you one."

Before Randy could answer, Hutchens squirmed through guests, making a beeline for the bar next to the back door.

Randy picked up a small pink plate and loaded it with hot appetizers.

Guess it's going to be a girl.

He hadn't eaten all day. He popped a spicy meatball into his mouth while standing there at the crockpot full of them. Impressed, he stabbed three more onto a long toothpick and plopped them on the flimsy paper plate that was becoming dangerously lopsided already.

Hutchens poked his head around the corner, scaring Randy. "Hey, man. Tables out back. I got you a beer." He raised it in the air and motioned for Randy to follow.

Randy grabbed a napkin and worked his way to the back door.

"Randy? Oh my gosh. Haven't seen you in forever. How are you?" Jessica wrapped her hand around his wrist in that way that always made him want to pull away. It was an irritating habit. She was like a boa constrictor, and if he'd just been one step faster, he'd have made it outside without bumping into her.

"Hey, Jess. I'm good. Busy."

"Still working too many hours, I bet," she said in her slow, syrupy accent.

It didn't sound like a compliment coming from her. "Love my job." He popped a meatball in his mouth for no other reason than to not have to talk to her. They'd dated only briefly, but those were a few months he'd have preferred to skip. He pointed to his full mouth, feigning regret, and then slipped outside.

"Did you see Jessica? That lady is smoking hot," Hutchens said.

"Yeah. You could've warned me."

He shoved a beer in Randy's hand. "Here. She's not as hot as that little number you brought to the softball game, though. I guess now I know why you can't let that case fall to the bottom of your stack."

Randy bristled at the comment. Sometimes Hutchens could be such a jerk.

The backyard was packed with people from work. It was humid, but a man would rather sweat than be in a baby shower, and the proof was right here. Had to have been a woman to come up with that coed baby shower idea.

He vowed right then and there that if he ever did have the chance to have a few kids, he would absolutely veto this idea. He'd spring for the fanciest ladies-only baby shower he could afford to avoid this situation. That seemed fair.

"Hey, Randy. Come meet my brother-in-law. He's a detective like you. He works down in North Carolina."

Randy walked over and shook his hand. "Randy Fellowes. Nice to meet you."

"Mike. You work with Caldwell, I hear," the North Carolina detective said, making small talk. "I'm married to Tess's best friend."

Hutchens bellied his way in on the conversation. "So, you a detective too, Mike?"

Mike nodded.

"Maybe you can give the youngest detective on our team some pointers on when to call it the end of a case." Hutchens slapped Randy on the back. "Poor kid's spending all his off time still trying to relentlessly track down some con who took advantage of this pretty woman that he won't admit he's smitten with."

One of the other guys from their precinct added in his two cents. "She is hot. Can't blame you, man."

"It's not like that," Randy said. He might not admit it to Hutchens, but he wasn't fooling himself. He knew full well Natalie was special. Had they only met under other circumstances, they'd be together by now.

Mike stuck up for him. "Give Randy a break. Maybe it's the real deal. Nothing wrong with working every angle possible on a case. They all are important to someone, and who knows, maybe she's the one."

Randy didn't like being the center of any conversation.

"When you know, you know," Mike said. "I met my wife when I first joined the force. I was a traffic cop at the time. Gave her a speeding ticket."

The guys all snickered and moaned.

"Couldn't get her off my mind," Mike said. "Had to keep myself from looking up her home address. That's how much she had me off-kilter. Luckily, I ran into her at the Strawberry

Festival while working extra shifts to buy a new truck. There she was. White shorts and these big wedge sandals that made her legs look like they never ended. I can still remember how that little belly-button ring peeked out from her shirt when she walked."

The guys mumbled their version of appreciation.

"I knew right then and there I'd marry her someday," Mike said. "So, see? Not impossible to meet the girl of your dreams on the job. It took me two years to get her to take me seriously, but it was worth it."

Two years? Randy hoped it wouldn't take that long to convince Natalie to give him a chance. He glugged back the rest of his beer.

The other guys peeled off, and Mike and Randy stood there. "Hey, don't let them give you a hard time. My dad always said we should take pride in making every case matter. We are what gives them closure and confidence in the system. Don't apologize for that."

"Yeah, I don't pay them any attention. And you know, it just sucks that those con men can get away with that stuff. I hate seeing a woman taken advantage of."

"Same here. I have a friend that's been working on a case like that. Guy wooed this woman out of her house and almost all her savings. There are a lot of those cases sitting around unsolved."

"It's frustrating."

"I'll get my friend to give you a call. Maybe y'all can compare notes. I don't know. Maybe he's tried something you haven't, or vice versa." Mike tossed his head back, raising his beer to the older detectives who were stuffing their faces across the way. "Those old guys probably aren't even up on the latest social media and stuff. Lots of new ways to crack a case these days."

"Appreciate that. Thanks."

"Sure. Just promise not to invite me to a wedding or one of these parties. Okay?"

"Deal."

Hutchens walked over and tapped Randy on the shoulder. "Hey, do you want to catch a ride home with someone else, or I'll drop you off back at the station now?" He lifted his phone into view. "I just got called in. Gotta run."

"Out of here, guys." Randy was happy for the excuse to leave. He dug a business card out of his pocket. "Give this to your buddy. Would love to hear from him about that case."

"Yeah. Will do. Good luck." Mike pushed the card into his back pocket and turned to talk to some other guys.

In the car, Hutchens had talk radio cranked up, and Randy was glad to sit quietly on the ride back to the precinct until they pulled into the parking lot.

Randy spoke up. "You can just let me out here. I'm going to run into the office for a few minutes and check on a couple of things before heading out."

Hutchens let him out at the back entrance. "Have a good night, man."

Randy stood there at the curb for a moment. Natalie's voice toyed with his thoughts. As clearly as if she was standing next to him, he remembered her saying, *If you can ever pull yourself away from your job long enough to get away, you should come up to Chestnut Ridge and experience it for yourself. The fishing is great.*

Maybe he didn't really need to go back into the office tonight. "Got to start somewhere." He reached into his pocket and took out his keys. He flipped them in his hand as he walked over to the parking garage.

I can do this.

And he reminded himself that all the way to his car and halfway home.

It wasn't like he got paid to work all the extra hours, and no one was pushing him to do it. Yeah, he was eager to prove himself, but he'd already done that.

It won't kill me to live a little. Or go fishing up in Chestnut Ridge some-time. Soon.

Randy had just gotten home when his phone rang. It was David from Bay Area Automobile Gallery & Tap House re-turning his call. He'd left that message before Natalie said she wasn't ready to let someone else take care of the Mustang.

"How've you been, David? You're working late."

"Yeah, we're switching out inventory on the vehicles tonight, so I wanted to be here when we closed to get things moving."

"That's actually why I was calling you before."

"You offering to come help?"

"I would."

"I'm kidding. What's up?"

Now that he was on the phone with David, he might as well get the additional details, in case she changed her mind. "I have a friend who has a classic Mustang in storage. It's really nice. I thought maybe she could put it in your rotation so that your guys would make sure it got started. I know it's not good for those older cars to sit around."

"Not good for any of them. Yeah, sure. A Mustang. You know my weakness. A Shelby?"

"It's not a high-dollar one, but it's in great condition. A little sixty-six coupe."

"I take it this is a lady friend."

"Yeah. It was her husband's car."

"Divorce settlement."

"No. She's a widow."

"Sorry to hear that. Yeah, sure. You just let me know when she's ready to bring it down, and I'll make room."

"What's the monthly charge?"

"Nothing for you, buddy."

"Thanks, David."

"Any time. Now bring your new friend and have dinner on me."

"We just might take you up on that." He hung up, hoping that he'd get the chance to take Natalie there one night.

Chapter Twenty

NATALIE HAD been antsy since she got back to Chestnut Ridge from Richmond. The push and pull of her feelings around Randy had left her feeling unsettled. What if he just felt sorry for her? Did that happen with detectives and their—? She wasn't even sure what she was. A case?

With her mind in overdrive over something that she knew shouldn't matter, she busied herself by writing a list of to-dos that she hoped would take all day and maybe spill over to tomorrow if she was lucky.

Her first stop was to pick up fishing gear. She didn't know much about fishing, but with the water within walking distance it seemed like a good hobby to take up. Plus, she could eat what she caught. Maybe. The thought of gutting a fish made her squirm. *Maybe I'm a catch-and-release kind of fisherman.* At least it would get her out of the cabin and into the fresh air.

Shopping for the stuff didn't take long. There wasn't that much to choose from in the store on Main Street, so she just bought a variety of things: a tackle box, two fishing poles, and a book about fishing.

With her purchases safely in the truck's bed she checked off NEW FISHING GEAR and then walked down the block to the hardware store to stock up on sandpaper and exterior paint. She couldn't wait to go wild on that rusted eyesore of a horse trailer. She might even paint the dull gray weathered outdoor furniture. She picked out a pretty aqua color for the chaise, eager to add some color to her life.

She was known for the beautiful colors in the note cards she sold online. It was time to bring more color to the cabin.

"What can I get you, young lady?" The man wore an apron that had more paint on it than fabric.

"I'm going to need a quart of exterior paint in each of these colors." She fanned the color strips she'd pulled from the display. Red, yellow, blue, white, black, green, and purple, because that was one color that she always found tricky to mix without it turning muddy.

"You want to come back in a while?"

"Sure. How long?"

"How big a hurry you in?"

"Not that big."

"How about tomorrow morning?"

Living on country time would take some getting used to. "That'll be fine," Natalie said with a smile. There'd be no painting this afternoon.

On her way back, she daydreamed about creating a series of cards with repurposed horse trailers on them. One like Courtnie's coffee shop, maybe an ice-cream stand, and one with birdhouses and feeders.

The cards she'd done with the retro campers were suddenly outselling even her best sales months. Must be the camping time of year.

With extra time on her hands, she stopped in to pay a visit to Orene.

"Well, isn't this a wonderful surprise? Come on in!" Orene held the screen door wide. "I've been wondering how you were doing up there in the cabin on your own. Everything going okay?"

"Couldn't be better. You were right. Tucker has taken great care of the place."

"No surprise there." Orene led the way to the sitting room. "I see you got something else to drive. That'll do you better up on the mountain for sure."

"Yes. It was perfect timing."

"How's that?"

"Uh, well . . ." Natalie searched for just the right words. "It's kind of a long story."

"I've got nothing but time. I'll put on a pot of tea." She headed for the kitchen. "Come on. Keep talking."

"Um, okay, yes, tea would be nice. So, I had some bad luck recently."

Orene stopped mid-reach for the teapot. "You weren't in a car accident, were you?" She swept her finger in the air. "Turn. Let me look at you."

"No. No. Nothing like that. Well, I suppose luck had nothing to do with it."

"You sit while I get the kettle going."

She flumped down into a chair, revisiting why she thought coming here was such a good idea in the first place.

"Okay, so what went wrong?"

"It happened a while back," Natalie said. "Before I ever came here."

"Well, whatever it was must've kick-started you toward Chestnut Ridge, so no matter how bad you thought it seemed, there's a bright side if you ask me."

"One would think."

Orene sat there listening, just waiting for her to start talking.

"I really don't want people to know about this," Natalie said. "It's really embarrassing."

Orene folded her hands in her lap and nodded slowly, encouraging her to continue, but not promising to keep it to herself, Natalie noticed. Still, Natalie continued. "I got into a relationship. With a man."

"Honey, you're widowed, not dead. Nothing wrong with that. Even in the Bible—"

"Well, that's not all of it. This man. He lied to me. He . . . well, it turns out the police believe he's a professional con man. He took me for almost everything I had. The insurance money. My savings. The house Jeremy and I worked so hard to buy."

Orene's mouth dropped open, and her eyes opened as wide as wooden nickels.

"Even that truck out there. It was Jeremy's truck. Gone. Thank goodness they recovered it when they did, but everything else is gone."

"Oh my goodness."

"I'd been staying with my best friend, and she didn't mind, but I was just sort of stuck, waiting for my problem to get solved by the police, even though they were pretty clear that it might never be resolved. Finally, one day I just had to do something besides wait. I realized I did have a place to stay."

"The cabin."

"Yes. The cabin here in Chestnut Ridge. Jeremy had once

again rescued me, even though he wasn't here. I was desperate when I came to Chestnut Ridge."

"And anxious. That's why you came that night without even thinking about where you'd stay?"

"Exactly."

"Natalie, dear, why wouldn't you want anybody to know about all that? It wasn't your fault. Not like you traipsed off to Vegas and blew everything rolling dice or something."

"Because I should've known better."

"Hmm-mmm. Nope. That is not the way it works, young lady. You just quit that way of thinking right now. There was once a saying. Let me see if I can get it right. It went something like: No thief, however skilled, can rob one of knowledge. That's why knowledge is the best and safest treasure to acquire."

"What does that even mean?"

"It means no one can take what you know, Natalie. That was all just stuff. Material things, and whatever it was, it can be replaced if it needs to be." Orene tapped the side of her head. "But you have all your memories. You have all the love you shared with Jeremy. You are the same bright, beautiful, loving woman you've always been. Now, that baddy who took your stuff. You can rest assured he'll get what's coming to him for his actions. Don't you give that situation a second thought."

"That's easy to say, but I trusted him. With everything."

"And you know what, when we are trustworthy, we trust others." Orene pursed her lips. "Don't say I can see that as a bad thing, either."

"You are very kind." No one could ever accuse Orene of being a glass-half-empty person. She found the silver lining in everything.

The whistle on the teakettle blasted, sitting Natalie up in her chair.

"Perfect timing." Orene jumped up to make the tea. "And isn't that where we started this conversation? About perfect timing."

"Yes. We sure did." Natalie knew this energetic woman was a big part of what was drawing her to Chestnut Ridge. She was an absolute delight to be around. "So, back to the perfect timing. A detective has been working on this case for months now. And suddenly I move up here, need a truck, and then it's not long after that he calls to tell me they've recovered mine. Well, Jeremy's. You know what I mean."

"I do. It means your prayers were answered."

"I guess they kind of were."

"This detective must be very good at what he does. I'd think that tracing a true con's trail would be very difficult."

"I'm finding that out. He's good at his job, and he's really nice. I think his captain would've had him push my case aside months ago."

"Maybe this detective . . . what's his name?"

"Ra—Detective Fellowes. Randy Fellowes."

"Perhaps Randy likes you a little. Hmm?"

"We're just friends."

"Oh. Okay." Orene poured two cups of tea. "Let's have this in the sitting room. It's so much more comfortable."

They prepared their tea. Orene had pulled out pretty sugar cubes with little flowers painted on them.

Another woman who loves sugar cubes as much as me. It's like we are related. "These are beautiful." She could imagine Jeremy rolling his eyes.

"Aren't they a treat? Each one is a teaspoon. Just pop them right into your cup."

"Got it. Okay. Aren't we snazzy?"

Orene breezed down the hall. "My husband used to say I was really missing an opportunity not opening up my little tearoom here. I do love all of this stuff so much. It's a shame not to share it, but I never wanted him to have to live with it night and day." She sat and leaned into Natalie. "He was a man's man. Ruggedly handsome right to the end."

"I can still see the love in your eyes," Natalie said.

"Still makes me twinkle," she said with an impish grin. "No doubt."

Natalie placed her hand on her heart. She'd never heard anything quite so sweet.

"Well, we are delighted you are here in Chestnut Ridge, no matter what brought you here. I do think it's fair to say that family brought you here. I mean, all family is not blood, and following Jeremy's path back to Chestnut Ridge seems to fit if you ask me."

"He was not only my family, but my best friend. My friend Sheila introduced us, and she's who was there for me when Jeremy died. I stayed with her when this big mess happened, up until I decided to come here."

"You'll feel like family here. Maybe living in the city has its limits." Orene giggled. "City limits. Get it?"

It was a silly pun, but Orene was getting a great little laugh out of it.

"I get it," Natalie said, "but I think when you have no family at all, you act and react differently to things. I guess that's why Jeremy and I connected immediately."

"I see." Orene paused, and then, almost as if she were deciding whether to say anything, she finally said, "What about Jeremy's grandfather? He never told you anything about him?"

Natalie shook her head. "He mentioned he was gone, but I don't think we ever talked about how he died. I guess I just assumed he died of old age. I didn't have grandparents. See what I mean about reacting differently when you don't have extended family? I didn't even think to ask."

"I'm seeing that. You believe that you and Jeremy were like two peas in a pod. Is that right?"

"We were, and he made me feel like I was the most precious thing in his life."

"I'm sure he did. There's something to be said for that. No matter what else, that is the part that keeps you together day after day."

"Yes." Natalie liked being able to share with Orene. She was such a good listener, and she wasn't forcing unsolicited advice on her like so many of her older patients, although she kind of loved them for that too. "Jeremy was a hard worker. Trustworthy. Always there for me."

"Just like his grandfather," Orene said in a matter-of-fact tone.

That caught Natalie off guard. "You knew Jeremy's grandfather?"

"Of course. I know everyone who happens through this town."

She leaned in. "What was he like?"

"Oh gosh, where to start about Paul? He was a brilliant kid. Too smart for his own good, I believe. He was always taking things apart and putting them back together. Had such a logical mind. The smartest kid in school, really. Loved to read. We went to school together, but then, everyone went to school together back then."

"You went to school around here, then."

"Where else? The schoolhouse was for all grades, and we closed down during harvests. He went on to college. That was rare for kids from 'round here. The town paid for his college on the commitment that he'd work here in Chestnut Ridge for at least seven years when he completed his studies."

"That was generous."

"We take care of our own, which sometimes means funding the future. We've sent kids to school for medical, dental, we've funded agricultural studies to have someone who knew what they were talking about to help our farmers. It all pays off."

"Wouldn't it be nice if it was like that everywhere?"

"It could be. Easy enough." Orene lifted her chin. "You know, I'd promised to give you that number of the guy looking for help with seniors around here. I let you leave without doing that. I'm so sorry."

"Not a problem. I've been busy."

"Let me write it down now before I forget again." She got up and scribbled a name and number on the back of an index card. "If it's not a fit don't feel bad. It's a start, though." She handed the card to Natalie. "The company offers not only nursing, but errands and driving seniors to appointments, well, pretty much whatever they need."

"That sounds like it could be perfect for me. I could meet people and learn my way around town simultaneously. Plus, I'd have time to keep up my card business. I do some artwork on the side and really enjoy that."

"That sounds so interesting. So you're an artist too?"

"Well, I never went to school for it, but I guess so. People seem to love the original drawings I've done. I turned them into prints and sell them in packs of note cards online. It's actually starting to build into a nice little income, but I'll need more."

Orene pointed her finger straight up. "This might just work out then, and give you some extra spending money while you're toodling around making new friends."

"I could volunteer to help occasionally."

"No, they pay a wage for it. Paid help works out better than volunteers."

Natalie could see how that could be the case. Volunteers were hard to get and harder to depend on sometimes. "Okay, well, a little paycheck will be a bonus then. I'll give him a call this afternoon."

"Actually, let me call Jesse right now while you're sitting here. Maybe I'll catch him at his desk, and a reference from me goes pretty far in this little town." Orene picked up her house phone and tapped in a number. "Hey, Jesse. It's Orene. How are you doing today?"

Natalie listened even though it seemed a little like eavesdropping, but a nervous excitement kept her leaning in.

"That's great," Orene said. "Look, do you still need a nurse or a driver for your special one?"

Natalie watched Orene listen, nodding with understanding.

"Yes. I thought as much," Orene said. "Uh-huh." She shook her head. "Yes, you may have heard about the new gal in town. The one staying up at the cabin?"

She nodded and looked at Natalie. "Yes, she's Jeremy Maynard's widow. Really sweet gal. Yep, that's her. She has some time on her hands and doesn't really know many people yet. No family at all."

Orene nodded and shook her head.

"Yes. I know." Orene smiled at Natalie. "It'd do her good to get to know people around here and learn her way around while she's at it. She's a geriatric nurse. Overqualified maybe, but I think it might be a good fit. She'd love to talk to you about the position.

"I know." Orene pressed the phone to her ear, switching her grip. "Mm-hmm. That's what I said. Yes, I think you're right."

Natalie wished she could make out the conversation on the other end.

"Great. Tomorrow morning at ten. Yes, I'll have Natalie meet you to pick up the car and a FriendsGiving shirt. I'll tell her."

Orene hung up and clapped her hands. "Easy as pie."

"That simple?" Natalie could barely believe it.

"Well, I told you they were shorthanded. The company is called FriendsGiving."

"Isn't that when friends get together for Thanksgiving?"

"Well, I've never heard of that. Isn't that what Thanksgiving is, anyway? Seems odd to have to create something else with the same purpose. I don't know, but it is most surely the name of this company that helps keep things moving in our county."

"Wonderful. I'm delighted. I thought it would take at least a week to get started."

"Are you busy this week?" A wrinkle formed above Orene's right brow.

"No. Not at all."

"Are you available at ten tomorrow morning?"

"Yes!"

"Good. Then that's settled. He said you might as well start, and try it on for size." Orene scribbled an address on a piece of paper. "You'll meet up with Jesse at this address. He'll give you the keys to the vehicle you'll use. They keep the cars parked there. You'll just pick it up and drop it back off each day. They refuel them and keep them clean for you."

"I can't thank you enough."

"You're going to love getting to know this town, and we're going to love you becoming a part of it."

"I know I will." Natalie got up and pulled Orene into a hug. "Thank you so much."

"You're welcome. This works out for everyone."

"I'm going to run to get a couple of things done today before I start this new job." Natalie couldn't believe how quickly that had happened. "I'll put my teacup in the sink. Is there anything I can do for you while I'm out?"

Orene was beaming. "Not a thing. Just enjoy this beautiful day."

Since the day Natalie set foot in this town, good things had begun to fall into place around her. She went back to the market and picked up a small cooler and some water to keep in the car while driving folks. She grabbed a box of tissues and a bag of individually wrapped sugar-free mints. At the last second, she grabbed a copy of the local newspaper and tossed it on the counter too.

"I'll need a bag of ice, please," she said to the girl at the checkout.

She piled everything into the truck and drove back to the cabin.

When she got to the bridge, she regretted having so much to carry to the house.

She wished she'd opted for two small bags of ice rather than the twenty-pounder. The first thing she'd save up for with her new paychecks was one of those UTVs to tote stuff back and forth, or at least a wagon.

She got the ice put away and then went back for the fishing gear. One thing for certain, she'd be in better shape living here, if for no other reason than the walk.

Home. Sweet. Home.

Chapter Twenty-One

NATALIE WOKE with the sunrise, which was getting a little later each morning. It always messed her up when the days got shorter, and it wouldn't be all that long before the clocks rolled back an hour and it would be dark even earlier. She stretched and got out of bed.

She stood in front of the window watching the birds and other critters she now considered neighbors—mostly squirrels, rabbits, and this morning a trio of deer.

She felt stronger here. Being this far away from her troubles had turned out to be a good thing.

Every morning, she recited her new mantra to remind herself that Marc was the one to blame.

Marc was never in love with me.

Not everything is what it seems, especially if it seems too good to be true.

It's okay to believe the best in people.

I deserve this new beginning.

Each day it got a little easier to believe too.

The sooner she truly believed that, the better off she'd be.

Maybe a little hard work was part of true love. She walked over to the mantel and took the photograph of her with Jeremy into her hands.

"I will always love you, Jeremy. I feel you here watching over me." She hugged the frame close, clinging to her memories.

She returned the picture to its place on the mantel. She wasn't due to pick up the car for hours, so she got her colored pencils and sat down in front of the window to work on some new drawings.

Flipping the pages back on her sketch pad, she delighted over the series of cheerful, chubby birds that she'd started sketching over the last few days. In the short time she'd been here, she'd seen so many different types of birds. Some were so colorful that they looked like they belonged in the tropics.

While in town today, she hoped she could get a good enough signal to place an order online for a few things. A *Birds of Virginia* book was going to be helpful to identify and learn more about the local species.

She'd planned to call this note card series "Birds of Chestnut Ridge."

Thank goodness she could work on her note cards from anywhere. When she was a kid she was always doing something artsy, but she'd never considered it something she could do for a living. Not until Sheila had talked her into setting up a shop online after making Christmas cards a few years back. A happy accident for sure.

Already this first drawing was coming together. She used several shades of green in the sprigs of the pine. She'd never realized just how colorful pine trees were. Light, dark, and even shades of yellow-green and rusty brown among the pine cones were complex and full of texture. She had a feeling taking note of the subtle changes through each season was going to be really special.

But a girl couldn't live on work alone, and with no internet and iffy television channels on a clear day, she yearned for something that would get her out and about.

This job was going to be perfect for her. And she hoped it would partner her with a few special seniors. She did miss that about her old job.

Mentally stronger these days, she could cope with the emotional part of that job again.

She sat back, looking at the drawing of the beautiful dark bird with bright orange bands on his wings. She set that one aside and started another, a bluebird.

The difference in the body structure of the two birds was noticeable even at a quick glance. If Natalie was lucky, maybe she'd catch a glimpse of an eagle someday. That would be something to see.

Satisfied with her morning production, she put her things away, and picked up the copy of *The Enterprise* she'd bought the day before. She took it outside and sat in one of the chairs on the deck.

The view drew her attention from the paper.

Will I ever get used to this? I hope I never take all of this beauty for granted.

The awe she experienced over the simplest details: the variety of greens in the landscape, different pitches of each birdcall, and even the cicadas with their mind-numbing stutter were pleasing and filled her heart with a joy her life had been missing.

She unfolded the newspaper and started to read the articles.

It was a good paper. Stories about the locals and celebrations scheduled for the next month. Even every arrest was posted in pretty good detail. There weren't too many. She could imagine the extra punishment of public humiliation kept the number of arrests under control.

That old adage about everyone knowing your business is alive and well in this town.

She would've known about the driver shortage if she'd picked up a copy of this last week. There was a whole article about how the good news of Agnew J. Fuller being accepted into the veterinarian program at Virginia Tech had left a gaping hole. There were dozens of notes from people who'd benefited from his service while working on his acceptance into the program at Tech.

Each note had a picture of the person next to it. Mrs. Martin looked cheerful, with her toothy grin and glasses so big they made her look a bit owl-like.

Reading the article in detail, she realized if she decided to go that route, FriendsGiving did have openings for people with her geriatric nursing skills too.

This part-time job would be a perfect test drive with the company and maybe lead to something bigger down the line if she wanted that.

I've got options, and I don't have to decide anything today.

Not one to be late, especially for a first impression, she put her things away and packed her new cooler of goodies to take to the truck. At least with just a few things on ice, the hike was more manageable this morning.

She climbed into the truck and drove back out to the main road.

When she pulled up to the address on Main Street, an older gentleman stood between a shiny black Cadillac CTS and a red Toyota Camry with a brightly colored FriendsGiving logo on the door.

"Hi. You must be Jesse." Natalie walked over to the man whose weathered skin told of years of hard work in the sun.

"That's me. You must be Natalie. Orene is always making connections where they need to be made. I hear a welcome to Chestnut Ridge is in order."

"Yes, sir. Thank you."

He opened the trunk of the Cadillac and gave her the once-over. "You a small or a medium?"

"I'll take the medium, please."

He pulled two shirts from a box and handed them to her. "This will get you started. I like to give folks a three-week trial. At the end of those three weeks, either of us can end the employment for any reason. Sound fair enough?"

"Works for me."

"Great. I just have a couple things for you to fill out. You do have a valid driver's license, right?"

"Sure do."

"Good." He handed her a clipboard.

It only took her a minute to fill out the forms and turn it back over.

The shirts with the FriendsGiving logo embroidered on the lapel were nice-quality polo shirts. She hadn't expected anything more than a screen-printed T-shirt.

Jesse glanced over the papers, then smiled. "After these first three weeks, I'll give you a list of recurring clients. You'll be able to work together with them on the scheduling if you want to adjust it. Mostly our customers need things like pharmacy pickups, grocery store, some need rides to church on Sunday, others just a little company and for someone to make sure they are doing okay."

"I can do all that. No problem."

"The schedule isn't too busy. It'll leave you some time to explore the surrounding areas, and some of our seniors are very active in county groups. Sometimes there are field trips you can put your name in the hat to help out with. Our drivers usually like those, since they get to go along for the trip too."

"That could be fun. Thank you for this opportunity."

He handed her a card. "My number's on there if you need me. The car always has a full tank of gas and is ready here in the morning. I'll trust you'll meet the commitments as they come in. If you have to decline one, just be sure you get a response from me that I've rescheduled it to someone else. I like to keep communication clear. Don't like leaving my neighbors hanging."

"Of course. I've got it, and if someone cancels and you need me to fill in, I've got a flexible schedule right now."

"Good to know," Jesse said. "You're welcome to use the car for your own errands while you're running these. We're pretty casual about it. Haven't had anybody abuse the privilege yet. Don't expect I will."

"Thank you."

"Guess that's it. So, here's the information on your two scheduled appointments. Mr. G. needs to pick up some prescriptions today, and has a doctor's appointment tomorrow."

"Great. I can handle that."

"Today will be simply picking him up to take him to the

drive-thru at the pharmacy, and then back home. Don't ask why he won't let you just pick them up and deliver them to him. I know it would be faster, but he's set in his ways. He's . . . Well, Paul is Paul. No one else like him in the world."

"Can't wait to see what that means," she said with what she hoped came across as a friendly laugh.

"He's very particular. Doesn't want anyone up on the hill either. He'll meet you at the gate at the foot of the driveway at that address. He rides down on his scooter. Very independent, he is. If he's not there, just wait. He'll be along shortly."

"Well, I guess we're lucky he has to go farther than the scooter will take him. Else he might be found cruising right down Main Street."

Jesse cracked a smile. "You think you're joking, but that's pretty much how it is. As long as you follow the instructions, you'll be fine. Oh, and don't be late." He tossed his head back and smiled. "You know, I think you two will find common ground very quickly."

"I'll take that as a compliment."

"As you should." He dipped his head in an old-fashioned how-do-you-do sort of way and then got into his car.

She waved as he drove off. There was still plenty of time before she had to pick up Paul.

At least driving and parking the Toyota wouldn't be a problem. It looked tiny sitting next to Jeremy's truck.

She unlocked the car and placed her cooler behind the passenger seat where she could reach it. It was a very nice car to be a fleet car. Leather interior, all the bells and whistles, even a sunroof. She got in and worked her way through all of the buttons and gadgets, then drove through town.

Checking her GPS for directions, she saw she had enough time to go out to the pharmacy at the other end of Main and then backtrack to pick him up, so she did.

She'd only been to the little market on Main Street until now. Natalie was delighted to see there was a big chain supermarket on the other side of town. It wasn't as big as the one in Richmond, but it was still a big step up from the country store.

It was only 6.8 miles from the pharmacy to the address Jesse had given her to pick up Paul.

The GPS took her down new roads with beautiful countryside. The streets twisted left and then right, and she had to brake to keep from going too fast around the curves until the path started going up. The car whined a bit as she pressed the accelerator to get up the incline. Pastures filled with cows and an old barn with a patriotic barn quilt brightened the landscape. Across the way, high up on a hill, a huge house rose with turrets like a castle. It looked oddly out of place.

That's got to be the castle house Stretch was talking about.

There was a mixture of little houses and larger farmhouses. A blackboard fence marked off acreage on the right as she got closer to the address on her GPS. The trees blocked most of the view here.

The GPS signaled she'd reached her destination, only there wasn't a thing there. She went around the next bend and then saw a big rural mailbox and driveway.

"That has to be it."

And sure enough, as she pulled up to the driveway, there was an elderly man in a suit and bow tie astride a bright red scooter parked next to the stone-pillar-gated entrance.

She put the car in Park and climbed out. "You must be Paul. Good morning. I'm Natalie. I'll be your driver today."

He cocked his head. "You're new in town."

"I am. Yes, sir. Is it okay that I call you Paul? Or would you prefer Mr. Grandstaff?"

"I'd prefer Paul, I believe."

"Paul it is."

"Hmmph. And what brought you to Chestnut Ridge? Not chestnuts, I suspect. They don't even grow them up here anymore."

She laughed. "No. It wasn't chestnuts. I don't think I've ever even had one, though I love that song."

"Oh yes." His face twisted, and then he puckered his lips and whistled the melody to the Christmas song.

". . . on an open fire. Jack Frost nippin' at my nose," Natalie sang along. "Hey, you're really good! Better than a band."

He shrugged, then got off the scooter. He tugged a crumpled paper bag out of the basket on the front and tucked it under his arm. Then he pulled a cane from a tube on the side, swinging it to the ground with his weight against it as he walked to the car.

"Very nice to meet you, young lady." He stopped, got his balance, and stretched out a wrinkled hand.

His skin hangs like he needs some fluids. Once a nurse, always a nurse. She just couldn't help herself. Hydration was so important. Just being a little out of balance could cause a host of problems in these older folks. At least he was using his cane, and his gait wasn't bad.

She'd find a way to impart some hydration wisdom kindly his way at some point. Blurting out her opinion on day one was probably not the way to impress him.

She shook his hand. His grip was good. That was promising. "The pleasure is all mine. It's beautiful out this way." She opened the door to the back seat and held it.

He climbed in without a word.

She closed his door, then went around and got behind the wheel.

"Is your scooter fine there? Do you need me to move it?"

"It's fine."

"All righty, then. We're off to the pharmacy." She turned around in the spot before the gated entrance. She wondered if there was a whole neighborhood up beyond the trees in the curve that she couldn't see from here. A good question to ask next time.

The metal gate was very decorative, with shiny black rails and tall pines with deer leaping over a fence. In two pieces secured to giant rock-faced pillars, they opened in the middle.

She glanced in her rearview mirror at the little gray-haired man in the plaid bow tie.

He looked longingly out the window.

She noticed the security camera on the pole as she pulled back out onto the road.

Chapter Twenty-Two

NATALIE DROVE down the mountain with Paul in the back of the shiny red car. The curves were a little more precarious going down the mountain, but the fleet car handled them with ease. The sun shone brightly and the cows were now grazing closer to the road. She reached for her sunglasses in the top of her handbag and slid them on.

"So what brought you to Chestnut Ridge, if I may ask?" Paul asked.

Why is that question so hard to answer? Maybe because it was a bundle of things.

She glanced in the rearview mirror. "Well, I lost my husband a few years ago."

He nodded but didn't let her off the hook with just that. He sat quietly as if waiting on the rest of the answer.

"I don't have any family, and neither did my husband, but he had a hunting cabin that he really loved." He was still watching her. "I needed a change, so I will be staying there for a while."

"A change, huh?"

"Yes, sir. Something positive."

"Well, I'm sorry for your loss. Losing a loved one is the hardest thing." He shook his head and looked out the window. "I know that firsthand."

His voice softened, and she instantly felt a connection with him. "I'm sorry for your loss. How long ago did you lose your wife?"

He lifted a frail hand, a slim gold band still on his ring finger. "It was eons ago. I was a younger man at the time, but not as young as you. It changed the course of my life, and some of it has been really good."

"Well, then there's hope for me."

"Yes, and you will be okay eventually. It's not an easy thing to go through. I'm sorry you're experiencing this so young."

"Thank you." She'd learned how to politely acknowledge the remarks about her loss with a gentle smile that no longer came with a bucket of tears.

Paul passed the crumpled bag he'd been carrying over her seat. "This is for you. They are fresh eggs. You're not one of those vegans who doesn't eat eggs, are you?"

"Not a chance. You brought me eggs?"

"I've got some chickens. They lay more eggs than one man can eat. Practically more than the town can eat, I think."

"Thank you. That's so nice of you, and there's nothing I don't eat. Oh, except black licorice. Just never could get the taste for that."

"Never cared for those black jelly beans myself."

"Well, we have something in common already."

"I was assured we would hit it off," he said.

Orene probably called and filled him in already. "Well, it's very nice to meet you. Can I assist you inside the pharmacy today, or will we just be picking up at the drive-thru?"

193

"Just a pickup."

"Drive-thru it is." She turned into the pharmacy and pulled up to the window. "We're picking up prescriptions for—" She couldn't even finish the sentence before the pharmacist looked past her and began a conversation with him herself.

"Mr. Grandstaff. Good to see you, sir. We have your order ready. Just one moment." The woman sprinted from the window, gathering little bags and stapling them together.

Natalie twisted in her seat and smiled at Paul. "Grandstaff. That's such a lovely name."

"Yes. It's a good name. Has served me well."

The pharmacist returned to the window and slid the stack of prescription bags out in the tray. "Here you go. You're all set. Everything has been posted to his account."

Natalie took the bags and the signature pad and handed them to Paul.

He scribbled across the pad and handed it back. "Thank you."

She set it back in the tray. "Thank you," she said to the pharmacist, then pulled forward and stopped in the parking lot. "Is there anything else I can take you to get today?"

"No. This is it."

"I'll get you back home then."

The ride back went fine. Paul didn't say much until she pulled into his driveway and parked next to his scooter. "You know I don't mind meeting you at your house so you don't have to ride that down the driveway, especially as we start getting into winter."

"I prefer it this way." He opened the door and pushed himself to his feet with a grunt.

"Have a good afternoon," she said.

He nodded and slid his cane into its slot as if it were a holster on the side of the scooter, then sat astride the seat and motored up to the window she'd rolled down.

"I have you down for tomorrow for your doctor's appointment. I'll see you here for that."

He nodded, then pressed a button, and those beautiful gates slowly opened in front of him.

She sat there until he revved that bright red scooter and went zipping up the drive and disappeared around the corner.

"Okay, so he's a little different, but sweet. Can't blame a guy for wanting his privacy."

She wondered how on earth FriendsGiving calculated pay for trips like that. It couldn't amount to much. Hopefully, after her three-week probation, Jesse would load her up. She had plenty of time, and this wasn't even like work.

She wasn't really ready to go back home, though. The whole process hadn't taken an hour. Returning the vehicle back to where she had picked it up, she got in her truck and decided to take another ride around town. She took the same route up to Paul's address and on past it about three miles. There was a lookout at the top of the mountain. She pulled to a stop and got out to take a look.

The view seemed to go on forever. The panorama across the Blue Ridge Mountains from this vantage point was spectacular. For the first time, she understood why they were called the Blue Ridge Mountains. The shades of blue and green were gemlike, more beautiful than she could've ever imagined.

To see this in autumn when the leaves are in full color will be magical!

Her heart pounded. Inspired, she ran back to the car and got her sketch pad.

She grabbed the pad from the back seat, and although she'd planned to work on the bird drawings, the view of the mountains was too pretty to waste.

Natalie walked over to the stone wall and perched right on top of it to sketch. For over an hour, she let her eyes transfer the scene to her fingertips, not even thinking about it.

The intricate curves of each ridge were as unique as the clouds above. Using pressure and hash lines, the scene finally came together.

She'd been so blessed to see many different things this year. The Atlantic Ocean in its shades of green, the crystal-blue waters of the Gulf of Mexico, the lush green mountains, and the hand-built cabin where she now lived in the Blue Ridge Mountains.

Natalie mindlessly sketched, letting her mind's eye take hold of the whole picture and transfer the details to the page. She flipped over to a new page to sketch an old barn on the top of a hill across the way that looked like it might fall in if a heavy wind kicked up. It had probably been there longer than she'd been alive, though, and would most likely hold strong a few more generations too. They didn't build things like that anymore.

The sun warmed her skin, reminding her of those beautiful sunny days in Cancún with Marc. Magical memories that were just a means to a bad ending.

Being with Marc hadn't been a total loss. He'd changed her in a good way. Her priorities were straight now. In the past, she struggled with compartmentalizing work and play, letting them blur into something that never felt like time off. She'd never make that mistake again either.

Marc had been a mistake. A regret, but it wasn't all bad.

Is it okay to keep the good parts in mind? It seems so unfair to lose everything. The material things are one thing, but memories? Experiences? Do I have to lose those too?

Natalie had met Marc Swindell in first class on her trip out to Texas.

She'd never flown first class in her life, and the only reason she was doing it at that time was because after Jeremy died she'd found he still had over 400,000 airline miles. Straight out of college he'd been a consultant and racked up so many air miles he'd never had a chance to use.

When they first met he had the craziest schedule, gone weeks at a time and working fifty and sixty hours a week. He left that job when they got serious, trading it for a steady nine-to-five position that wouldn't monopolize his life. He never wanted to fly anywhere after that. Any vacation was always a car trip, and Natalie had never really minded that.

It seemed frivolous, but she also hated to let the free air miles go to waste, so she'd used them on every trip she took that year. First class definitely had its perks.

It was nice being treated special while she was feeling so broken inside. The man she'd planned to grow old with was gone. Losing him had shattered her future.

It was a coincidence that she'd ended up on the same flight, and in the same row, with Marc Swindell three times before he finally struck up a conversation with her. He was pleasant, engaging, and so polite.

It still played with her mind that it had been an act—just part of a bigger plan. Randy believed Marc had targeted her because of all those first-class flights. Seeing her as someone with surplus assets.

It was a shame that one decision to splurge on first class with Jeremy's air miles had led to all of this.

It was a theory. No one would be able to prove it unless they someday located the man she'd known as Marc Swindell, and it looked less likely that would happen with every passing month. She couldn't give up hope, though.

Natalie laid her sketch pad in her lap, staring off across the mountains where clouds dotted the sky. Her mind wandered to the last day she and Marc were together in Cancún.

She'd recited the minute-by-minute account a hundred times to the police and detectives as they tried to unbraid fact from fiction and determine precisely what crimes had been committed. She'd become so tired of retelling that same story that she honestly hadn't thought much about those details since.

Maybe the natural beauty of the mountains today had made her think of that night in Cancún, because it had been a once-in-a-lifetime kind of night.

Marc had been frustrated with his partner over a phone call that resulted in Marc taking an early flight home the following morning to handle a problem at their office in Richmond. She'd expected to go home with him, but he'd insisted she stay and finish the vacation.

If only I'd known at the time what those few extra days of pampering were about to cost me.

They'd enjoyed dinner on the beach and then gone out with the resort biologist to help with the baby turtle release. Helping those tiny creatures to the water, knowing only a few would make it to adulthood, was heart-wrenching.

They'd learned that hundreds of leatherback and logger-head turtles came to nest along that stretch of beach each year, laying one to two hundred eggs at a time. Still, only one in one thousand baby turtles would survive to adulthood, and most would perish in their first hours.

Eager and determined, the tiny turtles worked tirelessly, moving through the sand, waddling with their new flippers under the moonlight that guided them to the ocean.

She and Marc had held hands watching as the first hatchlings began their journey. Only a few people at a time helped the turtles, to not cause more confusion. They waited for their turn, and Natalie was consumed with emotion as they did their part.

"Have you ever seen anything so touching?"

He'd pulled her close. "It's amazing. The only thing I know of as magical as this is the ponies that run wild along the beach in the Outer Banks. I will take you there someday," he'd said. Her heart had soared at that moment.

He leaned in, whispering the details into her ear. "The ground rumbles when their hooves dig into the damp sand, their manes flicking in the salty air, and the young colts run in awkward gallops and leaps trying to keep up. Even *I* cry at that," he'd said. "You are my beautiful one."

A tear slipped down her cheek at the memory of how emotional that evening had been. Marc had been so sweet, clinging to her hand as they played chaperone to their little batch of turtles. Wishing them well, she'd said a little prayer over them as if it were a family send-off, hoping it would make a difference.

It was probably the trifecta of the heavy food, the night air, and emotion that had left her exhausted that night. They'd gone back to the room, skipping the dessert and nightcap they'd been enjoying every other night. Slipping into bed, she'd hugged the pillow, and Marc had comforted her. His fingers swept down her arm and back up. Arm tickles. He knew all the ways to touch her heart.

He'd leaned in and said, "My sleeping beauty, this is everything it was meant to be." He kissed the nape of her neck.

Those words had buoyed her still-grieving heart. She'd thought Marc had meant they'd be together forever. She hadn't been in a place to return those words yet. She'd lain there clinging to his that night.

But now, at this moment, she realized he wasn't promising her forever. He'd been telling her it was over. She'd lain there quiet, letting him believe she was asleep, while he basically apologized for closing the deal. It hadn't been a promise of forever at all.

How did I miss that?

With joy in her heart she'd hoped her own feelings would catch up to his one day. What she'd heard as a promise of forever had really been goodbye.

Then he'd said, "You are more than I'd ever dreamed of, dear Natalie. My whole life has changed because of you. You dream of me and enjoy the rest of your trip. I will be dreaming of you just like this where the ponies run wild and every tomorrow there."

She shot to her feet. "He was telling me. Everything right there in plain sight. Just like his name!"

She raced back to the car to get her phone. She reached across the console, sending the phone spinning across the passenger seat. She crawled behind the wheel and thrust herself over to grab the phone. She pressed the button to call Randy, and after all that . . . there was no signal.

"Really?" *Take a breath.*

She was frantic, wanting to tell Randy what she'd remembered before Marc could get away. Her heart was pounding. She inhaled slowly, trying to calm herself.

Marc Swindell won't be any harder to find in an hour than he is at this moment.

Settle down.

Parched after sitting in the sun sketching all that time, she reached into her little cooler and got a bottle of ice-cold water, and slugged it back.

She'd drive back to town and call where she knew the signal was usually strong.

Bringing up the GPS on her phone, she typed in the address to the cabin, even though she was fairly confident she could find it on her own. So far, this town didn't seem too challenging to get around in.

She went back the way she came without looking at the GPS. Proud of herself for learning a couple new streets already, she turned and stopped to get a to-go order of barbecue from the Trout & Snout to take home for dinner.

Natalie hadn't expected to run into anyone she knew, but lo and behold, not only did the waitress, Amanda, remember her, but Orene happened to be sitting in the same booth they'd shared on Natalie's first night in Chestnut Ridge.

Amanda wrote down her order, then pointed over her shoulder. "Why don't you say hello to Miss Orene while you wait. I'll get this turned in to the kitchen."

"Thank you, Amanda. I will." Natalie walked over to where Orene concentrated on peppering a big order of something fried.

"Orene. How are you?"

Startled, she stopped shaking, and her head popped up. "Oh! Great. I'm good. You met Paul today. How are you?" She patted the seat and scooted over. "Come. Sit down with me. Can I order you something?"

"No. Amanda just put my order in, but thank you." She sat down next to Orene. "And I did meet Paul this morning. He's very sweet."

"Bwah!" Orene barked. "He can be a cranky old man some days. I guess you caught him on a good one." She picked up her fork. "So it went well?"

"No problem at all. It was quick and easy. Thank you for connecting me with Jesse. I think I'll enjoy adding these trips to my days."

"What about dinner? Want some of my trout?"

"No. I'm fine. I ordered the barbecue."

"Today's dessert special is apple dumplings. Might as well order two. They freeze, and I promise you will want another one tomorrow. They are that good. He doesn't make them often enough if you ask me."

"I'll be sure to add that to the order."

Orene raised her hand in the air. "Need to add two apple dumplings to Natalie's order," she yelled out.

Amanda called back, "Got it, Miss Orene. I was already

ahead of you on that one!" And it wasn't even a minute later that Amanda came out with a bag and waved over to their table.

"There's my food," Natalie said. "I'm going to let you finish your dinner. Thank you again. I'll check in on you later this week."

"Please do. I'm looking forward to it. I'll fix tea."

"Great."

She paid the tab—it was a wonder they could stay in business with prices that low, but she was grateful because it was easy on her budget.

She dialed Randy's phone to tell him about her last conversation with Marc.

The phone rang. Three. Four. Five times before it went to voice mail.

She pursed her lips into a pout. She should've called before she'd gone into the Trout & Snout. A message would have to do now.

She headed back to the cabin.

Under a hot sun all day, the dirt road kicked the dust into the air like clouds behind her. She slowed, but there was no escaping it.

A family of deer were grazing near the bridge.

She stopped the truck, hoping to not scare them off, but they all froze.

She sat still until they finally went back to grazing, but just then her phone pinged and the largest doe jerked up and darted off into the woods. The others followed in a blur of white tails bouncing through the foliage.

Chapter Twenty-Three

RANDY'S DAY had been lousy. Hutchens was out on vacation, so they were shorthanded, and the captain had been in a bad mood all week.

Randy hadn't even had time to grab lunch before being tasked with another call. One clear on the other side of the city, putting him right in rush-hour traffic on top of it all.

His caseload was climbing at a disproportionate rate.

He came in and dropped into his chair. There was at least two hours of paperwork to get through just from today. He jerked open the bottom drawer of his desk and snagged a protein bar. It would have to hold him over.

The blinking light on his phone probably meant more work, but he needed to knock this stuff out first. He powered through the reports.

Rolling his shoulders, his joints creaked in retaliation for the missed workouts this week.

He pressed Enter on the last updates and shut down his computer, then pressed the button on his phone to retrieve his voice mails. Anything urgent would've come straight to his cell phone.

His pen poised over his notepad, he jotted down the details and inquiries as he listened.

He paused when he heard Natalie's voice. A pleasant surprise. A great ending to an otherwise not-so-great day. She had something to tell him. Something she thought might be important.

It was close to nine o'clock. Randy hated to call that late, but it sure would be nice to hear her voice tonight.

He grabbed his keys and walked out of the building. It was a quick ride home, and all he could think about was her. He went inside, sat on the couch, and stared at his phone.

He found the number, hesitated only a moment, and then hit the green button. On the second ring, he was regretting calling so late and considering hanging up when she answered.

"Hey, Natalie. It's Randy. I got your message. I'm sorry to be returning your call so late. I had a grueling day."

"No worries. I'm just sitting here reading. I'm glad you called me back. It's good to hear your voice."

His heart hitched up a beat. He felt the same way. "How's it going up there?"

"Good. I've met a few more people. This is really a great little town. That's not why I called though. I remembered something this afternoon."

"Something important?"

"I think I might know where Marc is."

"Really?" He sat up. "Did he contact you?"

"No. Nothing like that. I don't know why it didn't come to me until this afternoon, but I was sitting there just kind of quietly sketching and it all came rolling back."

"It happens that way sometimes. Fill me in."

And she did, in detail. Every word. "Do you think he was bragging about his deception before saying goodbye?"

"You could be onto something. I mean, anyone would've made the assumptions you did at the time, but knowing what we know now, yes, this could absolutely be a lead."

"I was hoping you'd say that."

"I met a detective from North Carolina who connected me with one of the guys who's been working a case very similar to yours. We've been exchanging information. He's not far from that area."

"I'm almost afraid to get my hopes up," Natalie said.

"You've been more than patient. This could be the lead we need to finally find that guy." He stretched out on the couch and kicked his shoes off. They clunked to the floor. "This is good news. I needed some of that today." Talking to her was the best part of this day. "I have some news for you too. Not about the case, but I checked with my buddy that has the tap house."

"The place with all the old cars."

"Yeah. He said he can work your car into the rotation. He'll keep up the maintenance and make sure it's started. I know you weren't really ready to consider that, but if you ever decide you want to, it's an option."

"That's very nice of him. Something about letting it out of my control still makes me nervous."

"I understand. Maybe one night when you're in town I can take you to dinner there so you can meet the owner. It might make you feel better about the arrangement."

"I guess we could do that."

He'd hoped for a little bit more excitement in her voice, but he'd made it sound more like a favor than a date. Maybe she'd have reacted the same way if he'd asked her out point-blank. That sullied his mood. "It's late. I better let you get back to your book."

"Yeah, I have to get up early in the morning. I've got a job now. I'm driving seniors to appointments as a way to get my foot in the door, and it's been an easy way to learn my way around town. Anyway, they might have some openings where I can put my nursing degree back to good use."

From bad to worse. He wished he'd ended the call sooner, or maybe not called at all. There was no salvaging this day. He'd hoped she'd end up back in Richmond or at least closer, where they might have more of a chance to interact and build their friendship . . . or more.

"Today," she went on, "I found this great lookout point up on the ridge. I sat there sketching for hours. It was really inspiring. I can't even put into words how beautiful it was."

"You'll have to show me sometime."

"Definitely. You can see for miles. It was pretty spectacular."

You're pretty spectacular. But he kept that to himself. The bounce in her voice was new. She sounded relaxed. Happy. Maybe she was just excited about the new lead. He hoped the lead was more successful than his attempt to ask her out.

"Let's plan that visit soon," he said, unwilling to let the call end without something positive.

"You're the one with the busy schedule," she reminded him. "You let me know when and we'll make it happen."

"I'm overdue for some fishing."

"You know where to find me."

"I'll look into this lead. It makes sense that the truck was down in Williamsburg, and the storage place was in Virginia Beach if he's in the Outer Banks. That would be kind of between here and there."

"I hope so."

"Me too. I'm up to my ears in cases with Hutchens out of the office, but I'm going to try to make a couple calls on this in the morning. I'll check my calendar and we can set that fishing date too."

"Looking forward to it. Thanks, Randy. It was good talking to you."

"You can call me anytime you get bored in that sleepy little town and don't have anyone to give a ride to."

Her laugh was light. "I'll do that. Bye."

He hung up his phone and lay there. It would be easier to put in for a day off after the workload he'd been handling this week. Sooner rather than later. He needed to make that happen, and see if the feelings in his gut about this gal were real. Unable to shake her from his mind, he slept right there on the couch that night.

When he woke up the next morning, he was still on the couch in his dress pants and shirt from the day before. He didn't even remember falling asleep. Talking to Natalie had been a nice way to end his day.

Waking up with her on his mind was even better. Eager to make some calls about the information she'd given him last night, he sat up. He'd be lying to himself if he put Natalie in the same category as all his other cases. He was drawn to her in a way he'd never experienced, and maybe it was time to pass her case to someone else just to be sure it was done with a clear head. But then, what if they let it sit?

He had some things to figure out, and the sooner the better.

Since it wasn't quite five o'clock in the morning yet and it was still dark outside, he headed to the gym, which was about the only option at this hour.

He changed into workout clothes and carried a suit to change into.

There were perks to getting up this early. Randy finished his workout in record time with no waiting for equipment, and when he got to the precinct the break room smelled of fresh coffee.

He poured a cup and made the second pot so whoever came in next wouldn't have to wait either.

The stack of teetering folders on his desk made him sigh. At least the paperwork was up to date online. There was still a lot of paper in their precinct. Hopefully at some point they'd get everything online.

He sat down and took a slug of his coffee.

It was still too early to make calls, so he shot out a few emails including one to the detective he'd met at the baby shower. It was a long shot, but you never knew which rock you overturned would make the difference.

Chapter Twenty-Four

EVEN THOUGH Natalie arrived at Paul's address early the next morning, he was already sitting at the gate waiting on her.

Wearing a lovely gray suit this morning, he looked sharp in his red-and-gray-striped tie. Natalie took notice of his leather loafers. They looked high-dollar—the kind that lasted a good long time. She doubted the little store on Main Street carried those.

She'd pulled right up next to the scooter. She got out of the car and walked around to open his door. "Good morning, Paul. I saved you a couple of steps this time."

"I'm quite able to make it to the car."

"I know. I saw that yesterday." She resisted the urge to help him. "I *am* on time, aren't I?"

"You're early, which I appreciate." Finally, he treated her to a crooked smile that made one gray woolly eyebrow climb toward his hairline.

"Oh, good. I was afraid you'd been waiting."

"Not long."

He walked to the car, lowered himself into the back seat,

then swung his well-clad feet in with a grunt. He settled his cane next to him and then looked at her.

She smiled and shut the door. All this man needed was a little time. He was moving around slowly but just fine with no assistance.

Natalie got in the car and readjusted the rearview mirror so she could see him back there. "I have that we'll be going to the medical tower in Roanoke this morning. Is that correct?"

"It is."

"All righty. I'm just going to put that in my GPS, and we'll be off." According to her paperwork, his appointment wasn't until eleven thirty. They had time to spare. "Would you like me to turn on some music for the ride?"

"No, thank you."

"Okay. I enjoy the quiet too. No problem."

He wasn't very talkative, but then she wasn't here to entertain him, simply to get him from point A to B and back again. She'd try to keep to herself unless he spoke up.

It was a long, quiet ride, except for the input from the GPS voice, who thankfully kept her on track. The ride was mainly a divided highway with little traffic all the way to the town of Roanoke.

Just beyond the "Welcome to Roanoke, Virginia" sign they passed several antique shops. She made a mental note of them, knowing it would be a fun place for a day trip when Sheila came to visit. On the way to the medical tower, there were trendy restaurants and a supercute farmers' market area. *Maybe next year, I'll do a container garden and grow my own fresh veggies.*

She'd never had much of a green thumb, but then she never

thought she'd live in a cabin in the mountains, either. The funny thing was, despite the hot mess she was in, she felt stronger than ever being in this new place all on her own. Even if she made a few mistakes, there was nothing she couldn't correct on the second try.

The GPS announced, "You've arrived."

Natalie pulled into the parking lot. "Well, Paul, it looks like with the combination of me being a little early to pick you up and the cushion they added to the schedule, we've got some time on our hands. Can I treat you to a cup of coffee somewhere to kill some time?"

He shook his head. "I'm having some blood work done, so I can't eat or drink anything."

"Well, that's a bummer." She twisted around in her seat. "Especially this late in the morning."

"Yes, they don't seem to really care about that," he said.

"If you ever need someone to help schedule your appointments, just let me know. I'm good at that kind of stuff too. They don't care because they aren't the ones sitting there parched with a grumbling stomach at near lunchtime, but I'm great at fighting for your convenience."

His eyes widened with embarrassment. "Did you hear my stomach?"

"Oh no. I was just making a generalization. I was a nurse for years. I've seen it all."

He relaxed a bit. "I didn't think much of it when I scheduled the appointment, but I won't make that mistake again."

"Would you like to sit here in the car until time, or I can take you in now if you'd prefer."

"If you'll just drop me at the door, you won't need to accompany me inside. This appointment will take at least an hour, perhaps longer. I'll text you when I'm done."

"You have a cell phone?"

"Of course I have a cell phone." His brows drew together. "I'm old, not feeble."

"I didn't mean to imply—"

"I have your phone number already programmed in my phone." He pulled it from his shirt pocket. "Jesse gave me your number yesterday."

"He's good at his job, isn't he?"

"Completely reliable." Paul's chin raised. "He would never let anyone down."

She wondered how long they'd known each other. "That's admirable. I got that impression in the short time we spoke." She started the car and pulled to the front door of the medical tower.

"I'll be here in the parking lot waiting," she said.

"You should explore the town. Get some lunch or something. I'll text before I check out and make my next appointment. That'll give you a fifteen-minute head start, the way these folks work." He rubbed his wrinkled hands together. "This generation has no sense of urgency."

"Especially in the doctor's office, am I right?"

"Yes."

"Okay, I might take a look around town while you're busy. Thank you for the suggestion. I'll be watching for your text."

He got out of the car and slung the door closed behind him. As he hobbled up the walkway, leaning on his cane, he raised his hand in a backward wave over his shoulder.

Or maybe he was waving her off, not appreciating her waiting to make sure he got inside okay.

Pride.

She never liked to steal pride from her patients, or client, in this case. She eased off the brake, still keeping an eye on him from a distance for her own satisfaction.

She cruised around the block, but there really wasn't much of interest right here at the medical center, and she wanted to wait to eat lunch. Paul would need something to eat after his appointment.

A giant rooster that must have stood twelve feet tall in about every shade in a twenty-four-color box of crayons touted home cooking in front of a small diner. That looked like a great spot to take Paul.

She took a left at the light, hoping it would take her back to the edge of town where those antique shops were. One more left, and she was right in front of a cute shop with a myriad of milk cans and fun flags out front.

This looks promising.

She parked and went inside. The building was filled with antiques and lots of crafts too. Someone had made a cute flower arrangement in tiny pair of Western boots. Little silk daisies in yellow and white poked out from between the leaves of a silky green fern. A fun black-plaid bow wrapped around the boots tied it all together.

It would look charming on the front porch, giving it a little zing of color too. Natalie picked it up and carried it with her, afraid she'd never be able to find it again in the maze. She wanted to get through as much as possible before going back to pick up Paul.

An entire glass-front case was filled with pocket watches. Big and small, some very ornate. Next to that, tons of old jewelry glistened under shiny lights.

A cameo ring caught her eye, but she resisted the purchase. The last thing she needed right now was jewelry. The loss had made her realize just how unnecessary so many things were. Even though all of hers had been stolen, she'd never worn most of them anyway. Thank goodness she'd taken the pieces most important to her with her on vacation.

She checked her phone to see what time it was.

Despite Paul's instructions, she didn't want to leave him waiting. She paid for the boot flower arrangement, then put it in the trunk before heading back to the medical center. She parked in the very back and rolled down the windows to get some fresh air.

The temperatures were getting noticeably cooler this week.

Thinking of sweater weather made her smile.

Friday-night football games, campfires, marshmallows, and watching for shooting stars. Autumn was her favorite time of year.

Natalie's phone pinged. It was Paul letting her know they were about done.

She thought about Orene's comments about him. He seemed perfectly sane to Natalie.

Not wanting him to assume she'd ignored his advice to explore the town, she waited until she saw him come outside before pulling out of her parking spot and up to the door.

When she turned the corner, he waved from the curbside.

She maneuvered the car right to the ramp access, and Paul got back in the car.

"How'd it go?" she asked.

"Excellent," he said with a lift of his chin.

"Terrific." She pulled out from under the entrance canopy and pulled to a stop. "Now, I'm not trying to tell you what to do, but I saw this cute restaurant just a little way up the road. Something to Crow About."

He laughed. "The place with the giant rooster?"

"Yes. Doesn't it look fun?"

"It looks interesting. I've wondered about that place."

"You haven't eaten all day, and I'm getting hungry. How about we get some lunch?"

"I've never been asked that when I've been driven to an appointment before."

"Is there a rule against it? I'll pay for my own, of course," she said.

"No. No rules that I know of. Yes, let's do lunch, young lady."

"Great." She dropped the car back into gear and drove straight to the restaurant. After she had parked in the handicapped spot out front, he was out of the car before she got around to help him.

"I'm so glad your appointment went well," she said.

"Being alive to make it to the next appointment is an achievement in itself."

"Oh, stop," she said with a laugh. "You get around quite well."

"Yes. Well, I do work on that. When you're as old as I am, you'll realize that there's a new ache, pain, or bother every day. It's just part of getting old. It's not for sissies, I tell you."

"I've heard that before." She put her arm out without a word as he took the step up to the sidewalk.

He placed his hand on her arm and made the step. "Thank you."

"My pleasure." Not making a fuss was often the best way to be of service in these situations. She was glad to do it.

When she got to the door, he stopped her. "Let me, please." He opened the door. He looked a bit off-balance for a nanosecond, but she refused to flinch, trusting he knew his limitations.

"Thank you, sir." She dipped inside, and he followed.

"Two for lunch?" the hostess asked.

"Yes, ma'am," he spoke up.

They were seated in a booth near the windows in the back of the restaurant.

"Wow, I didn't realize we'd have a view too." She leaned forward, scanning the horizon. "It's so beautiful."

He nodded slowly. "I've always loved the mountains."

"I never knew I did until now."

The hostess brought ice water and menus to the table. "Your waitress will be with you shortly. The specials are on the wall over there."

"Thank you." Natalie read the specials out loud to Paul. "Let's see, today's specials are a tomato basil soup with half of a chicken and Brie sandwich, chicken and artichoke pizza, or stir-fried vegetables over rice."

"I'll have the soup and sandwich special," he said.

"Sounds like two."

The waitress must've overheard them because she was right over to take their order and off to the kitchen just as quickly.

"So, have you always lived in Chestnut Ridge?" Natalie asked.

He leaned back in his chair, folding his hands on the table in front of him. "Not at all. Started out here, though. I was born in Chestnut Ridge," he said. "Grew up there. Lived there until I went away to college."

"And you came back after college?" She remembered Orene saying something about that.

"I did. With a law degree and the most beautiful girl I'd ever met on my arm, too."

"That sounds romantic."

His face lit up. "It was. She owned my heart. In those days, you married a woman before living with her. I had a commitment to the town to practice law in Chestnut Ridge for a period of time. No matter how much I loved her, I couldn't move to where she lived, and I couldn't imagine leaving her behind."

"Did she like it here?"

"She did. She was one of those people that saw the beauty in everything. I think she'd have been happy anywhere."

"That's lovely."

His eyes danced. "Everyone loved her. There was no denying her sparkle."

"Do you have a picture?"

"Of course." He leaned forward and pulled a worn black leather wallet from his back pocket. The photo inserts had yellowed so badly you could barely see the pictures through the plastic. His knobby fingers worked a small picture from one of the holders and passed it to her across the table.

"Oh my gosh!" She looked at him and then at the picture again. "You look like a Hollywood couple. She was gorgeous." She handed the photograph back to him. "And you were *very* handsome!"

He chuckled. "It was a long, long time ago. Funny you should mention Hollywood, because I did end up there. I'll have to tell you all about it sometime."

"I'd like that."

The waitress brought their lunch, and they ate, enjoying the quiet company.

Paul insisted on paying for their lunches, so she let him, but she'd be careful of that in the future. She'd hate for anyone to think she was using her position to mooch off of clients.

"I'll leave the tip," she said to him at the register, then went back to the table to do so.

When she returned, he'd already walked to the door, heading to the car.

It only took a couple of minutes to get buckled up and back on the road.

They drove for about fifteen minutes when he broke the silence. "Why did you move to Chestnut Ridge?"

She'd answered that question before. Maybe he'd forgotten. "My husband owned a cabin there." She knew she couldn't just leave that open-ended like that. "I lost him in a car accident a few years ago." The exact number of days calculated in her brain, like they always did.

"My condolences."

She glanced in the rearview. He was looking right at her. His eyes spoke more than those two words. "Thank you." She choked on the words. It had been a while since it had hit her like that. She swallowed and repositioned her hands on the wheel before continuing.

"I'd only been to Chestnut Ridge a couple of times with him. Just to go fishing. Never overnight. I ran into some bad luck, and I needed a place to stay. A fresh start. This seemed like the right place."

"You're Jeremy's widow." Paul was stating a fact, not asking.

"You knew that already, didn't you?"

"Word gets around in a small town. Even to those of us who rarely get out."

"I guess so."

"You had a good marriage?"

"The best." She took a breath, not wanting to cry while she was driving.

"I'm sorry. Did I upset you?"

"No, it's just . . . I still miss him. We were perfect for each other. He was the most wonderful husband. I'd have done anything for him, and I know he would've done the same for me."

"That's special."

"Very."

Thankfully, he didn't ask anything else, giving her time to pull herself together before pulling back into his driveway.

She put the car in Park. "The drive back seemed faster, don't you think?"

"It did. Thank you for your service and for such a lovely day. I haven't enjoyed something like that in far too long." He placed his hand on the back of her seat.

"Thank you for lunch," she said. "That was unexpected, and you can't be doing that. People would talk."

"I'm fully aware of that." He gave her a wink. He opened the door and scooted toward it. "Next time you buy your own, as long as there is a next time."

"I'd really like that."

"Excellent." He got out of the car, but before he closed the door, he said, "And I'd be remiss if I didn't at least mention one thing. The area where that cabin is, well, it's still very undeveloped. There are bear, and coyotes. You need to be careful. I guess I'm just telling you to be armed and aware of your surroundings. Nature can be dangerous."

"Yes, sir. I will be." She hoped she portrayed confidence, but the truth was, that left her feeling a little vulnerable out there all alone.

He got out of the car and got on his little scooter. He honked the horn in a little *toot-toot* that sounded like a clown car. She hadn't noticed the bright orange flag flying in the air on the tall antenna behind him yesterday.

She giggled the whole time she watched him cruise up the hill.

I don't care what they say about him. He's a sweetheart, and I hope I'm that spirited at his age.

Chapter Twenty-Five

"HOW IS it possible that each day feels better than the last?" Natalie carried her coffee out to the porch, thankful for her little part-time job that added the perfect balance to her days now.

I owe Orene a big thank-you for making that call for me. Thank goodness I mentioned I was looking.

Paul's warning had echoed Tucker's about being prepared, which had her feeling slightly on guard. She'd stopped at the country store on her way home that afternoon, searching for something in case of emergency. She had considered pepper spray, an air horn marketed as a bear horn, and a can of wasp spray that claimed to spray twenty-two feet at one point, but that was still a little close for comfort, especially when talking about bears.

She opted for the bear horn over the pepper spray and promised herself she'd call Randy the next morning to see if he'd be willing to help her make a good decision on a gun and give her a few lessons. Jeremy had always wanted to teach her to shoot, but she'd never seen the reason for it. Maybe it was just one of those things a person living up here needed to know.

Picturing herself holding a gun in a stick-'em-up pose made her laugh. Maybe a shotgun would be easier to handle. Something that would make a lot of noise and send critters running without having to hurt them, and would reduce the need to be a good shot.

She had the bear horn in her pocket. It would have to do until she could learn how to handle a gun. She'd also picked up a pair of rain boots, a loaf of bread, and a pumpkin. No one else would see it on her front porch, but it would be a fun project. Maybe this afternoon she'd even try one of those fancy designs like the ones at Orene's.

It was eight o'clock in the morning when Natalie called Randy's office, hoping he would answer.

"Fellowes."

Today her heart raced at the sound of his voice. "Randy, hi, it's Natalie. How are you?" She paced the porch to expend the energy that had her on the edge of giggly.

"Great to hear from you. I'm good. Hope you are."

The uptick of his voice made her smile. "I just wanted to check in on things."

"Glad you did. I was going to give you a call today too. I got some information in overnight that I think you're going to find really interesting."

"Really?" She stopped. "Already?"

"I talked to a detective in the Outer Banks who is handling a case very similar to yours. I don't know if it's the same guy, but we're sharing information."

She sat back down. "That's great."

"Yeah. I'm hopeful. At some point, I will need to walk

through some of the details again and probably ask you a few more questions."

"Yeah. Absolutely."

"Are you going to be around this weekend? I could call you."

"Yes. Call me anytime. I called for another reason too." She heard him take in a breath.

"Sure," he said. "What's up?"

"I need a favor."

"Need me to bait your fishing hook?"

"Well, I can probably figure that out. In fact, I bought a few new rods, reels, and gear the other day, but if you want to come up and fish, maybe you could educate me on how to safely handle a gun while you're here. Two different people have mentioned bears and coyotes. I think I'd better be prepared rather than stupid about this."

"Happy to help you with that."

"I don't know if I need a pistol or a rifle. There could be a bear, or something smaller like a raccoon or a skunk, although I can't imagine shooting anything."

"Well, from experience, you don't want to shoot a skunk anywhere near your house. They spray when you shoot them, and you'll live with that wretched smell for weeks."

"Oh no. Is it that bad?"

"Badder than bad."

"Well, I'll pray no rabid skunks come crawling around."

"Do you have a rifle?"

"No."

"Shotgun? Pistol?"

"Not even a water gun."

"Maybe you could go ahead and get a water gun. A Super Soaker, for sure. That would at least buy you a minute."

"Yeah, I could rain on their parade." She laughed. It might actually work. It wouldn't hurt her feelings as long as it shooed them away.

"Tell you what, I'll bring a few different guns so you can try them out. We'll figure out what the best option is for you. When do you want to get together?"

"Sooner the better."

"How about tomorrow? A day trip will do me good. I could be up there by around ten if that works."

"Are you sure you don't mind?" Guilt crept in on her for asking the favor. She hadn't expected him to drop everything to come help, and she knew he usually worked on the weekends.

"Positive."

"I'll pay for the ammo and whatever else we need," she insisted. "How about I make a picnic lunch for us and we can work some fishing into the schedule too?"

"How about I bring something?" he said.

"Sounds good." She found herself looking forward to it, and not just to check it off her list.

"Can I bring anything else?"

"Nope, you're doing plenty, and I really appreciate it," Natalie said. "Do you still have my address?"

"I do, but if you want to text me with a pin drop from your cell phone, that'll save me looking it up."

"Absolutely. Also, the GPS doesn't bring you in the right way, so if you call when you get to Chestnut Ridge, I can talk you through the last few turns."

"I'll do that. Should be close to ten."

"Thank you so much. I really appreciate it, and I look forward to seeing you."

"Me too. Natalie, I'm happy you called me. I'll see you in the morning."

She said goodbye and hung up the phone with a sigh of relief. Hopefully there'd never be a situation where she needed to shoot something, but she wasn't about to take any chances. If this situation with Marc Swindell taught her anything, it was that anything could happen.

Randy had seen where she lived with Marc. This was about as far away from that lifestyle as a girl could get.

Why do I even care? I'm not trying to impress him. I'm happy here, and that's all that matters.

She set down her coffee cup and walked out to the small clearing beyond the deck. It looked so peaceful now. It hadn't taken but one night to learn that once the sun set, this side of the mountain was pitch black unless the moon was bright. Even then, there were dark, shadowy areas where creatures could lurk.

As she walked farther into the open area near the bridge, her eyes darted for signs of any wildlife. The grass swayed in the breeze and leaves drifted to the ground in a dizzy spiral.

It really was beautiful. Sure, she had a lot to learn, but she was ready.

Her phone rang. She tugged it from her back pocket, where she promised Sheila she'd always keep it in case she got into trouble. Sheila's picture smiled back at her from the phone. Natalie answered, "Hey, Sheila. Good morning."

"How's nature treating you? Are you ready to throw in the towel and come back to the city? It's no fun here without you."

"I miss you too, but no, thank you. I'm fine. It's definitely different, but I am enjoying the solitude." She let out a relaxing breath. "I really love this place."

"Are you serious? Wait, is that your nice way of saying I talk too much?" Sheila was teasing, but it was also true there was never quiet time in Sheila's house unless Sheila wasn't home.

"No, you stop that. I was referring to no road noise. No airplanes overhead. No music from the neighbor's house." There'd been a chorus of dueling coyote howls the other night, but she'd figured out she could lower the top part of the window instead of raising the bottom. She felt a lot safer that way. "I'm settling in."

"It's hard to picture you there."

It was a little hard for her to imagine at first, too, but she loved it more every day. "Wait until you see it in person. The pictures I sent don't do it justice. It's so beautiful and peaceful, and when you come up, you'll have to see for yourself. And the people. Sheila, they are the nicest people in the world. Thoughtful. Welcoming. It's like living in one of those Christmas-movie towns."

"It sounds like you're one hundred percent sure you don't need a place to stay, and that makes me a little sad, but I do think I'm going to downsize a bit. It's time I break free from my past and start doing something besides work."

Natalie walked back to the deck and sat in the chaise lounge. "Sheila? Is everything okay?"

"Yes. No. Kind of. I don't know."

"That covers pretty much everything."

They both laughed.

"Oh, Nat. I don't know. I was so glad the divorce was over,

and I don't miss Dan. I'm glad it's all behind me, but now that you're gone I'm realizing that all I do is work."

"Oh, honey. I've been telling you that for months." Natalie's heart clutched a bit. Sheila had been in self-preservation mode from the time she learned her husband had been cheating on her. It was sad that she was realizing all this, but good that she was coming alive again. "Sheila, you deserve true love and happiness. You're going to get it."

"Maybe. Maybe not, but I think getting out of the house we lived in together is a good start. I'm putting the place on the market."

"It'll sell in a snap. It's a gorgeous home, and you have decorated it like it's staged already."

"I don't want people peeking through my panty drawers during open houses, though. I was thinking of going ahead and moving into a furnished rental while I look. I could just store all my stuff until I find the right place."

"Move here." Natalie's hopes soared.

"That will never happen, girlfriend." Sheila's laugh made Natalie laugh too.

"It would be fun. Don't knock it until you've tried it."

"Some things you don't even have to try to know they aren't a fit," Sheila said.

"Fine."

Sheila yammered on. "I'm thinking a little downtown condo with no commute to work would be nice . . . for a while anyway."

"Change is good." Until now, those words had always been one of those empty consoling phrases she'd tossed out. But now . . . she truly believed it.

"Who are you kidding? We both hate change. Change sucks."

"I'm feeling differently about that now, Sheila. Change can suck when it's not what you want, but when it's your own do-ing . . . it's kind of nice. Still scary, but in a good way. I'm really enjoying my life right now."

"I think I'm actually ready for this."

"Shedding the old stuff to start fresh. It's going to be great," Natalie said.

"Oh my goodness. Natalie, you are just getting too positive. I don't think I can take the pep talk." But Sheila's heavy sigh was followed by a much more relaxed laugh. "I hear you. You're right."

Maybe Orene was rubbing off on her. And Randy too. "I'm getting pretty good at these pep talks. I give myself one every day." Not exactly a pep talk, but a prayer. Call it whatever, it was changing her life and her attitude, and if it helped Sheila too, that was a bonus. "Do you need me to come help you move?"

"I'm going to hire movers." Sheila's laugh was strained. "I just wanted to be sure I didn't move into some tiny place if you might need to come back."

"Nope. That won't happen. Even if I come back, I'm able to get my own place and take care of myself. I can do it. Don't forget I'm here for you."

"Of course you are. You're the best friend a girl can have. Why don't we set up some time to grab dinner with this Randy guy? I think he's good for you, but I want to get to know him."

"So I don't screw up like I did with Marc?"

"Well, when a guy sorts you from your herd of friends, it's a red flag." Sheila paused, and Natalie knew that Sheila was not passing judgment. "We'll be more careful to notice those in the future."

"I don't think Randy's that type, but yeah, I'd love your opinion. We'll plan something, or you could come to the cabin. We could all go fishing."

"Can you picture me in waders? Yeah, no, that is not going to happen, no matter how wonderful a friend you are."

"Takes one to know one." Natalie hung up her phone and set it on the arm of the chair.

She went inside to mark the dates on her calendar, circling the first weekend in November. Then she circled tomorrow on her calendar too. *My first scheduled visitor in my new home.* She was looking forward to seeing Randy and having her first shooting lesson.

A horn honked in the distance.

She looked out and saw a big black 4WD truck slide to a stop on the other side of the bridge.

Stepping back from the window, she put her hand to her pounding heart. It wasn't Tucker's truck.

They made themself announced by blowing the horn. Better than being snuck up on. It's probably fine. But what if . . .

She spun around, looking for something to use as a weapon. That flimsy fishing pole wasn't going to scare anyone. She stepped into the kitchen and grabbed the cast-iron skillet. The darn thing was so heavy she couldn't lift it with just her one hand. Swinging it wouldn't be easy.

The shopping bag on the coffee table caught her attention. She lunged for it and dug for the air horn. Hopefully, if it could scare a bear, it would scare a man.

Should've gotten the pepper spray too.

Why didn't I make a plan for this when I was clear-headed? Right now, her thoughts were running as wild as a kitten in a rainstorm.

"Hello?" The deep voice was followed by heavy footsteps in front of the cabin.

Her heart pounded as she scanned the house for her phone in a panic. She inhaled sharply when she realized it was still on the front porch, and the front door was wide open. All that stood between her and the deep-voiced stranger was a screen.

She backed up to the sink, unsure of what to do. She took a steadying breath, praying it would be okay. "Hello, can I help you?" She didn't move, waiting to see if he responded.

"Hello! Ma'am? I'm a friend of Orene's. You met my brother Jesse too, I believe."

The rush of breath she'd been holding expelled in a whoosh. "Coming." She felt like an idiot for overreacting.

"I'm sorry to just drop in on you like this, but when I heard we had a new neighbor in town, I wanted to say hello and let you know we're just on the other side of the mountain."

"Oh, okay. I'm Natalie. Nice to meet you."

"Will you be a year-round resident?"

"That's the plan. It's so lovely here." She stepped out onto the front porch. He was dressed in khakis and a long-sleeved Carhartt T-shirt in a rust color that saluted the season. An older gentleman, his curly graying hair looked more like a Halloween costume in the way it hung wild but was missing on the top and back from what she could see. His skin was weathered and dark, but his smile was white and genuine.

"It's a good town. I've lived here all my life. If you need some help or have any questions, I wanted to give you my number. I live and work over on the other side of this mountain. We're neighbors in a hikeable way."

"I'm not much of a hiker."

He let out a jolly laugh. "That's okay, miss. I wouldn't make you hike that mountain for a cup of sugar. Wanted to give you my phone number. If you need a cup of sugar? Or a chain saw? Or whatever, you just call me. I can be here in just a few minutes. You hear?"

"That's very kind. You don't even know me." She shrugged, trying to cover up her embarrassment for letting those last words come out.

"I know you're my neighbor, and I can tell you there's one thing about this place. People take care of our own. You're gonna be one of us now. We're here for you."

"That's very generous. Thank you." She extended her hand, and he gave it a firm shake, then handed her a slip of paper with his number.

"I'm Joseph P. Forrester. People 'round here just call me Joe."

She took his number. "I'll hang on to this, Joe. Thank you."

"That's all I wanted. I'll let you get back to what you were doing." He turned to leave. "Natalie, you should stop by the fire station tomorrow. It's black-pot chicken day. Just five dollars will get you the best chicken, beans, slaw, and dessert you ever had."

"Are you a fireman too?"

"Nope. Just a cook. I cook, and they serve it up. It all works out."

"I like the sound of that."

He jumped into a boxing stance, fingers pointing to her.

"Careful now. We'll have you helping collect money at the next one."

"I'm willing to do my part."

"Well, there you go. You just passed the first neighbor test. Welcome to Chestnut Ridge."

That's the kind of people Sheila needed to be meeting. She hoped she would come and experience it at some point, but she was definitely a city girl.

Chapter Twenty-Six

IT HAD been a long time since Randy took a whole weekend off work. Even longer since he'd done so to meet up with a woman. But as much as he'd like to think this might turn into a date, he knew she had reached out because she needed his help. He was just glad she'd called him for it.

His truck was loaded to the gills for the day trip.

Guns, ammo, targets, fishing gear, a cooler, a change of clothes in case they did go fishing, a nicer shirt in case he could talk her into letting him take her out to dinner, and snacks, because he didn't like to be anywhere without some healthy snacks. He had no idea what kind of food she enjoyed, when she wasn't downing half-dozens of Krispy Kreme doughnuts, that is.

His stomach grumbled. He reached into the grocery sack in the passenger seat until his hand landed on an apple. He pulled it out and took a big bite.

Good stuff, right there.

He chomped while he drove, the roads beginning to lift and curve the closer he got to the Blue Ridge Mountains. It was a pretty drive. It would be beautiful when the leaves were in full color in a couple more weeks.

He wiped his sticky fingers on his jeans and drank the rest of his coffee, which was only lukewarm at this point.

The sign for Chestnut Ridge welcomed him, and an arrow to the right led him straight down Main Street. He stopped and topped off his fuel tank, then called Natalie.

"Hey. I hope I didn't wake you. I made better time than I thought I would. I'm already here in town."

"That's great. You're fine," she said with a bounce in her voice. "I've got coffee on."

"That sounds good. We've got a beautiful day ahead of us."

"I'm so glad the rain held off. I was afraid you might have to teach me to shoot from the porch."

"We could do that."

She laughed, then rattled off the landmarks to get to her place. "I'll meet you at the red pole gate and lead you back."

"Is there more than one way in?"

"Well, no, it's just not a paved road."

"I'm in my truck. You stay put. I'll be there shortly."

"All righty then. Just park at the bridge next to my truck. The cabin is right across the bridge to the left. You'll see it."

"On my way."

He ended the call, excited to see her again. When he looked across the way, he noticed the potted mums in front of the little store next to the gas station. He put the fuel cap back on his truck, snagged his receipt, and then jogged next door. He had a brilliant orange mum in his hand at the register when he saw the cut flowers. "Can I get one of those bouquets instead?"

"Sure. Just set that down. Which do you like?" the woman asked.

"The one with the sunflowers."

She grinned. "That's my favorite. Aren't they just inherently happy?"

"Yes. I believe you're right."

Lifting a large bouquet of the cut flowers from a can, she wiped the wet ends with a towel. "Can I add a bow to this for you? Is it for someone special?"

He felt the heat rise in his cheeks. "A bow would be really nice."

"Are you going far?"

"Just up the road."

"I'm going to skip the plastic then. It's just a pain, and I can fluff the bow real nice with some pretty tissue paper for you." In a flurry of scissor snips and wispy ribbon, she had that bouquet looking fit for a beauty queen in about three seconds flat. "Tada! Just have your lady friend plop them in a vase, and you'll be all set."

"You've done that before," Randy teased.

"A couple times. I love growing and arranging flowers. It's my thing. And if you're looking for something fun to do we have a sunflower maze on our farm. You can ask anyone for directions."

"Well, thank you. I think she'll really enjoy these."

He paid and left her a tip on the counter for the extra care with the flowers, while she helped the next person in line.

He headed out of the parking lot and down the street with the flowers on the dash.

It was basically one street of businesses, but it looked like they had pretty much all they needed. Randy passed the sign to get to the fire station, two churches, and the restaurant Natalie had mentioned. It was a couple miles up a quiet country road before he got to the curve in the road. He turned on his blinker and slowed to look for the unmarked lane. He stopped and opened the pole gate, and closed it before he went on. His truck shifted down as he climbed the hill.

The incline was steep before the trees finally parted, and the road widened. Randy followed the path, wondering if this much seclusion was more than Natalie had bargained for. He didn't know too many women who would opt into something like this, but if he knew one thing about her, it was that she was determined.

She was right, it was a primitive trail back to the bridge.

He pulled his truck right next to hers.

Randy got out of the truck, and Natalie was already heading toward him across the bridge. He lifted his head in a nod, her smile contagious.

"Good morning!" She waved frantically.

He leaned back into the truck and pulled the flowers from the dash.

Her mouth dropped open. "You brought me flowers?"

He shrugged, questioning whether it was as good an idea as he'd thought at the time. "They were pretty. The lady said sunflowers were inherently happy. I thought you'd enjoy them."

She took them and pressed her nose into the bouquet. "I love them. They are happy. I'm happy. Thanks."

"You're welcome."

There was an awkward hesitation, and he rushed to fill the vacancy. "So, I brought guns. Several of them, and targets. I thought it would be a good way to measure which was a better fit."

"Cool. What can I carry?"

He opened the back door, shifted the rifle case onto his shoulder, and handed her a pack of small round targets, then some life-sized human silhouette targets. "I know you won't be shoot-ing people, but we don't carry a lot of bear targets at the police range. This is what they had."

She laughed. "Well, when a bear stands up, they are pretty much the size of a man, aren't they?"

"For your sake, I hope there aren't any that big out here, but you'll be in good shape if we can get you to hit any of these targets. It takes practice."

"Like anything."

"Pretty much."

"Come on," she said. "I'll show you my place, and then we'll figure out where the best place to practice shooting is."

"Sounds good." The narrow bridge crossed over a babbling stream. His work boots echoed against the planks, or maybe that was his heart pounding. He hadn't been this nervous since, well, maybe forever, but darn if he didn't feel like a schoolboy today. Unprepared, confidence waffling, and not quite sure what to say or do. He followed behind her across the bridge. There was a pavilion-type building across the way, probably where the hunters had tied up their deer and skinned them, dressed them out. A hunter's paradise for sure.

"The cabin is just around this break in the tree line," she said.

She looked cute in blue jeans and a three-quarter-sleeve T-shirt in bright orange. He wondered if she'd been trying to go for a blaze-orange safety look or if it had been an accident. "Wow, you really are tucked away."

"It is, but it's so cute. I love it here."

The cabin was nice. Simple, but clearly built to withstand time and weather. Natalie had already added a wreath to the door. "This is great."

"Come on inside. I'll show you around."

He grabbed the screen door before it slapped shut.

It didn't take but a minute to see it all. Small and tidy, it did have everything anyone would need. "Your husband shoot all of these?" he asked, pointing to the trophy deer that lined the wall. Six in all down the long wall of the cabin.

"Some of them. Not all."

He didn't even know why he'd asked. It wasn't like he knew him.

"That's the tour. Not even a nickel's worth."

"Oh, I wouldn't shortchange this place. It's small, but it looks very comfortable."

"Thank you. Welcome to Chestnut Ridge. Not much to it, but the people are welcoming, the food is good, and I've got a place of my own. I've already met more people in this town than I knew in the neighborhood I was living in."

"That says something."

"Would've been nice if even one of those people might have spoken up and waved a red flag while I was living there."

"I hear ya. Once everything unfolded, the neighbors had plenty of opinions, didn't they?"

She nodded, wide-eyed. "But that's the past. I'm not giving it any more attention. That is, until you crack the case and need me."

Randy laughed. He knew she was only half joking, and he wished he could tell her he'd made more progress, but he hadn't heard anything back from the North Carolina detective so far.

He was glad to be here with her. To see where she was living. It wasn't anything like he'd imagined.

He'd been waiting so long for this moment. To spend some

time with her that had nothing to do with police business. A chance to be with her just as two people, not detective and victim.

"No problem finding it?" she asked as she took a glass tea pitcher and filled it with water. "This is the closest thing to a vase here. Hope you aren't insulted. These flowers deserve better."

"They look good."

She looked fresh. Rested. Her skin was slightly kissed by the sun. He withheld commenting on how pretty she looked, afraid to put her on the defensive from the word go. This lady had been hurt. He knew it, and he'd never hurt her, but he knew it would take time for her to trust in that. He had to earn that trust.

It was hard to not stare at her looking so fresh and relaxed. "Your directions were perfect. The landmarks helped. Still, I didn't expect it to be this far off the road."

"I know. We used to come in from the other side. I think it's shorter, but it's really steep, and the guy that's been sort of taking care of the place said that road wasn't easy to navigate even with the truck."

"It's great out here. How long has this cabin been here? The craftsmanship. It has to be old."

"It was in my husband's family for generations. We only came up here a couple of times."

"He grew up in this town?"

"Yeah. I'd never even heard of Chestnut Ridge until Jeremy brought me fishing. It didn't make that big of an impression on me because I didn't even remember I had it. I got lucky. It's nicer than I'd remembered. The plumbing is inside the house now, a big plus. When he brought me here fishing, we had to go outside. I was not a fan of that."

He couldn't even imagine her camping, much less this, but here she was, and she was owning it.

"It's a little early for anything but coffee. Can I get you a cup?"

"That would be nice."

They carried mugs back out to the front porch, making easy conversation about the short amount of time she'd been here.

"You said you've never shot a gun before?"

"Never."

"I'll take you through some simple safety things first. I want you to be safe, and some of it is pretty logical, so bear with me."

"I'm an excellent student, and I want to know those things."

"Good. Some people just want to start shooting, and honestly, that's just not a smart way to learn."

They sat on the porch talking about gun safety, the differences between the types of firearms he'd brought along, and which ones were best in what kind of situations.

"There is a lot to learn."

"You don't learn it in one afternoon."

"What kind of gun do you think I should have?"

"We'll try a few different things. Your size, hand shape, and weight factor into what gun is right for you. You want to get the job done, but you don't need something with a big kickback either."

"No, I don't need a cannon."

They both laughed at that.

"I did some research on the GIS mapping in the area. It doesn't look like you have neighbors except down the mountain, so we should be able to set up some targets in that clearing just over the bridge."

"There's nothing but woods behind there."

"Perfect." He carried the targets and set up a few along the edge of the woods, then walked back over to where she was sitting. "Are you okay? You look kind of nervous all of a sudden."

"It's just that I'm not good at sports. Like, any sport except miniature golf, and even that's iffy."

"I'm going to help you. You're in good hands."

She pressed her lips together. "Okay. I know I have to learn this."

"Before you go shooting at anything, you should call it in to local law enforcement. Do you have your local sheriff department number on your phone yet?"

"No."

He lifted his phone and texted the number to her. "Just sent it to you. Generally, if there's a bear or coyote in the area, you'll have some signs before you ever see them. If they hear you first, they'll usually reroute. Of course, when they've got babies, you don't ever want to get between a mom and her cubs. So being alert is the number-one thing, and really that goes for anything. People, wild animals, and even domesticated dogs."

"Good point."

"You ready to try this?" he asked.

"Ready."

He first taught her how to load and unload a handgun, then the shotgun and rifle. It wasn't until then that they actually took their first shots.

"I'm going to start you with this little twenty-two rifle. It was mine when I was just a kid. I won several 4-H ribbons with this thing."

"Well, then it has to be good luck, right?"

"It's good luck as long as you have good aim," he said, enjoying her hope-filled way of thinking.

He stepped behind her and helped her find the proper position for the rifle. "You're going to place the butt of the rifle right here in the pocket between your shoulder and collarbone. Feel that?"

"Yes."

"You want it right there, so you protect yourself. This gun has minimal recoil, but you'll feel it."

She glanced up, her eyes catching his. She looked nervous.

"Now, take a breath. Just get used to how it feels. Lower it and try again."

She did, and reset the butt of the rifle at her shoulder.

"Excellent. It looks perfect."

She moistened her lips. "Can I shoot now?"

"Line up your shot. Right there on that blue ring on the target."

She let out a slow breath and then pulled the trigger.

"You stayed focused on the target. Great shot!"

She squealed. "I did it." She jumped and turned around. "That was sort of fun."

"You might enjoy some skeet shooting sometime. I'm a member out at one of the skeet clubs."

"You're putting pressure on me. Isn't skeet where they throw those things in the air? I just shot my first standing-still piece of paper."

She was right, that was a leap, but he'd love to take her. He explained, "Well, it's a lot of fun. Sort of like putt-putt but without the windmills, and guns instead of putters."

"So, nothing like putt-putt?" Her eyes were wide and challenging, but her smile was adorable.

"Yeah, nothing like it, except it's competitive and fun."

"Well, then I might like it. I do like a challenge," she said.

"Oh, I *will* be keeping score," he teased.

"I'm counting on it."

"Okay, quit the smack-talking. Let me see you hit the other target."

She took a moment, got into position, and took her time. Squinting at the target, she finally pulled the trigger. It wasn't a perfect shot, but it hit the paper edge, which was pretty impressive the first time out.

They spent the better part of two hours shooting. She didn't like the handguns, too much kick, but she was pretty good with both the shotgun and .22 rifle he'd brought.

"You're doing great." He was honestly impressed with her ability to not only follow the instructions but the way she took her time. "How's it feel?"

"My arm is about ready to fall off. I'm using muscles I've never used before."

He reached over, took the gun from her, and rubbed her shoulder tenderly. "That's probably very true."

"That feels so good."

He pressed gently against the knot in her shoulder, then patted it. "We probably have done all we should do today then."

"I've always been so afraid to even pick up a gun. Thank you for taking the time to help me. Knowing how to load and, more importantly, make sure the gun is unloaded has raised my comfort level like you wouldn't believe."

"And you're a pretty good shot."

"I am, aren't I? Who knew?" She smiled broadly. "Thank you."

"It's been my pleasure. I like a gal who can take care of herself."

"I'm starved. Are you?" she asked.

"My breakfast burned off hours ago. I brought some snacks." He'd been thinking about them for the last hour, but hadn't wanted to distract her.

"Quit holding out on me then. Bring on the snacks!" She looked around at all the gear he had spread out around them.

He reached over and pulled a paper sack out of his duffel bag. "How do you feel about peanut butter and jelly on the softest white bread I could buy?"

"Like you're my hero!"

He tossed his head back, laughing, and flung a sandwich through the air in her direction.

She snagged it in midair. "Oh yeah!"

"Nice catch. And you said you weren't athletic. I believe someone is sandbagging me."

"Believe me. It was luck."

They sat in the grass and munched on their sandwiches without another word. She was so easy to be around. Her enthusiasm left him feeling like he couldn't wait to breathe the same air she did. *I could fall in love with this girl. Maybe I already have.*

He watched her finish off the PBJ like it was the best thing she'd ever eaten, then slap her hands against her pants. "I'm ready for another lesson. How about you?"

"How about we get to fishing?"

"I thought you'd never ask," she said.

You are the woman I've always dreamed of. I wouldn't mind getting lost in a sunflower maze with you.

Chapter Twenty-Seven

"THAT WAS the best PBJ I've ever eaten." Natalie tucked the napkins into the top of the bag so they wouldn't blow away. "Thank you for bringing those. Can't say the last time I've had one, and the strawberry jelly was an unexpected treat."

"Don't give away my recipe. It's a family secret."

She liked his sense of humor. He was confident but not cocky, and that was nice. "What happens if I tell a family secret?"

"You have to become one of us." He gave her a wink, and she couldn't help but giggle.

"Do you cook anything else?"

"Oh yeah. Sure. I burn a mean hot dog and have mastered the medium-rare hamburger on my gas grill."

"You're speaking my language. I love burnt hot dogs. How did you know *my* secret?" She pulled her knees up, wrapping her arms around them and rocking back.

"I have a feeling we have more than that in common."

"I don't grill," she said. "I'm afraid of fire, and I swear no matter how much I spend on a grill, the igniter breaks in a month. I absolutely refuse to turn on the gas and flick the lighter between the grates."

"Those igniters are junk. I'm pretty comfortable with my barbecuing skills and a lighter."

"Careful now, else I might make you prove it."

His smile was easy. He plucked a piece of grass. "We could cook over a real fire. There's plenty of wood around here."

"Don't you come from the city and start chopping down my trees."

"I could prove my grilling skills to you at my house. You still know the way back to Richmond, don't you?"

"I do."

"Let me cook for you."

She was almost afraid to respond but finally said, "I'd like that. I will."

"That's settled then," he said. "You pick the date. I'll make it work."

"Giving me a lot of power, aren't you?"

"I've got more vacation and personal time saved up than some guys have on the job. It'll be fine."

"Great. I'll let you know, then."

He looked at his watch. "Wow, this day is zooming by. If we don't get these guns put up pretty quickly, there won't be time to fish. I'm not ready for it to end, though." He got up and started putting the guns back in their cases. "Want to check those to be sure they're unloaded for me?"

"I can do that. I learned from the best." She began checking them just like he'd taught her. "All clear," she announced after double-checking the last one.

He rechecked each one again before putting them away.

"Don't trust me?" She was only teasing, though, and she'd never been good at keeping a straight face.

"Always, always, always double-check." He realized she was kidding and lightened up. "Seriously. You can't be too careful."

"I understand." She watched him diligently go through the process.

"Which gun were you the most comfortable with?"

"I think the twenty-two rifle," Natalie said after careful consideration. "I like that it's not too loud, and there wasn't much recoil."

"A good fit. That's what I thought you'd like best." He put it aside. "I'm going to leave this one here for you to practice with until we can take you to buy one of your own."

"No, you don't have to do that. I can go buy one—"

"I haven't used that thing since I was a kid. Get a feel for it. I'd recommend giving yourself some time with it, and then we can try others again when you've got more experience. Then, when you're ready, you can buy one."

"Are you sure?"

"Positive."

"What if I leave town and you don't get it back?" she said.

"I know you better than that."

She smiled. "Yes. You do. Thank you, Randy."

He handed her the rifle case with the .22 in it. "Ready for that fishing excursion?" He zipped the duffel bag.

Her mood lifted. "Yeah, great. I can try out the new gear I bought."

He picked up the bag and the other gun cases. "I'm going to put this stuff back in the truck. I'll get my fishing pole and meet you back at the cabin."

"Sounds good. I'll make some lemonade to drink before we

go." She walked back to the cabin, proud of her accomplishments today and feeling better about her ability to take care of herself. She put the gun in the corner next to the door.

I actually shot a gun.

It was empowering, and she liked that feeling.

She boiled a pot of water to dissolve sugar and started cutting and juicing lemons. Since she'd already used the only pitcher in the place for the beautiful flowers Randy had given her, she made the lemonade in a big mixing bowl. She filled glasses with some ice and then scooped lemonade into them with a measuring cup, resisting the urge to hang a slice of lemon over the edge. Probably a wasted effort on a guy.

"Knock, knock," Randy called from the door.

"Come on in. I'm about ready." She handed him a glass of lemonade. "For you, sir." He immediately took a sip. "Wow, this is good."

"Homemade."

"Nice." He took another sip while she gathered her things.

Natalie changed into a pair of hiking boots. If she remembered correctly, the trail down to the water's edge was steep.

"Let's go," she said. "I honestly am not sure where the trail is to the stream. We'll just have to look for it."

"I noticed a cut-through just to the left of the bridge. Want to try that way?"

"I'll follow you."

He led the way. He was respectful in how he twisted the branches as he walked ahead of her, clearing a path. Some of the brush was pretty thick.

The land sloped off, and the descent to the water's edge was thankfully not nearly as steep as she'd remembered.

"I can hear the water. Do you know what body of water this is?" Randy asked.

"Cherish Creek. Hard to forget a name like that. We caught sunfish and some other stuff. There's supposed to be amazing trout fishing over in the river."

"Probably redear sunfish. They're good eating. We'll have to try trout fishing sometime too." The water rushing over the rocks became louder.

"I think we're getting close," she said.

And then there it was, right in front of them.

A bright red bird with black wings flew across the creek.

"Did you see that?" she asked. "I think that might be the prettiest bird I've ever seen."

"He landed over there on that limb. Look at the black on his wings compared to the brilliant red." He pulled out his phone, his thumbs working across the screen. "I think it might be a scarlet tanager. Says they are seen around the streams and creeks in this area."

"Gorgeous."

"Yeah." He set his things down and opened his tackle box. "I brought some worms." He lifted a small container in the air. "I have some spinners and jigs that'll work too. What's your pleasure?"

"Hmm. Can I use the spinner? That sounds pretty."

He laughed. "Did you pick that just because you don't want to touch the worms?"

"Maybe." She gave him a playful look. "Perhaps, but if I try it and it works, then maybe I can never touch one. I'd be okay with that."

"You got it." He put a spinner on the end of her line and

added weight and a bobber. "You're set. Know how to use this thing?" He flipped the rod around and tapped her on the head with its end.

"Real funny, mister." She grabbed the end of the rod and tucked it away from him. "I might need a little refresher."

He got up and helped her. Standing behind her, he placed his hands on top of hers and moved fluidly, practicing a cast. "Are you sandbagging me? You seem to know exactly what you're doing."

"No. I'm just sort of remembering."

"Just click that over and hold it, then let go to cast."

She did so.

"Excellent. Now reel it in slowly. The spinner will act like a wounded bug as you pull the lure through the water. Maybe you'll get some interest."

He threaded a small piece of a worm onto his hook and cast out in the other direction while she worked her line closer to shore.

No sooner had Natalie recast her line back into the water than she got a hit. "I got one!"

"Reel it in." He laid his pole down and came to her side to help her.

She cranked the reel for all she was worth. Her heart pounded like she was running for her life, but she laughed the whole time. Suddenly the fish splashed out of the water and then went back under. "I really have something."

"You sure do." The fish flipped its fins when she pulled it in, sending water droplets across her face. "I think he's not very happy with me right now."

Randy grabbed the line. "What do you say we catch and

release today since we don't have time to clean and cook them?"

"Seems fair enough."

After the sixth catch and release, Natalie finally had to ask. "Are we catching the same fish over and over?"

"No. We'd be able to tell if we'd hooked him before. This is just great fishing."

"I think I like this." She cast her line out again.

"Let's plan another fishing day when we can cook what we catch."

"As long as you're the one cooking, it's fine with me."

"You can make the side dishes." He pulled his line in and started putting things away.

"Fine by me." But she'd be lying if she didn't feel a bit of disappointment now that the day was wrapping up.

"We better pack up," he said. "The days are getting shorter, and we don't need to be out here in the dark with nothing but our phones for light."

"We'd look like a couple of giant lightning bugs."

"You'd make a cute lightning bug." His gaze hung tight to hers, making her catch her breath.

"Thanks." She gathered their things and grabbed the fishing poles. The hike back up the hill was trickier than the walk down.

Randy stopped about halfway up. "We could add a couple landings along here by putting a couple three-foot boards down to give you an easier route back up."

We? She could picture the two of them working on that together. Her foot slipped, but she was able to catch her balance. "I like that idea."

He stopped at the top of the ridge. The day was coming to an end and she wasn't ready for that. It had been such a fun and easy day.

The bridge was just past where they stood, and she dreaded him saying goodbye.

"I'm going to head on home," he said.

"It's nice here, isn't it? Can you see why I'm excited about a fresh start here?"

His gaze held hers. "I understand it completely." His lips parted, but whatever he was thinking, he didn't say. "It's like being in vacation mode without leaving your yard."

"Yes. That's it exactly. I'm creating, and motivated, and it's low-key. None of the material things that I lost even matter."

"It's special. You deserve this. I'm happy for you."

"I feel like me again. Maybe a better version of myself."

"Impossible."

"You're a flirt."

"I'm serious."

"I like it. Not just the place, but you being here. Thank you for coming. For helping me and for this day."

"Anytime."

She scanned the area. "Do you think I'll be safe up here?"

"I do. I don't know this area, but I did a little digging. Occupational hazard, I guess. There's no crime to speak of out this way. If you pay attention to your surroundings and keep your phone on you at all times, you'll be fine. A gun isn't a bad idea. I'm often cautious about advising people to have one, especially if they aren't confident in how to use one. Still, if you stay in practice, it's a good thing. If you're going to toss it in a drawer and never load it, clean it, or practice, you're better off with a whistle. Okay, maybe not *just* a whistle, but a good softball bat. You don't want to end up hurting yourself." He handed her the fishing poles.

"I get it. Good advice. If I decide to get a gun, I'll stay up on my skills. Thank you for letting me borrow the twenty-two. That's really generous of you."

"We could put up a couple target boards in the clearing for you to practice. I could help you with that."

She set the end of her fishing pole down on the ground. "You'd really drive up to help me, wouldn't you?"

"Absolutely." Then he folded his arms. "Of course, it's gonna cost you."

"Uh-oh."

"Mmhmm. Copious amounts of that fresh lemonade, hours of fresh mountain air, and fishing."

"I might even cook for you."

"If you're lucky, I'll bring PBJs."

"I'm happy we met. The circumstances sucked, but we may have never met otherwise."

He placed his hand on her shoulder. "I feel the very same way."

Her heart raced. Was he going to kiss her goodnight? But he didn't, and part of her wished he had rushed right in before she could think about it. "Well, at least come up to the house and get cleaned up before you go. You've been smooshing worms with those hands." She splayed her filthy fingers in the air like she was giving up.

"That would be good." He left his things at the bridge and followed her up to the cabin.

She went to the bathroom, while he washed up at the kitchen sink.

He was standing at the fireplace mantel when she came out.

He turned, looking a little caught. "Um, I guess this is a picture of you and your husband."

"It is." She walked over and stood next to Randy. "I found that picture in the bedside drawer when I got here."

"That must've been a nice surprise." His eyes met hers in a thoughtful way. "You seem really happy here. At peace."

"I am," she said. "I'd been sort of protecting myself. Not allowing myself to think about my husband much because I thought it would hurt too much, but now. Now it's different. I'm glad I found that picture."

"I'm sorry for your loss."

"Me too." She didn't want to dwell on it. "I think it's cooler outside." She headed for the door and he followed.

They walked to the bridge together.

"I'm going to go buy an air-conditioning unit this evening. Who knew the mountains could get this warm this time of year?"

"Wish you'd told me. I have an extra one in storage. My AC at the house went out last year, and it was going to take a couple of weeks to get it replaced. I bought it to get through. I could bring it to you."

She paused but then shook her head. "No. I'll just go buy one. It would cost you just as much in gas to go get it and bring it to me as for me to buy one. There's actually one of those fancy mini-splits in the shed, I just haven't had time to figure out who can install that and what all it's going to entail."

He followed alongside, and their hands grazed as they walked.

"Hey?" came from across the bridge, startling a yelp out of Natalie. Randy instinctively took her by the arm and pulled her behind him.

"Do you know him?" Randy asked.

Natalie caught her breath, realizing it was Tucker across the bridge. "Oh, yeah. He's been taking care of the cabin." She called across to him. "Tucker! Hey. You scared me to death."

Tucker trudged across the bridge.

"Everything okay here?" Tucker was puffed up like he was ready for a fight.

Natalie was taken aback. "Yes, of course."

Randy stuck his hand out. "Hey, man. Randy Fellowes. I'm a friend of Natalie's."

Tucker hesitated, then lifted his chin and, without taking an eye off of Randy, asked her, "That true?"

"Yes. We were just doing some target practice and fishing." Natalie was so embarrassed. She barely knew Tucker, but he seemed to think he was her guardian or something, and she didn't really like the way that felt.

Finally, Tucker deflated a little and shook Randy's hand. "We take care of our kind up here. Saw the strange truck."

"I'm glad Natalie is in a safe place with a good support system," Randy said.

"Yeah, you don't need to worry about that." Tucker folded his arms across his chest.

"Well, I do," Randy said. "I'm a friend, and that's what friends do."

"So, you'll be coming around?"

"As long as Natalie is here, I will be." Randy stood his ground.

Those words hung on her heart, which instilled joy and fear at the same time.

"All right." He nodded in an almost impolite way. Enough so that Natalie was getting a little mad with Tucker. *Are these two going to fight over me?*

She stepped forward. "And I can take excellent care of myself. So no one has to worry."

"Yes. You certainly can," Randy said. "We good here?"

"Yeah, man," Tucker said. "Natalie, you know how to reach me if you need anything."

She waved, and he turned and walked back to his truck.

"That was interesting," Randy said.

"Very." She didn't like it one bit. "I'm sorry about that. I don't know what it was all about. I barely know him, but he's a lifelong friend of Jeremy's. I think he just feels protective since I'm alone here."

"Does he know about the stuff with Swindell?"

"No. I don't plan on ever telling anyone about *that*." Although she had confided in Orene, but she was already more than a neighbor.

"It might help to talk about it with a few folks. You shouldn't feel embarrassed. You were a victim of a crime."

He looked over her head toward where Tucker was climbing into his truck. "He's acting like a protective brother, which honestly isn't a bad trait."

She laughed, patting him playfully on the arm. "You're great. You know that? Thank you for coming all this way."

"It's not that far. I found it to be a relaxing drive. It's beautiful up here. Just like you said."

"So you'd come back?"

"Any and every time I'm invited."

Her heart flipped. "You are invited."

He gave her a quick hug, then turned to leave. She watched him walk across the bridge.

"Hurry back," she whispered.

Chapter Twenty-Eight

THE FOLLOWING morning Natalie was still smiling from Randy's visit. She was even craving a peanut butter and strawberry jelly sandwich.

She was sipping her coffee, enjoying the crisp fall weather on the porch, when her phone rang. "Hello."

"Miss Natalie, it's Jesse."

"Good morning." It was odd that he'd be calling on a Sunday morning. She hoped she wasn't getting fired. Had he gotten wind of her allowing Paul to buy her lunch?

"I know we haven't quite made it out of the trial period, but I have a request for you if you are interested."

Interested? This is good news. "Absolutely. What can I do?"

"Mr. G. has asked if you might be able to drive him to church this morning, and ongoing as needed for errands."

"I'd love that. He's a really nice man. I enjoyed driving him. Does this mean I'm hired?"

"Definitely." Jesse laughed. "He can be a delight and he's a wonderful friend, but he's a handful at times. I'm glad you got to see the good side of him first."

"Where does he go to church? What time?"

"It's short notice. If you can't accommodate today, we can start that next week."

"I can take him this morning."

"Wonderful. The service starts at eleven sharp. You've probably picked up on the fact that he doesn't like to be late."

"I'm the same way. Maybe that's why we got along so well. What's the address?"

"It's the rock church at Mountain View and Chestnut Spring Road."

Rock church? That hardly seemed the old man's style, but who was she to judge. "I'll pick him up at ten thirty."

"I'll let him know. And Natalie. Thank you."

"My pleasure." She hung up the phone and did a little dance, happy for the extra work. She went to the closet, changed into a long sundress, and slipped on a pair of flats.

She set the alarm on her phone so she'd have time to switch out cars in town, pick up Mr. G., and have one more cup of coffee before time to go.

When Natalie pulled into the driveway, Paul got off his scooter and climbed in with a broad smile.

"Thank you for taking on the extra duties," he said. "I realize I didn't give you much notice."

"It's no problem at all. This isn't even like work. It's like helping a neighbor, and I love that."

"Do you know the church?" he asked.

"I don't, but Jesse gave me the address. I've got it set in the GPS." She tapped the dash. "Love those things. I haven't been lost in years."

"I'd prefer a good old-fashioned map. Then, that's me. Old

and old-fashioned. You're welcome to join me in church, young lady. Not required. Just if you like."

She lifted her chin, smiling in the rear-view mirror. "Thank you. That's really thoughtful of you." She headed down the driveway toward town. It didn't take long to make it to the church. She parked right in front of a brass historical site marker stating the rock-faced church was built in 1929.

Rock-*faced*. Now that made more sense. "It's beautiful," she said.

"Isn't it?"

She walked around to his side of the car. She hooked her arm, and he accepted it.

"Thank you for joining me. We'll go in through that side door," he said.

They walked up to the large doors, and once inside, he led the way to a pew that clearly he'd been sitting in for years. The people nearby all greeted him.

She took a seat next to him, trying not to insert herself into the conversations around them.

The organist began to play, and everyone quieted.

It was a good sermon, but she couldn't keep her mind from wandering as the pastor preached about family. Had Jeremy ever been to this church? How many people in this room knew that she was his widow? She'd bet most of them. A wave of anxiety came over her.

A rudderless boat. That's what having no family felt like. And Jeremy had been such a steadying force for her. She missed him madly at this moment. She clenched her hands together. People here, they'd never understand how huge losing Jeremy was for her. He'd been her everything.

At that moment, the preacher called for them to bow their heads in prayer. She did so, and thankfully the moment passed. She wiped her sweaty hands on her dress as she sat down.

After the service, she and Paul walked back out to the car. Orene caught up with her just as she closed Paul's door.

"How are you? It's good to see you," Orene said.

"How nice to see you here. This is a beautiful church."

"Oh, yes, and our new pastor, isn't he great? I swear sometimes he's reading my mind. Sometimes that makes me a little nervous." Orene nudged her playfully. "Why don't you come over for tea this afternoon? I'll make some of those little tea sandwiches for us. We can call it lunch."

"I'd love that. I just have to drop off my client first."

Orene squeezed Natalie's arm. "Lovely! I'll be waiting." Orene was off and running, waving her hand over her head as she rushed across the lot to chat with someone else.

Natalie got in the car. "You ready to go home?"

"Yes," Paul said. "Such a simple yet important message today."

She smiled politely. She'd only heard about half of it, getting caught up in her own history and feeling so out of place with all the family talk.

"I was really delighted you chose to join me in church. I hope you'll do that every week."

She smiled, appreciating his kindness. "It's been too long since I made this a regular part of my life. I'm thankful for the invitation."

She drove back to his house and stopped next to his scooter. "All set."

"Thank you. I'd like to go to the market tomorrow. Could we

do that in the afternoon?" His hand gripped his cane. "Would two thirty work for you?"

"That'll be fine. I'll see you then."

She waited at the end of the driveway until she saw him clear the corner. What a strange thing for him to insist on coming to the gate. Maybe he'd change his mind at some point.

Natalie stopped and switched out cars, getting back in her truck, which felt gigantic after driving the car. She stopped at the market to pick up something to take over to Orene's, because no Southern girl would purposely show up to tea empty-handed.

She scoured the baked goods for something that would do.

Finally, she settled on miniature pumpkin cakes filled with cream cheese frosting and topped with candied pecans. Two of those and two tiny apple tarts. The gal working the counter set them in individual pastry cups in a cake box.

"They look beautiful. Thank you." She carried them to the checkout and then set them gingerly in the truck's front seat. Then, nervous they'd slide or tip out of the seat, she placed them on the floor.

She made it to Orene's without incident.

From the front porch, she could hear Orene singing. She waited, enjoying her sweet voice until the last note, then knocked.

"Oh, goodness! I didn't hear you drive up. Come on in. What did you bring?" She took the box, her face lighting up. "You didn't have to do that, but boy, we will enjoy these."

"I know. Don't they look delicious?"

"I bet my friend Nelle made these. She bakes on the side for the market up the road. That woman. She's got amazing baking and cooking skills. The nicest woman you ever met and the biggest faith! Lord, girl, she's had some heaping trials in her life. Doesn't matter. She just keeps looking up and moving on."

"She sounds wonderful."

"You'll love her. How about you come over around lunchtime tomorrow. I'll introduce the two of you."

"That sounds nice. What can I bring?"

"Not a thing. Nelle's cooking."

"Don't you think we should at least ask her first?"

"No. She's open for lunch three days a week—Monday, Wednesday, and Friday."

"How does someone stay in business with such limited hours?" Natalie asked.

"Once you taste Nelle's cooking, you'll know the answer to that."

"I have an appointment at two thirty to take Paul to the market. Can we do lunch early?"

"Sure. Come on over tomorrow whenever you're ready."

An hour had passed with the two gabbing before they sat down for tea.

"How are things going at the cabin, Natalie?" Orene pressed her fingers against the teapot lid as she poured for both of them.

"Great. I'm getting my ducks in a row. I've been doing a lot of painting. This town inspires me."

"Chestnut Ridge is a special place. No crime to speak of, and there's just something freeing here that you don't feel other places."

"Most of the time. I had something strange happen yesterday, though."

"How so?"

"Tucker showed up out of the blue."

"Really? At the cabin? Well, he must've been checking on things. I'm sure old habits die hard."

"Probably." It still bothered her. "It was more than that, though."

"What happened? You seem bothered by it."

"I'm sure Tucker didn't mean anything by it, but he was rather rude with my friend who was here for the day."

"A friend?"

"Yes. The detective I told you about."

"Detective Fellowes. Randy," Orene recited from memory. "Yes. How nice that he came to see you."

"Tucker acted all out of sorts about him being there with me. It was very awkward."

"I'm sure he was just worried about you. Knowing you've never lived in the mountains. Kind of showing up out of the blue and all."

"It just kind of caught me off guard."

"He and Jeremy were like brothers. I'm sorry it offended you, but I can promise you this: Tucker is one of the best men I know. They don't make them like him anymore. An old soul, he's very special. I hope you'll give him a pass."

She'd keep that in mind, and Orene's opinion did matter. She vaguely remembered possibly meeting Tucker when they were at the cabin, but why didn't Jeremy ever talk about his past? "I'm sure that's all it was," Natalie said, waving off the subject. "It just made me feel kind of guilty. For no reason. Randy is just a friend."

Orene lifted her chin, a twinkle in her eye. "Tough problem

to have. All the men wanting to take care of you," Orene mused. "I'd heard you had company. Nothing wrong with that."

"Word gets around fast."

"Small town."

"Or Tucker is a blabbermouth."

"He is, but it'd get around anyway. It can be a good thing. We take care of each other around here."

"I can take care of myself." She said it with such conviction she almost believed it, and it had been a long time since she'd felt that way. "But yes, it's nice to have people you can count on. Not just men. People in general. Like you. I'm so thankful I happened onto your doorstep. We may have never met."

"Oh, we'd have met. That I know. Tell me about this man. Is he handsome?" Orene topped off Natalie's tea.

"Well, yeah, but that's not the point. He's a good person."

"Oooh. It must feel good to have someone like that willing to come all the way up here for you. You've been friends for a long time?"

"We haven't really known each other that long, but he's the kind of person you can count on. Why do you think that some people you just feel like you can trust right from the word go?"

"Well, I believe it's a little like what the preacher talked about this morning. Family isn't always blood. We are all God's children, after all."

Natalie had felt that way about Marc Swindell too, and he hadn't turned out to be trustworthy. What if Randy, Tucker, or even this sweet little old lady were tricking her too?

Orene pursed her lips. She lifted her teacup and took a sip.

"But then, who am I to say? My own family practically cheated me out of house and home with that darned B and B website. I've been running the offense on that for a year now. Good people trust others. I'm the same way. We don't expect people to be dishonest or use us."

Natalie couldn't respond without risking a tear, so she just nodded.

"A broken heart can possibly be one of the most powerful things in your life. A kick start, if you will . . . if you let it."

"It just made me vulnerable."

"Well, you could say that about me letting my granddaughter play me, but we won't. Uh-huh. Being emotional, even vulnerable means the past meant so much to you. But we can't stay there. Can we?"

"I guess not, but I've prayed to turn back time."

"Don't pray away your tomorrows. You need to move forward. There is more ahead. Things more wonderful than you could ever dream of."

Why are people always saying things like that? "Do you really believe that?"

Orene scooted to the edge of her seat. "I'm livin' proof, darlin'. You can be too. Sounds like you're already on a good path."

"What makes you say that?"

"For one, you were smart enough to uproot yourself and come to Chestnut Ridge. You're surrounding yourself with good people who truly want the best for you. I think your friend Randy is good too. Why else would someone drive in from the city just for a few hours?"

"He *did* do that." It was scary to think about it, but she found herself grinning at the possibilities.

"Trust him. An amazing story just might unfold. I know you were heartbroken to lose Jeremy. He was so young. You both are. It's very sad." She shook her finger in Natalie's direction. "But this is the gate to a new beginning. Just keep on walking."

"You make it sound so easy."

"It is." She put down her cup. "Did I ever tell you that two presidents of our fine country actually stayed here before? It could've been more, but I only have documentation to support the claim of two of them. That's pretty special."

Natalie let Orene tell her story again. As a geriatric nurse she'd become immune to getting bored hearing the same ones over and over, instead taking delight in the memories that stood out in their aging minds. "It is. This house is special. I felt it that first night I stepped through the door."

"Teddy Roosevelt and Woodrow Wilson both stayed here while they were in office. The fairy stones brought them to this county."

"I can't believe I've never heard of them until coming here," Natalie said. "And then within a couple of days of coming here, I'd heard about them twice! I've got to see these fairy stones for myself. If there even is such a thing. I'm picturing those little elves that make cookies in a tree, soldiering forth with lapidary tools between cookie cooling to make them in their spare time."

"It's a natural phenomenon. I have a whole collection of them. Come with me. I'll show you."

Natalie got up and followed Orene into another room of the house. One she'd never been in.

"See here." She lifted a large flat box with a glass top. It was filled with cross-shaped stones. "There are four types of fairy stones. Three are crosses."

"And they just come that way?"

"Yep, they form this way all on their own." She lifted the glass top and shuffled through the pile, setting a few out on the table, one at a time. "It's really quite amazing. There are just a few shapes, but they can range from a tiny quarter of an inch to two inches, like this one." She held up a large cross between her finger and thumb.

"I like the smaller ones."

"Me too. See, here's St. Andrew's cross. This one is a Maltese, and this one's a Roman cross."

Natalie held her hair back as she leaned over for a closer look. "It's amazing."

Orene lifted the small Roman cross and pressed it into Natalie's hand. "They are said to bring good luck. I want you to have this one."

Where was this before I met Marc Swindell? "I might need a whole pocketful of them. I've been pretty unlucky of late."

Orene tsked. "Oh, just one will do the trick. I promise. I've lived a lot of years in this county. I've seen them work firsthand."

"Who am I to argue? Do I have to wish on them or something?"

"No. Just have it. That's all there is to it."

She didn't feel any different, but what could it hurt?

Chapter Twenty-Nine

NATALIE COULDN'T wait to have lunch with Orene and meet her friend Nelle. She arrived at Orene's just after twelve so they'd have plenty of time before she had to take Paul on his scheduled grocery shopping outing.

When Natalie got to Orene's, she noticed the new decorations she'd put up.

"Orene. It's me," Natalie called through the screen door. There was a new wreath on the front door made of fall leaves in green, gold, and orange. Orene had added a row of deep wine-colored mums along the steps up the porch too. On each of the pillars she had tied colorful ears of corn with raffia. It looked so festive.

Orene came to the door wearing black capris and a fun T-shirt with a row of toothy pumpkins across the front. Her hair wasn't in her usual tidy bun; instead it hung down her back. Natalie had never realized her hair was so long. "You look pretty."

"Thank you."

"Are you ready to go? I can drive."

"No need for all that. It's just up the road apiece. Right here off Main Street. Let's walk."

As Orene pulled a pumpkin-colored sweater over her T-shirt, Natalie waited on the porch. Orene didn't tarry one second, walking right past Natalie on her way out the door. "Let's go. Maybe we can still beat the big lunch crowd," she said as she marched down the stairs.

Natalie jogged to catch up with the spry old woman, who was pointing out the spots where the concrete seams had risen and might trip an unsuspecting newcomer.

Other than that, Orene didn't have much to say on the walk to Nelle's.

Orene swerved into the hardware store's front entrance, which took up the better part of this block. A trio of bells rang as they walked inside and headed to the right, hoofing it toward the back.

Natalie puppy-dogged behind the little woman, who wove between the rows of bolts and hardware and paintbrushes. Throwing a hand in the air, she said, "Heya, Bobby Wayne. What's cookin' today?"

"Hey, Orene. She's got jambalaya that'll smack your lips for you."

Natalie had to process the accent and the slang. It tickled her that they seemed to have their own dialect up here. Would it be that she'd be talking like that a year from now too? She highly doubted it.

Jambalaya wasn't something Natalie had ever eaten before. She hoped that fairy stone would bring enough luck that there might be something more on the menu today.

There were a dozen tables filled with diners in the far corner of the hardware store. A kitchen was tucked behind a chalkboard that ran the length of the wall. In bold shimmery gold letters, "Nelle's" had been painted on a sign that hung from the ceiling.

Orene marched up to a heavyset woman wearing a colorful apron and stirring a pot as big as a witch's kettle with a huge wooden spoon. "Nelle. Need you to meet somebody. We got us a new neighbor."

Nelle never stopped stirring the bubbling cauldron. Her toothy grin, spaced like Chiclets, gave her an appearance that matched the jack-o-lantern faces on Orene's playful shirt. "Who do we have here?"

The woman's accent was thick. Not like the others in this town.

"Hi, I'm Natalie."

"I'm Nelle, and I'm happy to meet anyone who's a friend of my dear friend Orene here. How do you know each other?"

Natalie silently translated the thick accent, trying to decipher the question. Or was it just a comment?

"She's Nawlins to the core," Orene said with a nudge.

"Love Nawlins, but I'm Creole. It's different."

"And you run this kitchen. It smells wonderful."

"Cookin' like I always did back home, because it makes me happy, and my food makes them happy."

"I can see that." People at every table were devouring the food. "I've never had Creole food. Is it spicy?"

"Naw, girl. You'll love my food. You two go sit down. I'll bring it over in a jiffy."

"Nelle." Orene's voice had lost its play. She nodded toward Natalie. "She was married to Jeremy."

Nelle's eyes widened. "Oh. I'm so sorry. But it's good you're here. Finally. How wonderful. He's greatly missed around here."

"You knew him?"

"I did." Her Creole accent hung in the air as rich and spicy as the jambalaya. "Amazing what brings people to this town. Brings us together, yes? Family. It's the most important thing."

"Is that what brought you to Chestnut Ridge?" Natalie asked.

Nelle glanced over at Orene. "Oh, goodness, my dear. A hurricane blew me up here, but that's a very long story for another time. I've got cooking to do. You two go sit. I've got work to do."

"A hurricane? My goodness."

"Oh, but it's true. Devastating, my dear, but don't let that worry you. It was the best change in my life. It brought me here." Her eyes glistened, echoing the cheerful look on her face. "Go. You two sit. Get hungry. I'll tell you the whole story another time."

"I look forward to hearing it," Natalie said, but Orene was already pushing her toward an open table.

"You will," Orene said. "Trust me. You can't escape her stories."

Nelle tossed a hand towel at Orene. "You get on outta my kitchen, you can't be nice. Before I say something to get me in trouble." Her hearty laugh ended in a howl that sounded like the last hanging note in a song.

Before they even got settled at the tiny corner table, a young girl was bringing bowls of jambalaya to them. Without a word, the colorful bowls were set down, and another teenager brought glasses of sweet tea over.

"We didn't order this," Natalie said.

"There's no ordering here. We get what we get and be happy with it." Orene placed a paper napkin in her lap.

"Hmmm, I am not sure about this."

"Ever had it?"

"Well . . . no . . ."

"Eat up." She grabbed Natalie's hands and, in a quick sentence, had blessed the food, picked up her fork, and taken a bite.

"Okay." Natalie pushed the mixture around in her bowl. It didn't look too appetizing.

Glancing around the room, she saw people were enjoying the food. There was happiness in the space, and out of sheer politeness and a grumble from her stomach, she gave in and took a bite, albeit a tiny one.

Orene smirked. "You like it, don't you?"

She licked her lips, waiting to decide. "I think I do."

"Eat like you mean it." She tapped her fork on Natalie's bowl.

This town was a surprise at every turn. If Natalie had learned one thing in the short time she'd been here, it was to quit questioning what she thought she knew. It was time to start trusting the journey, because there was something new around every corner. So far, all of it had been good.

She walked with Orene back to her house and then hurried along to pick up Paul and take him grocery shopping. At least there wouldn't be any surprises there.

Chapter Thirty

TO HER surprise, Paul was *not* sitting at the gate waiting on her this afternoon. She took quiet jubilation in making it before him. She'd always prided herself on being early to be on time, and darn it if, up until this very day, he'd beat her to it.

"Aha! Not today, my friend." She settled back in her seat, anxious to see his expression when he saw that she was waiting on him today. She reached over and took her sketch pad out of her tote bag. She'd been thinking about that rusty horse trailer nonstop the last couple of nights. The way Courtnie had repurposed hers and painted it had inspired her. She wasn't going to open a coffee and tea shop with hers, but what if she used it as a kiosk? A mural showcasing her art and the note cards could be a really clever way to grab customers' attention. It might also give her an excuse to travel a bit. Now that she had Jeremy's truck back, she had a way to haul it.

She made a quick outline of a horse trailer, then started penning a mural on the page in front of her, incorporating many of the featured designs that were already bestsellers for her.

A smile played on her lips as she let her imagination take over.

It came together so fluidly that she could hardly wait to get started on the horse trailer with it. She'd have to find someone to help with the fabrication changes. Maybe her neighbor Joe would have some ideas.

It was then she glanced at her watch and realized Paul was late.

That wasn't like him.

Worried, Natalie wondered if she'd gotten the wrong date or time. She sat there for another ten minutes, then got out of her car and walked up to the gate. There was no intercom, only a keypad. A sign read "No Trespassing," clear as day.

Although she was a rule follower, her concern was stronger. She couldn't very well leave. She tried Paul's number, but there was no answer. Calling Jesse would just mean waiting longer.

She pressed 1234 on the keypad with no luck. Then 0000, but that didn't work either.

Finally, she pushed on the gate and squeezed her tiny frame between the massive fence panels. The climb up the driveway was much steeper than it looked. She was winded when she made it to the curve where she usually saw Paul veer off to the right.

A black fence ran along the left side of the driveway from the trees as far as she could see to the next bend. There had to be a mile of pastureland on the other side of that fence. It was still green and as manicured as if it were a golf course. Off in the distance, a golden horse grazed, in no hurry at all.

It was a good thing Paul had that cart, because this was a long climb.

A trio of birdhouses rose in varying heights from one of the posts. One sky blue, one orange, and the other a chartreuse green. She made a mental note to pick up a few birdhouses so she could paint them and put them near the cabin, or on the bridge, in a similar cluster as they'd done here. Maybe both.

She was worried about Paul. Hopefully, he'd just overslept.

As she walked around the next curve, her legs were tiring from the climb. *When did I get so out of shape?* She stopped, not because of the burning in her hamstrings and glutes, when the house came into view.

Not just any house.

This has to be the castle they were talking about. Natalie remembered Orene saying no one had ever been inside.

Paul Grandstaff can't live here.

There had to be a mistake.

Her heart raced, realizing she was flat-out trespassing no matter how sincere her motives were.

Just as colorful as those birdhouses on the path up the hill were, there was a long line of beehives in staggered rows, almost like a little solar farm in bright oranges, greens, blues, and golds. Some were tall, some short, like wedding cakes for different-sized parties. She'd never seen so many. The thought of that many bees making a home here made her itch.

A dog barked, luring her attention away from the buzzing activities to a towering tiered water fountain in front of the house. It wasn't a scary guard-dog bark, and it only took a moment to find the culprit.

Two beagles leaped into the air, then jumped into the water spraying from the fountain.

They ran out onto the pavement a moment later, leaving a trail of paw prints and water droplets. One pup raced after the other, trying to bite his tail. And if that wasn't funny enough, a duck floating in the pond, unnoticed until now, suddenly raised up and flapped its wings, scaring both pups off, with their ears back and tails tucked.

She laughed out loud. *Bravo, Mr. Duck! You just outmaneuvered bird dogs.*

The image of Mr. Duck outmaneuvering the puppies would make a cute note card too.

She tucked away that idea and focused on the house. The architecture was unbelievable. There was even an actual tower at the far end of the building like a storybook castle, Natalie could almost imagine Rapunzel letting down her long hair. Up close, the colors on the exterior were applied in a way that it gave the appearance of moving waters. Almost like a Monet.

She spotted something bright orange moving in the breeze.

It wasn't a bird but instead the flag on the back of Paul's scooter.

This has to be the right place. I can't believe it.

In disbelief, she forged ahead.

Dark, heavy wooden double doors with oversized iron nail heads continued the fairy-tale castle theme. Rapping her knuckles against the door wasn't very effective. The door was so thick, so solid, that it barely made a sound. She lifted the heavy cast-iron knocker and banged it twice.

Am I dreaming this?

The puppies raced around the fountain after the duck again, yapping and backing up every time the duck quacked.

A noise came from inside. She took a step back, expecting the door to open, but when it didn't, she could just imagine poor Paul on the floor, unable to get up. He could've been there since yesterday.

She rapped on the door again. This time with aggression. "Hello, is anybody home? It's Natalie."

She couldn't make out the noise, but someone was in there. She swallowed hard, gathering her courage, and then tried the door.

She held her breath, listening.

Hearing nothing, she called out again. "Paul? Hello? Mr. Grandstaff, are you in there? I was worried when you didn't show up. I'm coming in." She waited, praying for him to respond. "I'm coming in now."

She pushed the door hard and waited for it to swing open.

Natalie stood there as she let her brain comprehend what was before her.

A ladies' hat, white with netting, hung on a coat tree.

Her mouth dropped wide as she stepped inside.

This opulent property.

The amazing castle on the hillside that no one ever visited was just a shell like a movie set. Exposed beams and scaffold-like structures held up the facade. In this vast space, the size of a warehouse, hay lay scattered across a cobblestone floor.

She scanned the space. A creek about three feet across, ran through the middle, babbling over a rocky bottom in a beautiful Zen-like melody.

A few chickens suddenly took flight, scattering with squawked objection to her visit. Feathers and hay flew in the air and settled back on the floor.

She walked toward piles of wooden boxes stacked at the far end of the area, next to a pallet of lumber.

There was that noise again, the hefty sputter.

She spun around, coming face-to-face with a huge gray horse. His nose hovered above her head, which was mighty intimidating. She stood still, and he moved slowly, sniffing and blowing.

She raised her hand. "It's okay. I'm just here to check on Paul." Standing perfectly still, she tried to believe it would be okay, because she'd never stood so close to an animal as big as this one.

The horse dropped his head, his soft nose nuzzling her arm.

"Oh? You're nice. Thank goodness." She placed her hand flat on his nose, then scratched between his ears. "You're very handsome."

He lifted his head and then lowered it again.

"Where is he? And what is all of this about?"

The horse moved away and then clopped across the stone floor toward the other side of the space, stopping only briefly to slurp from the running waters that seemed to continue on past the edge of the building.

In the middle of the right wall, another set of double doors and windows looked like perhaps they were part of an original structure. Like the outside of a house, here on the inside. Very strange.

Okay, so maybe Paul Grandstaff is a little crazy.

As if reading her mind, the horse meandered across the way, then pushed his nose against the door and walked right inside like he'd done it a hundred times.

"Where are you going? Good Lord, is that horse some kind of Lassie in disguise? Paul better not be in a well." She walked briskly where the horse had gone. "Paul? Mr. Grandstaff? Are you in—"

She stopped in her tracks.

The horse neighed and stood there over him.

The old man lay stretched out on an ornate leather day-bed like something you'd see in one of those old movies where someone would tell their shrink all of their woes. *Do people really do that? Or is that all just for the movies?*

It was an elaborate office, fancier than anything she'd ever seen. Bookcases lined the entire room, even built around the windows. Colorful hardbound books lined up like soldiers of knowledge—too many to count—towering to the ceiling, which had to be fourteen feet. An old library ladder on a rail ran the whole circumference of the room, even over the double doors where she'd just come in.

A desk that had to be nearly five feet by ten took up one end of the room.

She raced to his side. "Paul? Can you hear me?" Lifting his wrist, she felt for a pulse, and then his eyes popped open.

She screamed.

Then, he screamed.

"I'm sorry. You scared me," she said.

"What are you doing?" His eyebrows danced above his eyes—startled. "Where? How did you—"

"I'm sorry. You were late. I was worried. Unlocked. I—The horse led me here."

Paul sat there looking bewildered. His silvery hair was mussed, and even his eyebrows looked out of control.

She could barely breathe. "I'm sorry. I?" She was definitely going to get fired for this.

Suddenly he started to laugh. "Oh, dear Natalie, I'm so sorry.

You must've thought I was a goner lying here." He laughed and seemed quite tickled by the situation.

She nodded. "Yes! Dead as a doornail!" Her heart still raced over the shock of him coming to life right in front of her. "You scared me to death."

"I'm sorry. I don't know what came over me this afternoon. I suddenly got so tired. I thought to call and reschedule, but then I lay down, and I guess I've been asleep for quite a while." His laughter slowed.

"I'm so sorry I trespassed." *I'm getting fired for sure.*

He waved his hand and shrugged. "You can't turn back time. What is done is done." He stood and walked over and hooked his arm up around the horse's neck. "I see you've met my best friend."

He looked so tiny standing beneath that huge horse. She silently prayed the horse wouldn't step on him.

"He's an old man, like me."

"What's his name?"

"My wife had always said if we had a son we'd call him Junior. We only had a daughter. My wife had always loved horses, I never knew much about them. Me and this guy, though, we bonded immediately so I called him Junior. He's my namesake."

"Why did you buy a horse if you didn't know anything about them?"

"I didn't. Someone owed me money, and this is how I got paid. Small-town living. Bartering is still alive and well," he said with a laugh. He leaned his head forward against the horse's long face. "He's been a faithful friend." He patted the horse on the shoulder. "We take care of each other, don't we, old man?"

The horse shook his mane and sputtered.

"Wow. This was unexpected," said Natalie.

"I'd ask that you didn't share what you've seen here today. Most of the folks in this town think I'm some kind of rich recluse who lost his mind anyway."

"Why the facade? I don't understand."

"No one has been upon this property since I lost my wife."

"What about your family?"

"Family can be strangely difficult. And 'no one' is a bit of an exaggeration. No one except for a few special friends and family, as you mention."

"At least you had one. I don't have any family. All I ever had was my parents, and when they died, there was no one. No cousins, no grandma. You can't imagine how lonely that is."

"Imagine this, young lady. That level of loneliness when you *do* have a family. Family that doesn't want you, or has to be apart because of circumstances."

That struck her, leaving her a bit off-kilter. "But how could that be?"

"A broken family can break people too." He ran his hands through his hair, tugging it into submission as if he'd had years of practice doing so. "I made mistakes. People do the best they can, and sometimes that isn't so good."

"People in this town love you. I saw how they reacted to you at church and at the pharmacy."

"Thank you. People are quicker to dispel their own family, I'm afraid. It happens all the time, and quite honestly, sometimes for a good reason."

"I can't think of one good reason."

He eyed her carefully. "Your situation is rare. It's very rare that a person would have no family at all. Not a second cousin or aunt, in-law . . . someone."

"I always thought so, but when I met my husband, he didn't have anyone either. You can't imagine the comfort I found in that. We needed each other. We were each other's family."

"And now there's only you?"

"Yes. I'd have given anything to have someone to call family. Especially since Jeremy is gone."

"You are a special soul, Miss Natalie."

"You are too. I don't understand why you're alone. I love your company."

"And I yours, young lady," he said. "For a long time, self-preservation kept me from letting anyone know what was going on up here. Then I knew people wouldn't understand why I did the things I did, and I didn't want to explain."

"I shouldn't have asked."

"No. I'll tell you. Someone ought to know, I suppose. Besides Jesse. Jesse and Junior here . . . they know why my family relationships abandoned me. Or me them—who could make that call?"

"I don't understand," she said.

"Because you've never been in that situation. I've had my share of missteps, misgivings, mistakes. Some I will die with."

"There's no one that visits you?"

"This town is full of people who would visit if I'd allow it. People I've helped. People I've hired. People I've known my whole life, but you know, when a person fails family, it's hard to forgive oneself, which can make one bitter."

"You don't seem bitter." She pulled her hands to her hips. "I'm here to take you to the market. Are you up to going?"

He smiled gently. "Probably, but do you think I could trouble you to go for me? I've got a list." He got up and crossed the room to the huge lawyer's desk. He pulled a sheet from a yellow legal pad.

She ran her fingers across the leather on top of the desk. "Was this your desk? When you worked?"

"It was. Not when I was a lawyer here in Chestnut Ridge, but when I was in Hollywood. A whole other world. A lifetime ago."

She noticed the pictures in the ornate frames situated between the books, some on small easels, others hanging in the spaces between the wooden shelves.

"Are these pictures of you?"

He sucked in a breath. "Like I said. A lifetime ago."

"You knew movie stars? Is that President Reagan?"

"Before he was president. Yes. I ran in some fancy circles in California. I represented some very famous people."

"Wow. I bet your wife loved that."

"Oh no, that was after she died. I went a little crazy, I suppose. A friend heard about my loss. He let me be for a year or two, then convinced me to come out West and join him representing movie stars and people too rich to make good decisions."

"I'm so sorry about your wife. You never remarried?"

"Never. Patrice was the love of my life."

"That's so romantic." She touched one of the frames. "You were very handsome."

He handed her the shopping list.

"I'd be happy to do your shopping for you. This time. Anytime. And I will always visit if you'll let me."

"I'd like that more than anything. But can I ask you one thing?"

"Sure."

"Why?" His chin set.

"Why would I like to visit you?" The question surprised her. "Well, I think you're a nice man. You're delightful company. I don't really know. Maybe because I'm lonely too."

He nodded. "Call me when you get to the gate. I'll open it for you. By the way, how did you get in?"

She felt the redness rise in her cheeks. "I pushed the gates and shimmied through."

He laughed. "Well, there's always that. How'd you know I didn't have ferocious rottweilers up here guarding the palace?"

"I didn't. I was just worried about you." She walked out and closed the door behind her. "Thank goodness those puppies weren't too terrifying."

I sure didn't see this coming.

"No, they are quite the opposite."

"They're adorable. I could've stood there and watched them play all day if I hadn't been so worried about you."

"My apologies. Now, move along."

She left with a smile in her heart. He was a kind man, and she enjoyed spending time with him.

When she got down to the gate, she was thankful he'd opened it for her so she didn't have to squeeze through it again like some kind of criminal.

Chapter Thirty-One

WHEN NATALIE returned from the grocery store, she dialed the number Paul had written on the paper, and the gates opened. As she drove up the hill, she noticed a tiny chapel. It was just beyond where she'd seen the horse in the pasture and no bigger than a one-room schoolhouse. Maybe it was just a facade too.

She pulled her truck right up to the front door.

Paul and Junior stood waiting in front of the house. One of the puppies played at their feet, the other still harassing that poor duck.

"I was able to get everything on your list."

"Excellent. I have a little wagon. It makes it so much easier to get things inside."

"Great." She spotted it next to the scooter. "I'll grab it." She rolled the little green wagon over to the car and filled it with the grocery bags. Thank goodness she'd opted for the heavy paper bags instead of a million of those plastic ones. She'd never understood why people liked those so much.

One of the pups climbed right into the wagon. "Oh my gosh, aren't you about the cutest thing ever?" She lifted him out and put him on the ground. "Run along."

"You're a dog person, aren't you?"

"I've never had one. Always wanted one, but as a kid my parents didn't let me and then as a nurse I was just gone too much. But yes, I'd say I'm a dog person. I love them."

"Me too," he said. "They are quite good company, and entertaining, as you can see."

"Yes." She pulled the wagon full of groceries and followed him inside. "I have a couple questions."

"I thought you might."

"I saw a ladies' hat when I came in. Are you here alone?"

"A ladies' . . . ?" A sly grin spread across his face. "The hat by the door?"

"A white one."

"That's not a ladies' hat," he said. "It's my beekeeping attire."

She laughed. "I guess I know how rumors get started in a small town."

"Yes. Assumptions just like that one." He clicked his fingers. "Any other questions?"

"What about the little church on the hill? Is that on your property?"

"Yes. I had that built when my beautiful Patrice died. She's buried on the hill. As is my daughter."

"I'm so sorry."

"I'll show you to the kitchen."

She wondered if it was like a movie set too, but thought it would be disrespectful to ask, so she withheld comment.

She was glad she'd kept that thought to herself, because there wasn't anything makeshift or superficial about the rest of the house, from what she could see.

Fine art hung in the halls like a gallery. The floors were

smooth stone in beautiful blues and grays, and when he opened the door to the kitchen and flipped on the lights, she couldn't hide her surprise. "Wow. This is beautiful."

"Should be. Straight out of a magazine."

"It looks like it."

Together they put the groceries away in the restaurant-quality kitchen. The cupboards were quite bare, although the space was opulent.

"Why do you live in such a humongous house?" she asked.

"We didn't always. We lived in a smaller house down on the edge of this property. You met Jesse. He used to live there. It's sitting there empty now."

"Oh." She had to wonder why Paul wouldn't move back there. It would seem lonely to live in this massive space by yourself, but it wasn't her place to judge.

"Jesse cares for some of my businesses, and me when I need help. We grew up together. He's a few years younger than I am. A brilliant home builder. We've known each other our whole lives. He did a lot of the work on this place. The real parts. This kitchen. My office. The bedroom and bathroom."

"I still don't understand why some of it is like a movie set."

"This was my wife's dream. When the doctors said there was nothing more they could do for her, I quit working. We thought we had a couple of years, and I wanted to make them the best they could possibly be."

"You wanted to make all her dreams come true."

"I did. Patrice had this whole folder full of pictures she'd pulled out of magazines. Beautiful rooms. I wanted her to have everything she dreamed of."

"And this castle was in there?" She blinked away tears. "That is so sweet."

He laughed. "Not exactly. The rooms, the interior design, all of that was all Patrice. The castle? It was a long-running joke between us. She used to say that I treated her better than a princess. I loved it when she said that, and I adored the love in her eyes that went along with those words."

She swallowed back emotion, her heart hanging as heavy in her chest as it had at its most profound sorrow for her own lost love.

"So, I had this idea to do the castle when I realized our days would be fewer than we'd ever imagined. I wanted her to know." He took a breath. "Beyond a shadow of a doubt." He looked away. "Only, for all I tried, I couldn't save her. She got sicker so fast."

"I'm so sorry. It must've been torture to watch that."

"Devastating."

She pressed her hand to her heart, aching for his loss. It seemed like losing Jeremy in the blink of an eye was the worst possible scenario, but saying goodbye repeatedly and watching the decline? She couldn't imagine how that must have torn this man apart.

"When she was running out of time, I called my buddy from college who worked in Hollywood and hired some guys he knew who built movie sets. They came out and roughed in all of this around the house Jesse had built. They did it in record time while Jesse worked on finishing the house that we'd planned."

"I bet it was a flurry of activity."

"You saw all those beehives when you came up?"

"I did. I've never seen so many."

"That team worked as hard as a hive of bees. We were working around the clock."

"She had no idea?"

"None. They are truly artists in their own right. They completed the project, and even I couldn't believe it. We somehow pulled off the move. Getting her from the cottage up here took a lot of help. Hospice helped manage moving everything, and they knew it was a silly husband's grasp at holding her heart forever, but I had to do it."

She pressed her hands to her face, tears falling. "Yes. You did. It's beautiful. And I know she was amazed."

"Oh, yes." A tear slipped down his cheek. "I will never forget her face when she saw this. Sure, it was all smoke and mirrors, and maybe she did know it. I'm not sure, but we re-created the most beautiful bedroom she had in that folder. Her eyes danced when she saw it. We cried in each other's arms that night. The kitchen. My office. Her bedroom and bathroom were all she needed to see, and Jesse had re-created the magazine pictures she cherished masterfully. The rest . . . is just a fantasy."

"Wow." She couldn't imagine a love so intense. "You are the most wonderful man I've ever known."

"No. I most certainly am not. It was all for her, because of her. She made me a better man."

"The truest and purest love."

"When she died, I buried her up on that hill and hired Jesse to build that little church around it. I spent every day in that little sanctuary. I'll never know why God had to take her from me."

She watched his tears well. Even after all these years—a

lifetime ago, as he'd said himself—he was heartbroken. He wore those scars still.

Tears spilled down her cheeks too. "We're a pair, aren't we?"

He nodded, removing a crisp white handkerchief from his pocket. "Here you go."

"Thank you." She dabbed at the tears, but they weren't going anywhere.

"I'd done my time practicing in Chestnut Ridge, and when she died, it was so hard for me to get back to work. To living. When my friend from college came to see all of this and how much pain I was still in a year afterward, he was relentless in trying to get me to leave. Finally, he talked me into coming out to LA to work as an agent in the movie industry."

"That had to have given you some relief. A new hope?"

"I'm glad I did it. With my wife gone and my daughter dating a guy I never approved of, she and I were at odds." He leveled a stare at Natalie that bored straight through her. "I never approved of him. Never, and he proved me right over and over again. He was a bad man, but she wouldn't listen to me. We'd wanted her to go to college, but she wouldn't go. I don't know if it would've been different had Patrice lived, but do wonder . . . all the time."

"I see what you mean about family being hard sometimes."

"So off I went. It was totally different. Quite swanky. Big parties. Big gossip. There were big cover-ups for some of those famous people, but I did my job. It was different. So different that it seemed like someone else's life. I know that probably doesn't make sense."

"No. I kind of get it." Not so different from her being able to live and escape in that little fantasy Marc Swindell had offered her. Because he was nothing like Jeremy, and that's where her heart was. "What made you come back?"

"I was tired. It's a hectic and unhealthy way to live, burning the candle at both ends. Then Jesse called me one night. My daughter's husband had beat her so badly that even though she begged Jesse not to tell me, he called. He was afraid she'd die, and I wouldn't be there."

"How terrible."

"They both drank too much, and it wasn't a healthy relationship. They had a son. A good boy. That man, though. He was pure evil. Didn't care about anything or anyone but himself."

"You can't fix everything, although you did pull off some magic."

"I tried. My daughter was so out of it that she never even visited during that time. She was hateful. I didn't even recognize her. I'd send her to rehab, and that man would drag her out and start the cycle all over."

"How about your grandson? Were you close?"

Paul stared at her, nodding but not saying a thing for a long time. "He came. He had to sneak over because his father would have beat him had he known. We worked on projects. Restored old cars. Built beehives because Patrice was a campaigner about bees before it was even a thing like it is now."

"All those beehives you made. Because of her?"

"Healing process. My grandson and I made a bunch of them, and when he left, I was like my own little factory. I enjoyed the monotony of it. It kept me sane. Which, by the way, you come fill that pickup truck with them if you'd like to do your part for the bees. I have plenty to spare."

"Really? I'd love that. You'll teach me?"

"Of course."

"Maybe it'll help you too. There's something wonderful about the life of bees."

"I'd like that. Thank you." She could already imagine painting scenes on them. "What happened with your grandson?"

"The only thing I could do to possibly save him was to send him away."

"Did you? Somehow?"

"I set him up financially, with the promise he'd never speak to his parents again. Leave everything he knew to go to college. Forget about all of this, and never ever treat anyone like he'd seen his father treat them. And he did."

"I bet he was so thankful."

"In his own way maybe. He was angry too. He didn't want to leave. When his mother died, he blamed me. Said that it wouldn't have happened had he been here. Our relationship never had time to repair."

"I'm so sorry."

"It's a long, ugly story. Her husband had been slowly killing her for years. The relationship was abusive, loud, and full of addiction. I'll never know for sure if she took her own life or if it was at his hand, but it was very hard to watch it unravel over time."

"I'm sorry."

"It's hard to outlive a child. Even one who was as broken as she was. I'm glad my wife didn't have to bear that. It would have killed her had the cancer not taken her first."

"You said your daughter had a son. Do you still see him?"

"He too passed. Yes." He shook his head, lowering his lids. She suspected he was crying, but her vision was blurred from her own tears.

She took his hands in hers. "I can't even imagine what that must've been like."

"You didn't want children?" he asked.

"I wanted them desperately, but my husband wasn't quite ready. And then when he died, well, that was that."

"I'm sure you were a good wife."

"I tried to be. It was easy, though. I loved him more than anything on this Earth."

"You could still have children. You're young. There will be another chance for you."

"I'm not sure. It's hard to imagine starting over after sharing your life with your soul mate. We were everything to each other."

"Don't discount it." He pulled back his right hand and patted his heart. "Natalie, love is why we live. Don't cheat yourself from that."

"You never remarried," she said.

"I'm different. I had done everything I ever dreamed of."

"It's hard to trust people. I've run into some dishonest people of late. I'm not trusting my instincts like I used to."

"There are the bad ones. You'll see through them. There are more that are good. Sometimes people hide things, but for reasons they believe are honorable, which is a whole different story."

"Like you and all of this? Do people in town know that it's like a movie set?"

"Oh, heavens no. I don't let anyone come up here. They'd think I was completely cuckoo, and maybe I am."

"But they are your friends. They'd understand."

"I've let it go too far now. Now I'm town lore. The eccentric hermit who lives on the hill."

"In the castle."

"Yes."

It was sad he felt like he had to lie to these people about such a silly thing. "Honesty is still always the best policy. Sometimes the truth is hard to explain, but true friends would understand."

"Much easier to see that now. At the time, I was protecting my pain by hiding. I didn't want to share it." He reached for her hand and held it. "You are a kind and understanding woman. Wise beyond her years."

"I don't know about that, but I do know that you're a good man."

"Miss Natalie, I'd love to be your friend."

"I'd love that. I believe we're off to a very good start. I really enjoy your company. Your stories. I can't imagine what living in Hollywood and rubbing elbows with the rich and famous must've been like."

"It was like living a dream. I was a small-town man, and yet I was acting as if I'd been born into it. It was like Gatsby or something."

She laughed. "My, now that does draw an image. I guess you were sort of starring in your own movie."

"It would have been the most epic love story. We never lied to each other, never cheated, never went to bed angry. Not once."

"As it should be." Her phone rang. It was Randy, but she let it go to voice mail.

"Was that your new man friend?"

"Is anything a secret in this town?"

"Only my house."

"Goodness gracious. I feel like everyone is so suspicious. I don't even know if it would turn into anything, but with everyone talking about it, it makes me feel like I'm doing something wrong. Something I have to explain."

"But maybe it could be something very good. You can't stop living your life."

"But I had the perfect love already. You know how that is."

"And maybe there will be a second one for you." He looked at his watch. "You better get home before it gets dark. That road to the cabin is tricky at night."

"That's true."

"Why don't you take one of those puppies with you? Jesse has a habit of rescuing abandoned hunting dogs. A little beagle would be good company for you."

"Really? I hate to separate them."

"Take the one torturing that dastardly duck. They're going to get split up eventually anyway. We have to find them homes."

They walked out, and Paul gave a whistle. The puppies, white-tipped tails in the air, came running.

She picked up the little boy pup and snuggled him. "I've never had a dog before."

"Nothing to it. I'll give you a bag of dog food. They are already house trained."

"Hey, little guy. You want to come home with me?" She stooped down, petting him. He climbed up against her body and licked her chin, making her giggle. "I think he likes the idea too." She picked him up, and he quit squirming. His little heart pounded, but he seemed happy, and she felt happier just holding him. "Thank you."

"Thank *you*. One less mouth to feed for me. I'm more the horse and chicken kind of man."

A big red rooster strutted right out the front door, seeming to say, *That's right*, in his cock-a-doodle-doo way.

They both got a kick out of that.

"Laughter is good for the soul, Natalie. You've had me smiling more than I have in years these last few days."

"You're so sweet. It's been good for me too." She opened the door and let the puppy climb in. He circled and settled into the passenger seat.

"You have family now."

She could hardly contain the emotion she was feeling. She looked at that little tricolor pup in the passenger seat. "You might just be right."

She drove home feeling connected in a way she never had before. Resting her hand on the little dog's body as she drove, he slept the whole way home.

Once they got home he had more energy than she was prepared for. He raced ahead, and then, scared, came back and circled her.

"You'll learn your way around here. I have," she said to him. His ears set back, then he took off running again.

She sat on the porch and let him run and wear himself out. She mused over all the things she'd seen today. The duck, these pups, a horse in a house. It was beginning to sound like all the makings of a children's book.

There'd been something simply comforting about it all, though. Sure, it was a little off-the-wall, but in a good way. Like living in a fairy tale.

She went inside and grabbed the gel markers she'd bought recently. She hadn't experimented much with them but had seen some work by an artist who used them in watercolor fashion, and she'd been dying to try it out.

Soft watercolors matched the mood today. She couldn't wait to translate her experience today into a new set of note cards. She worked on the duck first, then one with the duck and puppies.

Her phone rang and she tapped it, letting it pick up on speaker mode. "Sheila! Hi."

"How are you?"

"Great. I'm working on a new set of cards that I think you're going to love. This guy I've been driving around, Paul, his place is magical. Like a storybook, and I am so inspired."

"That's great! You know I think you need to quit thinking about going back into nursing and focus on your gift. It's special."

"So is nursing. But honestly, I'd rather just keep helping seniors by driving them around and spending time with them and work on this. With almost no overhead, I can totally do that living here in Chestnut Ridge."

"Then do it. You should."

"You've got to come up and see me. It's so much better than you can imagine."

"I hope so," Sheila said, but Natalie knew she was kidding. "I was just checking in. Get back to that artwork and send me some pictures. I can't wait to see them. I'll be your first order."

"You always are. You and all of your clients."

"Well, sharing is caring." Sheila had made Natalie's note cards part of every closing gift she gave when her clients finally bought their dream home. From there it had been word of mouth and online marketing that had started the sales trickling in.

She hung up the phone, closed her eyes, and smiled, so thankful for the good that was following the storm she'd gone through.

"I'm trying to use the gifts you've given me, Lord. Every ounce of them."

Chapter Thirty-Two

RANDY HAD hoped Natalie would call back last night. He must've checked his phone twelve times throughout the night, looking for a missed call or a text. Or maybe it was just that he wanted a reason to call her back. To hear her voice.

It was a big day for this case, and maybe it was just as well he hadn't talked to her. If the whole investigation turned up nothing, she'd be disappointed. Hell, he'd be disappointed.

He was feeling optimistic, though. Finally, working with the North Carolina detective, Randy had been able to untangle the LLCs and ghost corporations that, like spaghetti, eventually led back to one common name.

A lot of the evidence aligned between the two cases. It was likely they were connected. Randy was almost sure that the man they were closing in on in the North Carolina case was the same man Natalie knew as Marc Swindell. The list of aliases was getting longer as they pulled each thread.

Adrenaline rushed through him, and there was no getting back to sleep.

He hit the gym early, sweating every bit of anxiety from his body and spending an extra fifteen minutes in the sauna to meditate.

Dressed and eager for news, he headed to the office. As he walked through the parking garage, his phone rang.

"Fellowes."

"I sent photos over this morning," the North Carolina detective said. "He's definitely our guy. Hope he's yours too."

"Me too." He fist-pumped the air. "Great."

"She confirmed it's him in the picture. I've sent over the details. Circumstantial, some of it, but others are tangible and concrete. It'll be interesting to see if your vic zeroes in on the same things mine did."

"This is great news."

"I wonder how many women this jerk has taken over the years," the detective muttered.

"Me too. When you add it all up, the money, the property, cars, it's a bit staggering," Randy said as he walked down the hall to his office.

"Yeah. He's living the high life too. Wait until you see his house."

Just talking about it left a bad taste in Randy's mouth. "I'll talk to Natalie today and see how this all fits together. I'll let you know."

"Yeah, keep me posted. We're planning to get everything together and make the arrest tonight. Any corroboration to help make this stick would be great. The timing is critical. I don't think he's going anywhere, but the way he comes and goes for weeks at a time, the opportunity window could close."

"I hear ya. We're going to work with the sheriff's department in the town where Natalie recently moved. I'll interview her today and get back to you."

"I'll stay tuned."

He ended the call and set his phone on the desk. "Yes." He dropped into his chair, and slapped the desk with zeal. "Yes!" He wanted more than anything to solve this case for Natalie. He'd been hoping for this kind of breakthrough for months.

It took Randy about an hour to download and print all the reports, photos, and case files. After bringing the captain up to date, the captain agreed it would be best for Randy to conduct his interview and take Natalie's statement at the Chestnut Ridge sheriff's department. The captain was able to quickly arrange that.

Randy headed to the mountains. Some things were better done in person. He needed to tell her about their progress, which he was dying to do. Asking the right questions and recording her responses to ensure he conducted his part of the investigation to the letter was key. He had to keep this part all business. He was so excited to tell her on a personal level too. It took all he had not to speed to Chestnut Ridge.

He stopped at the county sheriff's office headquarters to discuss the details with the sheriff, then headed over to update Natalie.

When he got to the turnoff to the cabin, he pulled over and texted Natalie.

> RANDY: Would you believe me if I said I was in the neighborhood?
>
> NATALIE: Not likely, but if it was true, I'd say come on over.
>
> RANDY: I was hoping you'd say that. Around the corner.

When he pulled up, Natalie stood on the bridge with her hands on her hips, wearing a big smile.

She stood on tiptoe and waved, then stuck her thumb out, pretending to hitchhike.

He pulled up alongside her and lowered his window. "Need a ride to town, lady?"

"You going my way?"

"Always."

"What are you really doing here?"

"Had to talk to you." He shut down the truck and got out. A beagle puppy came running from the bank, ears flying. "Who is this?"

"I have a new friend," she announced. "More like family, probably."

"You're replacing me already? Man, that was fast."

"Not likely." Their eyes held.

He'd never noticed just how blue her eyes were until that moment. "Good."

The pup started jumping and running between their legs.

"Don't let him jump on you," she said. "He's been playing in the water."

Randy squatted down to interact with the puppy. "What'd you name him?"

"I'm still working on that. We're just getting to know each other. I got that little bundle of joy yesterday."

"He's a cute little guy." He stood and let out a breath. "What's that?" He peered over at the painting she'd finished.

"Oh. That. It's a new set of designs for my note card collection."

"It's great. Wow, you're really talented."

She felt the blush rise in her cheeks. "Thank you."

"No, really."

"I was so inspired by some things here in Chestnut Ridge. I'm doing some mountain scenes, and these were from a visit with one of my seniors."

"Farmer?"

"Not exactly."

"Well, I have news." He clapped his hands together. "I've been dying to tell you, but I wanted to do it in person."

She cocked her head. "Good news?"

"I think so."

"About the case?"

He nodded. "Can I take you down to the sheriff's office?"

"Am I in trouble?"

"No. I need to show you some things. Get a statement. See if this is your guy."

"Oh my gosh." She clasped her hands around her mouth and nose. "Really?" Tears fell to her cheeks. She leaned over, trying to catch her breath. "I can't believe it."

"Well, let's see if it's him. By the book. There are procedures we have to follow. Bear with me. You ready?"

"Yes. Definitely. Let's go." She ran to the other side of his truck.

"Let's put the puppy up. Don't want to leave him in the truck. I don't know how long this will take."

"Yes. Of course." She ran back over and had to chase the puppy to catch him.

She had her arms full of the squirming bundle, who clearly thought it was a game.

He grabbed the puppy by the nape of the neck and pulled him into his arms. "I'll carry him."

The puppy barked.

"Yeah, yeah," Randy said. "I hear ya. We'll be back. Might even bring you a toy if you're good."

"I'm so excited. I can barely breathe. My heart is pounding so fast."

They put the puppy in the cabin and then drove straight to the sheriff's office.

There was no buzzer and no reception area. Six desks filled the room, but only one was occupied.

A portly older man walked out. "You made it back fast." The sheriff walked over to Natalie. "Hello, young lady. I'm Sheriff Brothers. We can use the interrogation room over there. I've already put all the files in there for you."

"Thank you," Natalie said.

"Thank you, Sheriff."

"Let's see what we've got," Randy said. He walked through the evidence provided by the North Carolina team. Letting Natalie draw her own conclusions. The first picture was from a distance, the work of a private investigator.

"His hair is darker in this picture, but it looks like him." Her smile faded. "It's been a while. I'm not as clear as I was months ago. I guess I've pushed those memories aside a bit." She put her hand over the hair. "The glasses too. He wasn't wearing glasses, but the smile? The set of his chin? It looks so much like him." She let out a sigh. "I think? I don't know."

"It's okay," Randy said. "Don't stress. Take your time. I have more pictures."

One by one he laid them out. The sheriff looked on.

She didn't say anything else, just sat there, nodding and taking it in, until he laid down a picture of the subject with a woman at his side.

She pressed her finger to the picture. "That's the same necklace he gave me." Her mouth shaped a perfect O. "That can't be a coincidence. I still have it in my things. I had it in my bag when I came back from vacation." She shuffled through the pictures again. "Those shoes. I hated them. They are like woven leather loafers, and they squeaked when he walked. It's him. I know it is."

The sheriff gave an approving nod.

"Excellent," Randy said. "There's more."

He went through the details of the corporation Swindell had used as a cover, and the supposed charity Natalie had been funneling her money into, which they'd been able to trace to the mortgage payments on the huge beach house on the Outer Banks where he resided with his wife.

"He's married?"

Randy nodded.

"Insult to injury." She pressed her hands together. "How?" She shook her head. "Never mind. It doesn't even matter."

"It's how he makes his living. You're one of at least three others we know of so far. Two in North Carolina and one in Texas."

"He must've been going to see her when I met him on the flight to Texas."

"I don't have all those details yet, but I think we'll see many things begin to fall into place quickly now."

She sat there nodding.

"Are you okay?" He placed his hand on her arm.

"Yes." Her voice was quiet. "Thank you. I don't mean to not sound elated. I am. It's just a little . . . overwhelming."

"I'm sure it is." Randy sat back in the chair. "You did good."

"You did," the sheriff said. "We'll need you to write a statement and a few signatures. This will surely help in that North Carolina case, and then we'll wallop yours right on top of that one. He might just go away for a long time."

"I hope so," she said.

"And thank you, Sheriff, for helping," Randy said.

"You're one of us now. We take care of our own around here, and you helping this little lady makes you extended family," Sheriff Brothers said. "If you're ever looking for a new job, Fellowes, talk to me. I'm retiring as soon as I find a sucker . . . a candidate . . . who will toss his hat in the ring."

Randy laughed.

"Wasn't kidding." Sheriff Brothers stood and walked out of the room.

"I've got to relay this information to my boss and the guys in North Carolina. They are arresting him this evening."

"What's his real name?" she asked.

"The one he's living with his wife under is Clayton Bellamy."

"I don't know why I wanted to know. It's not like it matters. One lie just leads to another."

"That's how they operate. I'm going to take you back home. I've got a ton of paperwork to do, and I need to do my part to be sure all this happens and sticks."

She placed her hand on his arm. "Randy, thank you. I know this is your job, but you've done so much. I'm so grateful."

Gratitude wasn't what he wanted. He wanted more. "Come on, let's get you out of here before the locals start making up stories about you being arrested," Randy said.

"You think you're joking. These people know everything," Natalie said as they walked out of the room.

"And that's what makes my job so easy," the sheriff said. "Nothing goes unnoticed around here."

On the way back, Natalie asked, "Would you mind if we stopped in for just a moment at Orene's? I want to invite her to the cabin to visit and meet the puppy. I think she'd love that."

"Absolutely."

"Right here." She pointed to the driveway, and he swung in. "I won't be but a minute." She jogged off, turning once to give him a little wave that made his heart skip. He'd never seen her so happy.

Chapter Thirty-Three

NATALIE STOOD at Orene's front door, ready to knock. She paused when she overheard raised voices.

"You still haven't told her?"

That sounded like Tucker's voice.

"It's not our place to do so," said Orene.

Natalie smiled. Just like Orene to keep others from judging. Such a sweet woman.

"You've had plenty of chances. You see her all the time. You can't just lie to her."

Natalie blinked. *That* is *Tucker. Lying?* Her skin crawled.

"This whole thing will blow up in your face," he said. "I'm telling you. It's not going to stay quiet for long. She's driving Grandstaff around like they are best buddies. People are talking."

Is he talking about me? Tucker's strange attitude that day with Randy came flooding back. Every nerve in her body tingled.

"We owe him the chance to tell her himself," Orene said.

He? Is this about Randy? Why does Tucker seem to think he needs to protect me?

"That crazy old coot is out of his mind. Family is important, but you can't expect people to just change their history."

"That history was ill-informed." Orene's words were stilted. "You need to just settle down, young man."

Anxiety swirled in her chest, pressing so hard that she could barely inhale.

Natalie backed away from the door and ran back to the truck.

Randy was smiling when she hopped in the passenger seat. "She wasn't home?"

"Um. Yeah, no. Let's go." She buckled her seat belt.

"Are you okay?"

"Go. Drive. Please." She smiled, but she could tell by the wrinkle on his forehead he wasn't buying her less-than-Oscar-worthy act.

They drove back to the cabin in complete silence. Randy got out of the truck.

"You don't have to walk me back," she said, anxious to find a spot to just let this all sink in.

"Of course I do. What is going on?" He put a lazy arm around her waist. "I haven't seen you like this in a long time. What's wrong?"

She found comfort in his touch. "Overwhelmed, I think. I'm fine. Thank you for everything. Really." When they opened the door, the puppy raced out of the house and did a full circle in the open field before coming back, tail wagging for a hello.

"I wish you would tell me."

She shook her head. She couldn't. She'd completely fall apart, and she just couldn't do that right now.

She grabbed the puppy and pulled him up into her arms, where he assaulted her with kisses as fast as his little tongue would go. "I can count on this little guy, can't I?"

"You can count on me too."

"I know." She felt her lip quiver and hoped he didn't notice. She buried her face in the pup's fur.

"Then tell me what's going on. You were on cloud nine, and now it's like everything is crumbling. What's on your mind?"

"I can't . . ."

He took the puppy from her and put him on the ground. "You can." He put his hands on the sides of her arms. "Look at me."

She did, and her lip trembled as she tried to hold in the thoughts racing through her mind. "Something is going on."

"What? With me?"

"No. You're perfect. It's this town."

"What? You love this town. You've said it like a hundred times."

"I do, but I overheard Orene talking to Tucker. They're lying to me about something."

"No. Wait. What did you hear?"

She went through the conversation she'd overheard.

"'Lie' can mean a lot of things. It could be a little white lie. Don't get upset. And that Tucker, he's kind of a hot bag of wind if you ask me, the way he got all puffed up when he was over here that day could go either way. I think he has your best interests at heart though. He didn't seem sinister. It's probably nothing."

"He *was* odd that day." She steadied her breathing. "Why do people want to lie to me? Am I that naïve?"

"No. Stop that right now. Natalie, what happened to you was not your fault. And this has nothing to do with that. I promise you."

"You aren't going to want to believe this, but here are the statistics." He turned her face toward him. "Look at me. Listen."

She nodded.

"Women who are targeted like you are cherry-picked because they are highly intelligent and empathetic, and in a weird way that's a compliment. You are smart, caring, and so special. You should be treated that way." He stopped, and took her hands into his. "If you've been taken for a ride by a manipulative liar, all that means is that you're an honest person. Nat, that's a good thing. I love that about you."

She hated it, though. She was tired of being a victim. "See what that got me."

"He was dishonest, arrogant, lacked empathy, and exploited others for his own gain. You can't distance yourself from people. You'll let the liar change who you are and how you live in this world if you do. His lies do not deserve that power. You are stronger than that. I'm here for you."

"I know. You're amazing. You're too good to be true and probably in a good way, but I'm terrified I'll make another mistake."

"I know. I know. I would never." He pulled her into his arms. Holding her. "Slow down. We've had good news today. One thing at a time. Right?"

She nodded, sniffling back a tear.

"Let's get this guy behind bars, and we'll tackle the other stuff together. No one is going to hurt you on my watch."

"You can't watch me twenty-four/seven."

"I can if you'll let me. Natalie, please give me a chance."

"But could I ever let my guard down? It wouldn't be fair to you if I didn't." How her heart wanted to believe that she could love him the way he deserved, but her heart had fooled her before. She put her hand on his chest. "Go do your job."

"This is more than my job, Natalie. Don't go letting an overheard conversation turn into shrapnel that blows everything up. I care for you. This is not *just* doing my job."

"I'm sorry. That wasn't fair."

"Do you want to ride back to Richmond with me? We can bring the puppy. You could stay at my place."

"No. I can't do that. I do love this place. You're right, it has to be a misunderstanding. Eavesdropping, overhearing, it's probably not the whole story."

"Exactly. We're okay, right?"

"Absolutely."

"I'm going to head back, then. There's a ton to do. Call me. Any time. I'm here for you."

"Okay."

"And if you need me to come to get you, I'll drive straight back. Got it?"

"Yes. You are so sweet. Thank you. Thank you so much for everything. I can't believe I was so lucky to have met you through all of this."

"Everything happens for a reason. I didn't know what I was looking for until I met you." He turned and left on that note.

She stood there, letting it sink in, as he walked away.

She spent the next several hours with the puppy, practicing a few commands in between playtime. "Sit" was going well, "shake" was coming along, but "stay" was nearly impossible.

"What am I going to name you?"

It was easy to set her concerns aside with this little bundle of joy entertaining her. He ran, ran, ran, ran, and then would fall asleep. Most of the time on his back, with his little feet in the air; it was adorable. She already had at least ten pictures of him sleeping, and it was only their second day together.

She sent a puppy picture to Randy. He hearted it immediately.

Her fingers hovered over her phone.

I want more with you, she whispered. She was tempted to type it but then laid down her phone. She was too emotional to make any decisions right now.

She lay down on the floor with the puppy and fell asleep until her phone woke her. "Hello?"

"Natalie, it's Jesse."

"Hi, Jesse."

"Mr. Grandstaff asked me if I could contact you and have you drive your truck over to his place. Says we're going to load you up with beehives." Jesse's laugh touched her. "I hope you're ready for all that."

"I think I am. I have absolutely no idea what it involves, but I love the idea of painting them. I think they'll look really cute. I just hope the bees will love them too."

"I have a feeling he'll make an apiarist out of you if you're not careful."

"An apiarist?"

"Bee-loving beekeeper," Jesse said. "I'm headed to Mr. Grandstaff's now, if you're not busy you could meet me there."

"Sure. I'm on my way." She got up and grabbed a couple of water bottles and a bowl to take with her for the dog. "We're going for a ride."

He yawned and plodded along behind her.

In the truck, he resumed his nap.

The gate was open when she got to Paul's, so she drove on up to the house. Jesse and Paul stood in front, talking.

"How are you two today?" she called as she got out.

"Good to see you." Paul waved a bony hand. "I'm so happy you're interested in the bees. I'll teach you everything you need to know."

"I'll try my best."

"I know you will."

Jesse loaded her truck with beehives until she got nervous. There were so many they might just go tumbling out into the street around the curves down the mountain. "I can come back for more if I need them. Let's not go stacking them too high. I'm not comfortable driving this truck even when it's empty!"

"You'll be fine." Jesse slammed the tailgate shut.

"Good old truck," Paul said. "I have something for you." He held up a finger and went inside.

Jesse walked around the truck, pushing on the boxes, ensuring everything was secure.

When Paul came back out, he was carrying a hat with netting. Not the white one she'd seen, though. It was a muted blue with tiny pastel raised dots.

"That's pretty."

"I want you to have it. Patrice made this. Never got the chance to wear it or use it, but I think she'd like you having it and putting it to good use."

"Are you sure? This is so special."

"I'm positive. Please. Take it."

"I'm honored. Truly." She tiptoed and kissed his cheek. "I'm so thankful our paths crossed and connected." She looked over at Jesse. "Both of you. Really."

"Life is good," Jesse said. "Trust the journey. I believe you have many bountiful and beautiful days ahead of you. Believe in your destiny, my friend."

"Yes, sir," she said. *How could there be anything dishonest going on around all of this?* It was hard to imagine. Part of her wanted to ask Paul and Jesse what they thought about what she'd over-heard Orene and Tucker saying, but she wasn't sure she really wanted to know.

One thing at a time. Natalie trusted Randy was right about that. A lot had taken place in a short period of time. She needed time to just let things settle. She couldn't wait until he came back.

She drove home believing Jesse's last words.

The cross-arm was down blocking Main Street. It was the first time she'd been stopped by a train, and this was a long one. She counted each colorful railcar as it rumbled by until it seemed that they might go on forever.

She pushed the gear shift into Park and picked up her phone to look through her emails.

There were a few emails from her website. She danced in her seat. Sheila had been right to suggest she put up a preorder page for the new designs. This was good.

She kept scrolling through her emails, and then back up to be sure she wasn't miscounting. Sure enough, there was a stack of orders. Her heart leapt.

Tilting her chin to the sky, she said, "Okay, Jessie. I'm be-lieving it now."

She downloaded the orders so she could print them when she got back to the house.

Natalie couldn't wait to tell Sheila, and Orene, too. They'd both be excited for her. Yes, they were like family. She'd never realized just how many people were part of her close circle. People she could trust and count on. Randy was among them too.

She remembered Paul's words about family. *Sometimes family can be strangely difficult.* And she was realizing that a small town was like one big family, and living here maybe she'd never feel alone again.

Randy had called Natalie every single day since he'd left. When the story finally broke three weeks later on the evening news, he'd been unable to be there for her in person, so they'd sat on the phone together and watched the cons Bellamy had pulled off against multiple women play out.

Bellamy was shown in handcuffs being taken into custody, and his days as Swindell and at least six other aliases were all over the television. Natalie watched from her phone, and it was hard to tear herself away from the commentary all over social media.

Two more women had come forward already. One of them whose case went back ten years. Rumors had it his net worth was in the millions, and none of it could be traced to anything legit.

So far, it appeared his wife had truly been clueless about who he was and what he was doing right beneath her nose. Natalie felt sorry for her.

She dialed Randy. "I can't believe all of the attention this case is getting on the news. I'm really thankful I'm able to help and keep my name out of the media."

"It's a pretty horrible thing he was doing, and the number of people he conned is still climbing," Randy said. "It'll take a long time to sort out all of the impacts, but there's enough to put him away easily."

"I'll make a statement. Not public. I don't want to be part of this media swirl, but I'll share the details needed to help make sure he goes away for a long time."

"If you hadn't told me about the ponies, he may have gotten away with a whole lot more."

"Yeah, it was so strange how those memories came at such a random time, and then *bam* it all made sense. People are strange."

"Tell me about it."

She laughed. If anyone knew that, it was Randy. "I don't know how you trust anyone, with all you see every day."

"Because good people are good. I surround myself with the few good ones. And for every bad guy I take down, I meet lots of good ones too."

"Perspective, right?"

"Exactly. So focus on the good stuff, okay?"

She knew what he was talking about. It was that conversation between Tucker and Orene. Her mood had been low ever since and she just couldn't shake it. "I'm trying."

Chapter Thirty-Four

RANDY WAS thrilled to have gotten what he needed to get Bellamy out of circulation. It was even better that they'd already recovered some of Natalie's things. The money would be harder to solve for, could take years, but there was hope. Despite all the good news, though, Natalie wasn't able to shake her concerns about what she'd overheard at Orene's.

The detective in him couldn't let that go.

He traced the facts he knew and the hunches he had about the people of Chestnut Ridge.

It wasn't that hard to unbraid once he started connecting dots, and he was pretty sure it wouldn't take but a few conversations with people in Chestnut Ridge to confirm his suspicions.

He looked up the number for Orene and called her.

"Orene. My name is Randy Fellowes. I'm a friend of Natalie's."

"Hello! I've heard all about you."

That sounds promising. "I'm sure you have. I'd like to come up this weekend and surprise Natalie, but I'll need a place to stay. I know you don't run an inn anymore, but do you think I could trouble you to rent a room from you for the weekend?"

"You most certainly cannot, but you are welcome to be my guest."

"I couldn't impose."

"You won't, and you won't have a place to stay unless you do it my way."

Her response didn't surprise him, from what Natalie had told him about the old woman. "You are one tough cookie."

"I like to think so."

"I'll take you up on that, then. I thought I'd come up tonight if that is okay with you."

"The sooner, the better." Orene hung up without a goodbye.

With that settled, he called Natalie. "Hey, gal. How are you?"

"I'm great. I'm out here in the field painting beehives. I have quite a kaleidoscope of beautiful colors going on. Like my own painted field of wildflowers."

"Are you going to be raising hippie bees?"

"Maybe. Got a problem with that?"

"Me? Nope. Whatever makes you happy makes me happy. I'll even paint the peace signs for you."

"I'll let you." He hoped she would.

"I was hoping you might be able to tear yourself away from all these painting projects you're working on to spend some time with me. Not detective work. Just us."

"I think I'd like that."

"Like a real date?"

She paused and he hoped she wasn't going to say no.

"I think I'd really like that too."

He withheld the verbal elation, but it was pulsing right through him. "That's great. I'll be up there tonight. I wrangled a room at your friend Orene's house."

"Well, you were pretty confident I'd say yes, weren't you?"

"I was very hopeful."

"You know the way." Her laugh was lighthearted. "Randy, I can't wait to see you."

"Anything I can bring you from the big city?"

"Yes, as a matter of fact. A dozen Krispy Kreme doughnuts. We'll put them in the microwave and pretend they are hot off the press."

"You got 'em. I'll see you later."

"I can't wait."

There was one more call to make. There was no telling how this one would go, but showing up in person to talk about it wasn't an option.

He dialed the number, which Orene had been kind enough to share with him, and hoped for the best. "Hello? Mr. Grand-staff. You don't know me, but we have a friend in common. Someone very special."

"I'm listening," he said, with a hint of question in his voice.

"Our mutual friend is Natalie Maynard."

"She's quite special."

"Yes, sir. She is, and she's been worried. I'm a detective, and I did some digging. I think I understand what's going on, and I'd like for us to connect these dots together if you'll allow me to help."

They'd gotten to the details Randy needed to understand, and together they made a plan that would straighten it all out with Natalie that evening.

Randy dropped the phone back in its cradle. "Wow."

"You look beat." Hutchens stood at his office door. "Thought you'd be gone by now."

"Working on it."

"Go, already. If anyone needs a life, it's you," Hutchens said. "Seriously. Go. You look like you need a break."

"I do." He turned off his computer. "I'm gone."

"Good luck."

Randy hoped he wouldn't need it. He pulled out of the parking deck only fifteen minutes later than he'd planned, which was still much earlier than Natalie would expect him.

He coasted along the dirt road, dust billowing around his truck. It was dry, but the trees were putting on a show that would be impossible to match.

Up ahead, Natalie sat on the bridge with her feet dangling over the side. For a girl with a fear of heights, she was making strides in that area.

He parked and walked over.

"You're here!"

He knelt beside her. "I wanted to surprise you."

The puppy ran over, barking out a greeting and backing up at the same time.

Randy clicked his fingers, then pulled a dog treat from his pocket. "Brought you something, little guy."

The puppy pranced over, took the beefy-scented rawhide from him, and ran off.

"I'm puppy-approved," Randy said.

"Natalie-approved too. That was thoughtful."

"I do what I can." He looked over the edge. "I remember the first day we walked over this bridge together. The spring water trickled over the rocks, gurgling and splashing to who knows where in a hurry."

"There's barely any water now."

"Seasons."

"If we don't get some rain soon, I'm afraid it will just be dirt. Then what will happen to the fish?"

"We won't need fishing rods," he said, joking.

"The leaves are so crunchy I can hear them crack when they hit the ground."

"Can I take you somewhere?"

"Now?"

"Right now. We have to name that dog, by the way."

"I had an idea."

"Yeah?"

"Buzz. Kind of goes with the bee theme, and he is a busy bee."

"I like it." He turned and slapped his hand on his jeans. "Come on, Buzz."

The pup came running toward him. "Think that has more to do with the rawhide than the name?"

"Definitely."

He picked up the dog. "Come on. You two get in the truck."

"You're kidnapping my puppy and me?"

"Nope. That's against the officer's creed to honor and protect. I'm taking you on a little field trip."

He started the truck, and took off down the dusty road toward the state route.

Once they hit the main road, a few rocks pinged the fender wells as they released from the tire treads.

Natalie rolled down the window and let Buzz catch the air in his teeth.

They drove down Main Street and then took a right up the mountain. "Maybe I should've asked where we're going," she said.

"Perhaps."

"You're not going to tell me?"

"You didn't ask."

"I'm asking."

"A friend of yours has invited us over."

"Now *you* have friends in *my* town?"

He shrugged, pleased with himself and praying all would be okay when she heard the truth. "Can't you share?"

She laughed, shaking her head. "I'm an only child, but I do know how to share."

"We'll see." He winked.

As they drove, she turned to him and said, "Are we going to the castle?"

He nodded.

"How did you ever pull that off, Randy Fellowes?"

"I'm one of the good guys. Remember?"

"You must be, because he doesn't let people in. He's very private."

"He thinks a lot of you."

They pulled into the driveway, and the gate opened as they approached. "I'm shocked."

"I told you we were invited."

"Okay," she said, but her tone was doubtful.

At the top of the hill, Randy pulled off onto a gravel road between two board fences instead of going toward the castle.

"This isn't the way," she said, pointing up the driveway.

"It's the way to where we're going."

Nothing but green fields lay on either side of the road. Ahead, the tiny church rose from the hill. When they pulled up, she saw the bright orange flag from Paul's scooter on the side of the building.

"What is all this?"

He took the keys from the ignition and turned to her. "Have you not figured out yet, that I would do anything for you?"

"You really are a true friend."

"Aren't we more than friends?" He held his breath. "Could we be?"

Her lips parted, but she didn't answer.

"I've never felt so alive since I got to know you. Well, not the first day. I thought you might be off your rocker then, but you're not. You're a sweetheart. An angel. A good person right to the core."

"I'm not perfect," she said.

"But I think you're perfect for me." He took her hand and squeezed it. "No matter what, I will always be honest with you. No secrets. No half-truths. Nothing to hurt you."

"You're scaring me."

"I know what they've been keeping from you, Natalie."

"You knew?"

"No. I didn't know all along, but you were so upset, and the detective in me just couldn't let it go. It didn't take me long to figure it out. We're going to get this all settled here and now."

"Should I be worried?"

"Not one more minute of your life." He opened his door. "Come on."

She got out, and they walked to the tiny chapel.

Grandstaff sat on a pew toward the front, his hands folded in his lap.

"I'm going to wait right here," Randy said. "Okay?"

She nodded and walked toward Paul, as Randy slid in the back pew to wait with his heart pounding.

"Hello." Paul patted the bench. "Sit. I've got some explaining to do."

She looked over her shoulder toward Randy.

He gave her an encouraging nod.

Paul pointed to the beautiful headstone. The shiniest stone Natalie had ever seen.

PATRICE GRANDSTAFF

LOVING WIFE, MOTHER, GRANDMOTHER.

QUEEN BEE. BEE THANKFUL PSALM 100:4

"My daughter's ashes are there in the urn next to it."

She took in a long breath, then took his hand. "It's lovely."

"Natalie. You are special. I told you about my grandson."

"I know you loved him very much."

"So did you."

She held her breath. "I don't—"

"Natalie, Jeremy had a family. He was my grandson, and the trauma he went through was greater than any child deserved. Family can be strangely difficult."

"I remember you saying that, but he would never—"

"He didn't lie to you." He fervently shook his head, raising a finger to hold her back. "Listen to me. He made a promise to me. A promise that he struggled with, but he did the right thing. Your love for each other was pure. Real. He told me about you. You were the best part of his entire life. You gave him happiness."

"I don't understand."

"I sent him away from here to protect him. Made him promise he'd never come back. We compromised on the cabin. His trips there weren't just for hunting but for us to reconnect too. His father was a bad man. Dangerous, and he was evil to my daughter and my grandson. It was so hard to watch."

He patted her hand. "We were going to tell you. He felt horrible that he let you believe he had no family, and yet he didn't want you to live with the fear and terrible pieces of his past."

"Why? I would've understood."

"It was not who he was. It was what was done to him. He had to move on to find a good life with you, and he did. Please don't be upset with him. This doesn't change one moment of your time or love for one another."

"He lied to me?"

"No. He was completely truthful with you. He loved you more than the air he breathed. You were his happiness. The family he'd been dealt was broken. Hurtful, and it would have hurt you if he'd shared it."

She leaned forward, sobbing.

He leaned over, stroking her hair. "Sometimes we make decisions that we think protect the ones we love. They aren't always right."

Grandstaff pulled a handkerchief from his pocket and handed it to her. "Natalie, you do have family. We are family. And there are people in this town that feel like you are family."

"Family can be strangely difficult," she said between tears. "In a wonderful way. I'm glad we're family."

Grandstaff turned and gave Randy a nod. "Your friend,

Randy. He's a good man. He took a chance putting this all together. For you."

Randy sat in the last pew, barely able to stand the way his heart was breaking for her.

He wanted more than anything to rush in. To rescue and console her.

Please let this have been the right thing to do. He held his breath. He'd forced this to happen. Believed it to be the right thing, coming from the right place in his heart.

"I saw why Jeremy loved you so much when your kindness touched me."

Her shoulders lifted as she dragged in a breath.

"I've mourned him silently for so long. I want to be here for you. For us to remember and honor him together, as family."

She raised her head. Sniffling. "Everyone knew?"

"No one meant malice, my dear."

Shaking her head, she swept at tears with a trembling hand. "Why, then?"

"I promise you. No one took any joy in not telling you." His voice strained, as if he was holding back a flood of emotion. "We wanted you to love this town. To feel closer to your husband. To find your own way, before there'd be a right time *if ever* to fill in the blanks for you. When you showed up, it was as if my prayers had been answered. Please. Please tell me you'll forgive me."

She got up and ran out of the church.

Grandstaff crumpled in that first pew, and Randy wasn't sure which one to check on first.

"Go to her," Grandstaff yelled. "I'm fine. Please. Take care of her."

Randy turned and ran outside looking for her.

She was in his truck holding the puppy, rocking.

"Natalie?"

"Please take me home."

He got in the truck and drove her to the cabin.

She turned to him, eyes swollen, looking exhausted. "I need some time alone. It's all just too much."

"I don't want to leave you." He blew out a breath. "I'm going back to Orene's. I was trying to help. Natalie, this is good. You've got family. People love you. The past is the past, does it even matter? I just want to make your future good and honest and no secrets and—"

"I know you're trying to help. You are. Please. I'll call you later. I promise." She clamored out of the truck and ran across the bridge.

His heart hung heavy. He prayed this had been the right thing to do.

"I love you," he said. When she was out of his view, he backed up the truck and drove over to Orene's with only a hope for forgiveness on his mind.

Chapter Thirty-Five

NATALIE CRIED. Hurt and angry, she threw things, screamed, and scared little Buzz, who had just run under the bed with his tail tucked tight beneath him.

Get yourself under control.

Perspective. Look at this from another angle.

Just when she thought things were going so well, all of this was feeling like more than she could handle.

Buzz poked his head out from under the bedspread, a dust bunny hanging from one ear.

She drank some water and apologized to the puppy.

"I'm sorry. It's just too strange to even believe."

Buzz settled down on her lap, his chin resting on her leg.

"I hope Randy will forgive me as easily. He meant well. Maybe I overreacted a little."

Buzz barked and nipped her chin in an awkward kiss.

"Okay, overreacted."

She sat there for a long time, then got her keys and drove out to the castle.

She'd never even noticed that gravel road before. She took that path and pulled in front of the tiny chapel. She got out and walked inside.

Not a sound but her footsteps.

She knelt in front of that very pew where she'd sat with Paul. Heard the truth. And she could imagine Jeremy and his grandfather together. Could even see the resemblance in that old picture she'd seen of Paul and Patrice.

No wonder Jeremy had been so afraid to have children.

It made sense now.

An abusive father, an alcoholic mother, and he was caught in the middle.

Peace fell over her. It wasn't about her at all. She loved Jeremy. She loved how he'd loved her, and together they enjoyed a blissful existence that neither could have experienced otherwise.

We were blessed.

She got up and drove to the house.

Paul sat on the bench by the front door. The puppy, duck, and rooster marched about as if trying to snap him out of the heartbreak he must be feeling.

"Hey."

"I'm sorry I didn't contact you and tell you when he died. I didn't know what he had or hadn't told you. It was wrong."

"It's fine. A wise man once told me that family can be strangely difficult."

He laughed.

"And then there was you," he said. "You changed my grandson's whole life. He deserved you."

"I don't regret a moment of my life with him. Except that I didn't get to know you before. Get to see you two together."

"Oh, Natalie. He was a light so bright. A good, good boy."

"A wonderful man." She sat down next to him. "Now, we're family."

"I'd love that so much."

"But you have to promise to not be strangely difficult," she said, leaning her head against his shoulder.

"I'm a bit of a difficult fellow at times, but with your help, and with the help of your fellow, Randy, I believe you and I will be just fine." Paul gave her a sweet wink.

"Me too."

"We didn't know for the longest time even where Jeremy had gone. Thank goodness for technology. When the obituary was released, it triggered an alert to the attorney here in town."

"That's how the will all came about. I knew he had one, but we'd never discussed it."

"I helped him put all of that together to be sure the cabin would remain in the family and cared for with no burden on you."

"That makes sense now. Did you two decide to have his remains cremated? I'd never heard him speak of that before."

"We did, and I'd like to move them here to this church if you'll allow it."

"With his family," she said.

"Your family too, my dear." Paul paused, then resumed.

"I treasured the time we got to spend together when he came to the cabin. We shared a love for cars, for fixing things. He was a smart young man. Gentle in spirit despite his father's hatred."

"I guess he had to cope, and sometimes things are messy. I just wish he'd told me. I'd have been there for him."

"He loved you, and those lies were not meant to trick you or keep anything from you."

"I don't understand, but I accept it. In a way, I feel more

peace about him being gone, weirdly, because of you," she said. "I am believing now that family is more than the people that we are related to. I'm glad we're related, though."

"Me too." Paul pulled her into a hug.

Chapter Thirty-Six

RANDY PARKED in front of Orene's house, feeling the weight on his shoulders of what all just went down. He'd only meant to bring the pieces together for Natalie. He just hadn't expected her to be hit so hard with all of this. He picked up his phone and made the call he should have made before he came and talked to Paul.

"Sheila? This is Randy Fellowes."

"The handsome detective. Hey. You're not calling to ask for my best friend's hand in marriage, are you?" She belted out a laugh.

"No." *Maybe someday, but not yet, anyway.* "I need your help."

"What's wrong?"

"Nothing we can't all get through. Together. Can you come up to Chestnut Ridge? I can send you the address." He filled her in on the day, and how hurt Natalie was at the moment. "I want to be here for her, but I think she needs you."

"She needs us both. I'm on my way."

"Meet me here at the inn and I'll drive us up to the cabin."

"No. You get your butt over and fix this. My heart is telling me you two were meant to be together. I felt that the first day

in the hospital. Go to her. I'm on my way, and I'll find y'all."
Sheila's phone disconnected.

He walked up to the house.

"You're back," Orene said. "How are you?"

"It's been a day," he said.

"Oh?" She looked concerned. He wasn't good at hiding his feelings and he felt like hell at the moment.

"I think we need to talk," he said.

She nodded. "I'll put on some tea."

"Actually, do you have anything stronger?"

She grinned. "A cold beer? I've had a few kidney stones. I swear a few good beers a week keep 'em at bay. Always have a good cold beer in this house."

"That was unexpected," Randy said. "I'll have one."

"I'm going to have one with you."

"The perfect hostess," he said.

"A Southern requirement," she teased as she left the room. A moment later, Orene was back in the living room. She handed him a cold one. "What's going on?"

"You knew something was up."

"Wasn't born yesterday."

"She knows." He paused.

Orene froze. "She?"

"Natalie knows Grandstaff was Jeremy's grandfather."

"Holy . . ." She guzzled her beer. "How did you know?"

"I'm a detective."

"Yes, you are." She swept a hand across her mouth. "A good one, apparently."

"I like to think so."

"You know, our sheriff has been looking for a replacement. You could move right into that position. I just so happen to have a lot of pull in this town. And Grandstaff has the rest."

"Somehow, I don't doubt that. Right now, though, I'm just hoping I didn't ruin my chance with Natalie. She was distraught when I dropped her off. She insisted that I leave."

Orene patted his leg. "You're going to be just fine. It all needed to be said. All is right when it's the truth." She stood. "Wait right here."

She nearly ran, as fast as an old lady could, up the stairs. Her footsteps came back down so quickly that for a moment, he found himself craning to make sure she hadn't tumbled, but just then she popped around the corner.

"Here," she said. "Put out your hand."

He did.

She pressed a fairy stone into his palm. "You carry that. Fairy stones can only be found near here. They will bring you good things. Not luck. The thing He wants you to have." She nodded to heaven. "Trust me. It's all going to be okay. I've seen it work a hundred times."

"Thank you." He squeezed the little rock in his hand.

"Don't drag your feet, boy. You go win that lady's heart."

"You're right." He got to his feet. "Thank you for being such a good friend to her when she got here."

"Honey, that was not my doing. God made that happen. She's an absolute delight. I'm happy He chose me as a vehicle to the truth. And even happier He chose you to be a part of it too. Go."

He got up, went back to his truck, and drove to the cabin.

Disappointed that Natalie's truck wasn't there, he settled back to wait for her.

The beauty of the countryside was nice. He hoped she saw him as something more than just the detective who'd been assigned to her case. Or, more importantly, not the man that brought out a lot of history she might not have wanted to know.

If she was considering a change, he wanted to be part of that equation.

She pulled up in her truck beside him.

He waited to see what she did before making a move.

She got out and walked to his side of the truck.

He lowered the window. "I meant well. I'm so sorry."

"No. Don't be. It's the truth, and it's all out in the open now. I'm tired. Really tired. What an emotional drain."

He got out of the truck with his nerves all over the place. His mouth was dry, his hand shaking.

She walked over and stepped close to him.

He relaxed and wrapped his arms around her. "Natalie, please don't ever run from me. I'm in love with you."

"It was the fairy tale," she said. "How appropriate that there was a castle involved."

"Yeah, that's kind of ironic, isn't it?"

She looked into his eyes. "You are my knight in so many ways."

"You forgive me?"

"Forgive you? I'm so thankful for you."

"Is there room to be more?"

She ran her thumb across his cheek. "Yes. I think there is.

I have love to give. I loved being married. It doesn't hurt as bad as it once did, but I do still miss him. I always will, but you . . . you are so special to me, and my heart says there is more. Much, much more."

He leaned forward and kissed her full on the mouth.

"I'm completely in love with you, Natalie."

"I feel it too."

He stepped back and opened the back door of his truck. Then turned with a smile. "It's not an engagement ring or anything like that, but I think these will make you happy for now."

He handed her the box of doughnuts. He'd all but forgotten about them until this moment.

She laughed. "Happy forever!" She lifted the box. "It's been a wild ride. So many strange things, and then there was you. Fixing everything."

"You inspire me. By the way, Orene said something very interesting to me."

"Really?"

"I'd like your take on it, and feel free to tell me if I'm moving too fast."

"What?"

"She said if I wanted to run for sheriff, she was pretty sure I'd get the votes. That would mean I'd have to be a resident of Chestnut Ridge."

"You'd move here?"

"If you're staying here, then this is where I want to be."

"I love it here. This is where my family is."

"Speaking of family, my sister is hosting Thanksgiving this

year. I'd really like you to meet the rest of mine," he said. "We're having it at Courtnie's house. I'm frying the turkey."

"I'll make something to bring," said Natalie.

"That's a yes?"

"It is, but do you think there's room to invite a couple people from here? Maybe Orene and Paul?"

"Yes, and Sheila too."

"You already thought of Sheila too. Of course you did. You're so thoughtful."

"When you were upset, I called her to come. I thought you might need her," he admitted.

"She's on her way?"

"Yes. She should be here any minute. There's always room for family even if we have to use a card table and a tent. We'll make it work."

"Don't you make me sit at the kids' table, future sheriff." She grabbed his hand and squeezed it. "You do have a certain sheriff aura about you."

He tilted his head. "You think?"

"I do."

"Save that *I do* for something more special in our future."

At that moment, Tucker's truck rolled up and he and Sheila piled out of the truck, heading their way.

"Family." She nodded with a huge smile. "Are you tempting me with a good time?"

"One that'll last forever," Randy said. "Seriously, I want to make a life together in Chestnut Ridge with you, Natalie. No matter how long it takes, or what comes our way."

He kissed her on the forehead.

"I want to be part of your family." She hugged him, then nodded toward Tucker and Sheila. "I think we have some explaining to do."

"We do. I hope you don't mind a little long-distance dating until we get all this worked out."

"I'd wait forever for you," she said. "I used to think the most important thing in the world was having a family, and then you showed me how anyone special can be family too."

Acknowledgments

T HIS BOOK and the beauty of the town described as Chestnut Ridge were inspired by the lovely setting of Patrick County, Virginia. This community is filled with faithful, giving kindness, and I'm so grateful for the new friends I've made in the short time since I've moved here. It was fun to include many tiny snippets that are special to this region, gleaned from the generous storytelling by welcoming neighbors.

Thank you to my agent, Steve Laube, for ongoing support, personally and professionally, through the writing of this story during a time when my life became a bit unraveled. I'm forever grateful for your guidance and kindness.

As an author, I know that I'm only a small part of the stories that land in the hand of my readers. Without my editors, Eileen Rothschild and Lisa Bonvissuto, and the entire SMP team, these words wouldn't shine and stand out in such a special way. I'm so honored to be a part of the St. Martin's Press family.

Heartfelt gratitude goes to my family and friends, who are always there, every step of the way. Thank you for the many shining moments you've shared with me on this journey. I can't wait to see what's ahead for all of us.

About the Author

ADAM SANNER

USA Today bestselling author NANCY NAIGLE whips up small-town love stories with a whole lot of heart. Several of Nancy's novels have been made into Hallmark movies, and most recently *The Shell Collector* was adapted as the first Fox original movie to stream on Fox Nation.

A native of Virginia Beach, Nancy now calls the Blue Ridge Mountains home.